PALM BEACH TABOO

A CHARLIE CRAWFORD MYSTERY (BOOK 10)

TOM TURNER

JOIN TOM'S AUTHOR NEWSLETTER

Get the latest news on Tom's upcoming novels when you sign up for his free author newsletter at **tomturnerbooks.com/news**.

JOIN TOM'S FACEBOOK GROUP

Chat with Tom and other Palm Beach Mystery Fans in the **Tom Turner - Crime and Mystery Facebook Group** at **https://www. facebook.com/groups/tomturnerbooks**

ONE

"HELLO?"

"Dispatch call you?" It was Charlie Crawford's partner, Mort Ott.

"No, why?" Crawford asked, squinting at his bedside clock. 1:15 a.m. "What's up?"

"A horizontal"—which was Ott-ese for a dead guy, usually in a supine position—"all the way up on North Lake Way. 1450." Some said Ott was direct. Others said irreverent. A few said heavy-handed. Many said all three.

"All right," Crawford said. "I'll be there in twenty."

"Okay," Ott said. "Just wish people would be a little more respectful of our sleep. You know, like maybe do their killing during the day?"

———

OTT GOT THERE FIRST. Crawford, who walked into the house at 1:35 a.m., was directed to a second-floor bedroom by a uniform at the front door. There were two other uniforms in the foyer. He nodded to them, then walked past and into a large living room. He was surprised to see most of the chairs and sofas filled with people: two women on a sofa wearing bathrobes, speaking softly to a fully dressed man facing them. A woman in blue pajamas sat in a leather club chair, staring out the window into the black of night. A middle-aged woman on another sofa was being comforted by a younger man with his arm around her shoulder. Another younger woman wearing a sheer negligee and an older woman in a white terrycloth bathrobe, sitting side by side in a love seat, both texting on their iPhones. Who were they waking up at this time of night, Crawford wondered? And, finally, a man in jeans and a white T-shirt, who looked to be in his thirties, pacing back and forth in front of a large picture window. A gas fireplace cast flickering light around the room.

Crawford proceeded directly up the staircase to the second floor. He heard voices at the end of the hall and followed them. He stepped through an open door, onto a thick carpet, and saw Mort Ott talking to a crime-scene tech named Sheila Stallings. He was happy to see her on-scene because she was thorough and experienced, second only to Dominica McCarthy. But then maybe he was biased.

Ott and Stallings were staring down at a man's bloody body lying in a king-sized, four-poster bed. The man's head rested on one of four pillows. Judging from the straight cut on his neck and the blood matted on his chest and neck, his throat had been slashed.

"Knife, huh?" Crawford said.

Stallings, who hadn't seen him, jumped. "Jesus, Charlie! Don't sneak up on me like that. I'm still half-asleep."

"Sorry." Crawford patted her on the shoulder.

"Yeah," she said. "Multiple stab wounds but a severed artery was what killed him."

Crawford turned to Ott. "Who is he?"

"Name's Christian Lalley," Ott said.

"And who are all those people downstairs?"

"No clue," Ott said. "They were here when I got here. Eight of 'em, right?"

"Nine," Crawford answered. Then to Stallings: "Find the murder weapon?"

"No, and I've been all over the room. It's not here. Maybe somewhere else in the house or outside. I'm gonna do a tight search."

"Hawes on his way?" Crawford asked, referring to the medical examiner, Bob Hawes.

Stallings nodded. "Dispatch said they called him right before me."

Ott shrugged. "Guess he's a slow driver," then under his breath to Crawford, "slow thinker, too."

The ME was not high on their hit parade.

"I'm going to go interview the people downstairs," Crawford told Ott.

"Decent chance one of 'em did it, wouldn't you say?" his partner asked.

Crawford shrugged. "Who knows? It's just kind of weird. Nine grown people all living together in the same house."

"Yeah, used to be ten," Ott said with a grim expression.

A theory had popped into Crawford's head.

Hatching theories was basically what he did for a living.

"I'll be down in a few," said Ott.

Crawford walked back down the stairs and into the living room. Most of its residents glanced over at him. He raised his voice and said. "My name's Detective Crawford." All eyes were on him now. "The man upstairs, whose name I understand is Christian Lalley, has been murdered." Typically, Crawford went light on the euphemisms, avoiding terms liked *deceased* and *passed away*. "You have my condolences. Now, I would like to interview all of you individually in that room, the library, I guess it is." He pointed to a smaller space off the living room. "But first, if you don't mind, I'd like to take a look at your hands."

And, if they did mind… well, *tough.*

The seven looked around at each other—then back at Crawford—with expressions ranging from surprise and disbelief to curiosity, irritability, and annoyance, but no one displayed what he was hoping to see: fear.

"If you'd all get in a line, please," Crawford said.

Slowly, they did, and without being told, held out their hands.

Crawford walked past them, inspecting the seven sets of hands. Aside from one obvious nail-biter and another with a slight tremor, he saw nothing out of the ordinary, and zero blood. Not that it meant they were off the hook.

"Thank you very much," Crawford said as he reached the end of the line. His gaze went to the woman who had been staring out the window and was now eying him with great interest. "Ma'am, how 'bout you and I talk first?"

Without saying a word, she stepped out of the living room and into the library, which had floor-to-ceiling bookshelves on three sides.

Crawford followed her to a beige wing chair and sat opposite her in a love seat. He pulled out his iPhone, which he used to take notes. "What's your name, please?"

"Jennifer Parker, but I'm known here as Belletrix."

O-kay, thought Crawford. "Please tell me what you saw or heard earlier this morning."

Belletrix was around forty and had long, dark hair with a few strands of grey mixed in. She had intense blue eyes and a small scar above her lip. "I didn't see anything. I just heard Christian scream bloody murder," she said, hitting the nail on the head, "and naturally, I was terrified. I didn't know what to do so I got up and locked my door and hid in my closet."

Crawford nodded. "Besides him screaming, did you hear anything else?"

Belletrix cocked her head. "I heard lots of footsteps, then I heard another scream. A woman's scream."

"Do you think that may have been her discovering Mr. Lalley?"

"I guess so. Maybe. I was just so scared. I was just trying to protect myself, to be safe."

Crawford nodded. "I understand. Do you happen to know who it was? The woman who screamed."

She frowned. "No, I don't."

Crawford tapped a note into his iPhone. "So, what happened next?"

"Well, about ten minutes later, someone knocked on my door. I didn't say anything. I was still so terrified. Then I heard a man shout something, but I didn't understand what he said and didn't move. Then I heard a crash and a man shout, 'This is the police!' He'd knocked in my bedroom door, broken the lock. It was a policeman in uniform, so I came out of hiding. He told me to go down to the living room."

Crawford was dying to know whether his theory was correct.

"Ms. Parker, who are you...people?" he asked. He couldn't think of a better way to ask the question.

"We're a congregation."

"A congregation?"

She nodded. "Dedicated to the advancement of society through altruistic sacrifice and illuminating a productive path to others less fortunate and less intellectually gifted than ourselves." She laughed. "Sorry, I know that sounded like a canned speech. Well, it kind of is. Put simply, we're a group of people who live together and do our best to help others."

Belletrix was careful not to say it was a cult, but it sure as hell sounded like one to Crawford.

TWO

NEXT TO BE INTERVIEWED WAS the woman in the sheer negligee, except she'd gone somewhere—Crawford guessed to the coat closet in the foyer—and put on a trench-style raincoat to cover up.

She told him her name was Samantha Mayhew but that she was known as Cressida, and she had long, red hair, with jet-black eyebrows. Not a combo you saw every day. Like Belletrix, she claimed she hadn't seen anything but heard footsteps running down the hallway on the second floor immediately after she heard Christian Lalley's scream.

"So, you think that might have been his killer? The person running down the hallway."

She shrugged. "Maybe. Or could have been someone responding to his scream. Trying to help, you know. I couldn't be sure. But I heard it right after the scream."

"Tell me about Mr. Lalley. I mean, do you have any idea why someone might have done this? Did he have any enemies that you know of? Anyone at all who might have had a motive to…kill him?"

"I have absolutely no idea. Until a while ago, Christian was number two in the congregation. He had a lot to do with how everything ran here," Cressida said, looping a strand of hair over her ear.

"Number two? Who's number one?"

Cressida turned as she heard footsteps.

Ott walked into the library, a paper cup of coffee in hand.

"This is my partner, Detective Ott," Crawford said. "This is Ms. Mayhew. To catch you up, Ms. Mayhew heard what she thinks were feet running down the hallway above right after she heard Mr. Lalley scream." Ott nodded. "Oh, and these people here are part of a... congregation, you call it, right?"

Cressida nodded.

"Which, as I understand it," Crawford said, "means you're a group of people who basically try to make the world a better place. And help disadvantaged people. Is that pretty much it?"

Cressida nodded again and smiled.

Ott nodded. "So, you mean a cult, right?"

Cressida frowned. "I resent that characterization."

Which didn't seem to bother Ott, whose expression didn't change.

Crawford kept going. "So, Mr. Lalley used to be second-in-command here to a someone I was just about to hear about." He extended a hand for Cressida to continue.

"His name is Crux," she said.

"Say what?" Ott said.

"His name is Crux."

Ott nodded as an impish grin cut across his face. "So, you're saying the head of your cult is named Crux? As in, crux of the matter?"

Her face hardened. "That's an insult. It's *not* a cult. Far from it."

Ott put up his hands. "Okay, sorry, congregation."

Cressida looked back to Crawford, her expression now sullen and tense. "For the third time, yes, his name is Crux. His real name is Lucian Neville."

"I'm just curious," Ott said, "where the name Crux comes from? Do you know?"

Cressida was ready with the answer. "It's one of the best-known constellations in the southern hemisphere. It's also known as the Southern Cross because of the formation of its five brightest stars."

Crawford nodded. "So, where *is* Crux? The man, I mean."

"He's up at 1500 North Lake Way. We own five houses in the area. All pretty close to each other."

Crawford was caught off-guard. He figured that any local religious group that owned five houses in Palm Beach would have crossed his radar at some point. "So, how many members of... sorry, you haven't told us the name of your congregation yet."

"SOAR."

"S-o-a-r?" Crawford asked.

She nodded.

"Is that an acronym or something?"

"No, it just means, you know, ascend, rise... mmm, climb."

"Gotcha."

Crawford heard footsteps and turned toward the library door. A short man with a neatly trimmed beard walked in. He was wearing khakis and a pressed, dark sports shirt.

Cressida ran to him and threw her arms around him. "Oh, my God, it's so awful what happened to Rigel."

Crawford got to his feet.

"I know, I know," the man said, patting Cressida's head, then turning to Crawford and Ott. "My name's Crux. Do you have any idea what could have happened to my brother, Christian?"

Crux had a slight accent, which Crawford pegged as Australian.

"In plain English, his throat was cut while he was in bed," Crawford said. "I'm Detective Crawford and this is my partner, Detective Ott. How did you hear about it? It's Mr. Neville, correct?"

"Yes, it is, but just call me Crux. Josie called me on her cell. She's one of the women down in the living room."

"And as I understand it, you live in one of the neighboring houses."

"Yes, I do," Crux said. "1500 North Lake Way."

"And you were there—at your house—when this happened..." Crawford glanced at his watch. "Approximately an hour ago?"

"Yes, I was." Crux cocked his head.

"Not in this house?"

"No," said Crux, squinting his eyes. "Wait, you're not thinking—"

"We're going to be asking everyone where they were when it happened," Crawford said.

Cressida stood. "I'll go make some coffee. I'm sure we can all use some."

"Thank you," Crux said as she walked.

Ott stepped toward Crux. "Let's get right to it. Do you know if Mr. Lalley had any enemies? Anyone who may have threatened him? Someone he may have had a dispute or disagreement with?"

"No, I do not. Rigel, the name he was known by, was a gentle, mild-mannered man. He'd be the last person I'd expect to be a victim of something like this. I mean, this is just inconceivable."

"Rigel," Ott said, scrunching his eyes. "That's an unusual name."

"It refers to a star in the night sky."

"Like your name does," Crawford put in.

Crux nodded.

"How many members are in your congregation?" Crawford asked. "And can you tell us a little about it, please?"

Crux ran his hand through his beard. "I'm not sure exactly how that's relevant, Detective."

Ott inhaled to speak, but Crawford subtly waved him off. "We just want to understand a little better what you do and who you all are."

"Why is that?"

Ott gave him a look; even Crawford was starting to lose patience. "Because the most likely killer is someone in SOAR. It is highly *un*likely that someone from the outside broke into this house then made their way upstairs and killed... Rigel."

"Yeah, and I was told all the doors were locked and could only be opened by a resident here," Ott said. "So, obviously, the most likely suspect is someone who was in the house tonight."

"By the way," Crawford asked, "do other members, specifically ones who live in your four other houses, have keys to this house?"

"I had one," Crux said. "But then I have keys to all the houses. I'm not sure if other members have keys for this house. And, as for your question about the congregation, we have forty-three members. Without going into a lot of detail, we are a philanthropic organization and every one of our members belongs to the Mensa society."

Whoa, that was a major curveball. Crawford's eyes darted over to Ott's.

"No kidding," Ott said. "So, does that mean that all of you have IQs of like 175 or something?"

Crux rolled his eyes. "They don't get much higher than 162 unless you're Charles Darwin or Bobby Fischer. You just have to be in roughly the top two percent to qualify."

"*Just*," Ott repeated with a nod. "That's a pretty tall order."

"And how long have you been here in Palm Beach? In the five houses?" Crawford asked.

"Bought the first one four years ago and the other ones every year or so since then."

Crawford's burning question was how they got the money to buy all the houses? But he didn't ask, because his gut was telling him that was an answer that could wait. Someone would tell him. Or he'd figure it out himself, in time.

On the surface, there appeared to be nothing wrong with SOAR— smart people supposedly doing good deeds. But one of their members had been brutally murdered.

That was a seriously *bad* deed.

THREE

TURNED OUT CRUX, who Crawford guessed was no more than five feet six inches tall, was actually from New Zealand. He made a joke about his height, explaining how his namesake, the Southern Cross constellation, was the smallest of all eighty-eight of them. Crawford and Ott spent another half hour interviewing him and got more information than they bargained for. And it felt as if Crux was willing to go on for another hour. He told them his parents had moved to New York from New Zealand when he was twelve. And that his father had been president of ASB bank, headquartered in Auckland, when he was recruited to take over a UK-based bank.

Crawford and Ott spent two more hours interviewing the other people who lived in the house.

At 5:05, Crawford and Ott finally walked out the front door of 1450 North Lake Way. Crawford turned to Ott as he opened the door of his car. None of the Mensa-member residents struck him as being the killer, but then, being as smart as they reputedly were, they could probably hide it pretty well.

"So, what do you think?" he asked his partner.

"I think they probably all have IQs fifty points higher than your normal, run-of-the-mill murderer," Ott said. "I don't know, man, they all seemed pretty tense and uptight, but I guess that was to be expected. What did you think?"

Crawford looked down at the pebble driveway, then up at Ott. "I got the feeling from a couple of them that they might be holding back. Like we were only getting ninety percent."

"I know what you mean. What about Crux?"

Crawford pushed a few pebbles with his shoe. "Umm, more like fifty percent. Like he might have a few secrets he wants to keep to himself."

Ott nodded. "Yeah, I got that too," he chuckled as he opened the car door, "By the way, what's with all these funky names? They get 'em from *Star Trek* or something?"

———

CRAWFORD CONKED out as soon as his head hit the pillow, even with three cups of coffee coursing through his veins. He set the alarm for nine-thirty and was at his desk by ten. As he always did with his homicide cases, he first went to Google, because, in the past, anyway, almost all his murder victims had been, if not famous, then at least pretty well known to others, even outside of Palm Beach. His most recent victim was Thorsen Paul, who had started the high-flying NextRed pharmaceutical company and was worth three billion one day, then bankrupt two months later. A year before had been Knight Mulcahy, the $60-million-dollar-a-year talk-show-host blowhard, who had more enemies than grains of sand on the beach behind his house. A little further back, there'd been the ruthless Russian gangster brothers living in a knock-off Hugh Hefner Playboy Mansion, complete with a harem of beautiful women. The list went on.

When Crawford Googled SOAR, all he got on Wikipedia was a brief sentence in red that said, *We have insufficient data on this entity.* When he Googled Christian Lalley, nothing at all came up. That wasn't a surprise to Crawford and only confirmed his belief that SOAR was highly secretive. And that Crux did not encourage his congregation to be the least bit talkative or forthcoming, even though he was quite willing to talk about himself.

Next stop was Rose Clarke, the most successful real-estate agent in Palm Beach, and Crawford's former *friend with benefits*. (She was still a good friend, but the benefits had dried up. That was a long story.) He dialed her cell.

"Hi, Charlie, whatcha up to? It's been a while."

"Too long. Are you busy?"

"I've got a showing at 11:30. You can come over now if you want?"

"Thanks, I will. Want me to pick you up your Starbucks special?"

Rose had some pretentious-sounding Starbucks coffee she swore by. It was called Aged Sumatra Lot Number 593.

"Oh, yes, would you, sweet boy?"

"Sure. See you in fifteen minutes."

He got there in thirteen, since there was a short line at the Worth Avenue Starbucks, and he double-parked in front.

He handed her the coffee. "Is this the equivalent of some fancy French wine?"

"Exactly," she said with a chuckle. "It's the Chateau Lafite Rothschild 2010 of coffee."

Crawford smiled. "I'll stick to the Gallo brothers of coffee. Dunkin' Donuts."

She batted her lashes. "Man of the people, Charlie Crawford."

He sat opposite her in her stylishly appointed office. She was the only one in her company who had an office, besides the manager. The other agents worked in cubicles in an open bullpen area.

Rose Clarke was Crawford's go-to when it came to learning more about the diverse people and personalities of Palm Beach. It was almost as if she possessed a vast, alphabetized catalogue of every one of the ten-thousand-odd citizens residing in the island paradise. Of course, that wasn't true, but Crawford had only ever come up with a few dozen names she didn't know personally or, at least, know *of*, during his years with the PBPD.

"So, what is the subject of today's little get together?" Rose asked.

Crawford came right out with it. "A guy named Crux and a... congregation named SOAR."

"Why? Did something happen there?"

Crawford nodded slowly. "I'm amazed. Something that didn't hit your radar five minutes after it happened." He leaned back. "A man by the name of Christian Lalley was murdered at one of their houses early this morning."

Rose leaned forward and put her coffee container down. "You gotta be kidding? How?"

"He was stabbed to death."

Rose put her hand up to her mouth and shook her head. "Oh my God, I actually met him once. I showed him the house they bought at 1450 North Lake Way. He made the offer and negotiated it."

"What did you think of him?"

Rose sighed and thought for a few moments. "Kind of a humorless guy. All business, no small talk. Straight-shooter, though."

"And what do you know about SOAR?"

Rose took a sip of her designer coffee. "Supposedly they do good things. I think they teach poor kids in West Palm. Dropouts and, you know, challenged kids. Something like that. They're pretty secretive, though."

"Yeah, no kidding. How much did they pay for 1450 North Lake Way?"

"Eight point five million." Rose always knew the numbers.

"So, the question is, where'd the money come from to buy that house *and* their other four?"

No hesitation from Rose on that. "Rich women. The first was Marie-Claire Fournier, daughter of the second or maybe the third richest man in Canada."

"So, she's a member of SOAR?"

"Was. She died last year. Less than fifty years old, as I recall."

Rose's cell phone rang. She looked down at it and turned off the ringer.

"Do you know what she died of?"

"No, but I remember seeing her at a charity thing a couple nights before it happened. Looked pretty healthy to me."

She had Crawford's full attention now. "So, you're saying it was her money? She paid for the houses?"

A knock came at Rose's door.

"Who is it?"

"It's Sylvia, can I come in?"

Rose rolled her eyes. "I'm busy, Sylvia, what is it?"

"I just got a really good offer for your listing on El Vedato."

Rose sighed and put her hand up to her mouth. "Come back in half an hour."

"But—"

"I'm sure the buyer's not going to change his mind in thirty minutes." Rose said and smiled at Crawford. "That's the first time I've ever told an agent with an offer to cool her heels."

"I appreciate it," Crawford said. "Just another few minutes. You were talking about Marie-Claire—"

"Fournier. Yeah, so what I heard was all the houses were in Marie-Claire's name and when she died, they were willed to her two daughters. One of 'em lives in Palm Beach."

Crawford nodded. "So, what did that mean? Crux and the SOAR members might be faced with having to vacate them?"

Rose held up a hand. "You'd think. Except out of the blue come two new SOAR members who offered the two daughters sixty-five million for all five houses."

"And?"

"They accepted it. It was a fair offer." Rose looked down at her silenced phone, which was flashing. "That's another offer," she said with a smile. "You're costing me a lot of money, Charlie."

"I'm sure the buyers aren't gonna change their minds in thirty minutes." He shrugged innocently.

Rose raised her Starbucks. "Touché."

"And who were those new SOAR members who bought the houses?"

"I knew you were going to ask that. It was kept very hush-hush for a while but eventually leaked. A woman named Fannie Melhado and her brother, Freddie. Members of the most exclusive club in Palm Beach."

"The Poinciana, you mean?"

"No, the forty-three billionaires who own houses here."

Crawford nodded. "Back to Marie-Claire Fournier, do you remember there ever being any suspicion about her death?"

Rose thought for a moment. "I just remember there being a lot of silence."

"You mean like…deadly silence."

Rose smiled. "Guess you could call it that."

Crawford thought for a second. "What's strange is, I never heard anything at all about her death," Crawford said. "And, presumably, if it was thought to be anything other than natural, I'd know about it."

"Why don't I nose around a little and see what I come up with?"

Crawford stood. "I would really appreciate that."

"For you, Charlie, anything." She flashed her best coquettish smile. "Well, almost anything."

He moved to give her a kiss on the cheek, but she turned at the last moment and it ended up landing on her lips.

"Kisses on the cheek are for aunts and sisters," she said. "Now get out of here."

FOUR

CRAWFORD CALLED Ott into his office. "We really need to interview all the SOAR members from all the other houses," he told his partner.

"Just line 'em up like a production line?"

Crawford shrugged. "I don't know any other way to do it."

"Any more thoughts on the ones we interviewed last night?" Ott asked.

Crawford thought for a few moments. "The problem was it was a high-stress situation in the middle of the night. Understandable that all of them would be, you know, jumpy, tense and keyed up."

Ott nodded. "Yeah, I agree, but what did you make of that guy Pollux?"

"I'd say he was the most jumpy, tense, and keyed up."

Pollux, who didn't give his actual name, reminded Crawford of Washington Irving's character, Ichabod Crane. And not the Johnny Depp version. He was a tall, lanky scarecrow of a man, mid 40s or so, who had the most prominent Adam's apple Crawford had ever seen. It stuck out at least two inches and looked like it was going to pierce the skin on the front of his neck at any moment.

"Yeah, no shit. Dude never made eye contact with either of us,"

Ott said. "Kind of creepy. Had one of those shifty looks common to used-car shysters and Wall Street guys."

"Watch it," Crawford said, "you're talking about my old man and my two brothers... the Wall Street guys,"

Ott put up his hands. "Sorry. Cam's a good dude. Never met your father or your other brother," he said. "Did you ever wonder what these SOAR people do all day long?"

"Good deeds, supposedly. But I'm not exactly sure how or what that actually means."

Ott swung a leg up on Crawford's desk. "So..." he said, "you think the killer's gonna out*smart* us?"

Crawford didn't understand the question at first, then: "Oh, you mean, the Mensa thing."

"Yeah, so I looked into it a little. The Mensa society. Know who's in it?"

"Who?"

"Well, the only names I recognized were movie stars. Steve Martin and Geena Davis were two of 'em."

"Steve Martin I can definitely see. Geena Davis... was she Thelma or Louise?"

"Louise. The one Brad Pitt banged."

Crawford chuckled. "You think that'll be on her tombstone?"

"Yeah, here lies *Geena the Mensa... who Brad Pitt banged in a cheap motel room.*" Ott shrugged. "Tell ya what, man, she never seemed all that bright to me."

"Hey, she was acting."

Crawford's office line rang. It said Unknown on caller ID. He picked up.

"Hello?"

"Inspector Crawford?" The man had a British accent.

Close enough. "Who's calling."

"I'm not going to give you my name, but I will tell you why I'm calling."

That was a start.

"Okay?"

"I used to be a member of SOAR." Crawford hit speakerphone. "Let's just call me a disgruntled former member."

Crawford mouthed *get a trace* to Ott.

Christian Lalley's murder had made the early morning TV news and was all over the radio too. Getting a call like this so soon almost seemed too easy.

Ott hustled out of Crawford's office.

"Anything you can tell me would be greatly appreciated, sir. How long ago did you... leave SOAR?"

"Five months ago. I didn't like what it had become."

"And what was that?"

"A bunch of people sucking up to Crux. He's the head of it, as I'm sure you know by now. He turned into a complete autocrat."

"Do you have any idea who might have killed Christian Lalley?"

"Not really. But I could theorize all day long. I'd recommend you ask Cressida. She knows where all the bodies are buried in that happy little island paradise."

"How do you spell that name?" Crawford asked. He knew the woman from last night but needed to kill time for the phone trace to kick in.

"C-r-e-s-s-i-d-a."

"I would really like to come and talk to you. I can assure you that no one will ever know we spoke."

"That's what you think. Those people have ways of keeping an eye on everyone they want to."

Ott was back in Crawford's office, now, scribbling something on a sheet of paper.

"What can you tell me about Crux?" Crawford asked as he read the page Ott slid to him. *Got it*, the note said.

"A lot," the man said. "But isn't that your job to find out?" Abruptly, he hung up.

Crawford looked up at Ott. "Now there's a guy we need to talk to."

"Yup. And through the miracle of modern technology, we're gonna."

FIVE

THE MYSTERY CALLER'S name was Simon Petrie and he lived in a modest, stucco, ranch-style house just over the bridge in West Palm. He was not happy they had found out he was their mystery caller.

Crawford and Ott knocked on his door, identified themselves, told him they'd traced his call, and asked if they could come in. Reluctantly, Petrie let them in after being assured that no one from SOAR had followed them or was watching from a car or a house across the street.

"You're sure about that?" Petrie asked as they sat in his living room.

"Not unless they have a satellite," Crawford told him.

"I wouldn't put it past them," Petrie said. "Those people are omnipresent."

Leave it to a Mensa, Crawford thought... use a fifty-cent word when a simple *everywhere* would do the job.

"Mr. Petrie," Crawford began, "you told us you were 'a disgruntled former member'... Why?"

"Disgruntled or a former member?"

"Well, I assume they're related."

"You are correct," Petrie said, then he got up and walked over to a window and peered side to side across the street. "You may think I'm paranoid"—the thought had indeed crossed Crawford's mind—"but you don't know who you're dealing with."

"Tell you what, Mr. Petrie, would it make you feel better if, after we leave, we have an undercover cop keep an eye on your house?"

Petrie cocked his head. "I might just take you up on that."

"Let me know; we'll arrange it," Crawford said. "Now, do you know whether SOAR or Crux have resorted to any kind of physical violence in the past? I ask because it seems as though you're fearful they might do something to you. Harm you in some way, I mean."

Petrie thought for a second. "I don't have any hard evidence, but after what happened to Christian…"

"We understand," Crawford said. "So, are you assuming that his killer was someone in SOAR?"

Petrie nodded. "Yes, from the moment I first heard about it. I don't know who, though. But I have a couple of guesses."

"Who?"

"I'm not going to say."

"Why not?" Crawford asked. "I assume you don't want the killer on the loose."

"Yes, but I just don't want to speculate without any proof whatsoever."

"Hey, look, Mr. Petrie, it's just between us. We're not going to tell anyone," Ott promised.

"No, sorry."

"How long were you in SOAR, Mr. Petrie?" Crawford asked.

"From the beginning," Petrie said. "I was one of the four originals. Lucian—I never could bring myself to call him Crux; it sounded so, so… I don't know, grandiose." He chuckled. "No, *pretentious* is a better word. Anyway, it was Lucien, Louise Bourne, Marie-Claire Fournier and me."

"Tell us about all of them, please, starting with Neville," Crawford said.

And for the next twenty minutes, Petrie rambled on.

He started by explaining that Neville and he had been best friends in college but, in the last few years, had kind of drifted apart. When Crawford asked why, Petrie explained that Neville seemed to increasingly lavish his time and attention on people who were rich and could advance the cause of SOAR, adding, "And that *certainly* was not me." Then he went on to explain how when Neville's father moved his family to New York City from New Zealand, Neville was only twelve. It was the summer and Neville's parents were able to fast-track their son into a prominent private school in Manhattan called Buckley. The headmaster was impressed that Neville never earned less that an A, not even an A-, in his prior three years of school in Auckland. Neville spent one year at Buckley—again achieving nothing but straight As— then moved to a school in Connecticut called Hotchkiss when he was fourteen.

His father, despite making a hefty salary at the bank that had recruited him, was wildly extravagant and a total stranger to the concept of saving money. He also was a closet gambler who went on three-day poker binges to London, Las Vegas, and Nassau casinos. He looked down his nose at the nearer Atlantic City casinos, even though they were just down the road, Petrie explained with a shrug.

Then, when Lucian was sixteen and a sophomore at Hotchkiss, two life-shattering events occurred simultaneously. One, his father lost over a million dollars in an all-night poker session at the Grosvenor-St. Giles casino in London, and two, and far worse, financial advisors at his father's bank were accused of engaging in fraudulent and illegal conduct, including misappropriation of client funds and charging fees to thousands of clients without providing them with extra services. Henry Neville was never personally charged with any of the crimes, but it didn't matter: those offenses had happened on his watch. He was summarily fired, and the bank paid a forty-five-million-dollar fine that went toward customer compensation.

Lucian never made it back to Hotchkiss for his junior year. His father informed him that he could no longer afford the expensive tuition, even though he secretly continued to gamble recklessly. Lucian ended up going to Eleanor Roosevelt High School in Manhattan. The only good thing about it, Crux had told Petrie, was that it was only ten minutes from his parents' co-op apartment. Lucian's grades slipped and he ended up with a B average. He had little interest in going to college anymore, but his parents pressured him. He was fortunate to get a scholarship to McGill University in Montreal based on his unusually high IQ of 150, not his grades at Eleanor Roosevelt High. McGill was where he met both Petrie and Marie-Claire Fournier, who became his girlfriend and, not insignificantly, his meal ticket.

Crawford glanced at Ott. "So, I don't know about you, but I have a million questions."

Ott nodded and held out his hand. "After you."

"So, Marie-Claire Fournier. I understand she died at around fifty years old. Seemed to be in good health one minute, dead the next."

Petrie shrugged. "I don't know what to tell you? Supposedly, an aneurism. Do I agree with you that it seemed suspicious? Yes, I agree with you it *did* seem suspicious."

"But what was the reaction of other SOAR members?" Crawford asked.

"Just that… you know, it was sad and unfortunate. And that she'd be sorely missed."

Ott leaned toward Petrie. "But nobody suggested it seemed fishy? No one was suspicious about her death?"

"Not really. It was more like everyone was all concerned about what was going to happen to SOAR."

"You mean because it's major benefactor was dead?

"Exactly."

"But then along came the Melhados." Crawford said.

"I'm impressed," said Petrie. "You men have done a lot of home-work already."

"Mr. Petrie, you recommended, when you called, that we speak to Cressida because 'she knew where the bodies are buried'… That's an interesting figure of speech. What exactly did you mean?"

"I just meant that there's always someone in any group or organi-zation—a very observant person usually—who knows just about everything that goes on. Cressida's one, Vega's another."

Crawford tapped the name Vega into his iPhone. "Vega? That name hasn't come up before."

"It will."

Crawford nodded. "Were you and Mr. Lalley friends?"

"Yes, we were. I even saw him a few times after I dropped out of SOAR. He was a good man, but not without flaws."

"We did briefly speak to Cressida last night. She told us Christian used to be number two at SOAR, right behind Crux," Ott said. "So, two questions: what specifically did Lalley do, meaning what was his specific job, and two, why did he 'used to be' number two... and not anymore?"

That was actually Crawford's next question.

Petrie leaned back in his chair. "Christian was the treasurer of SOAR. He had been a CPA in his former life, so he was kind of a natural... except he wasn't."

"What do you mean?" Ott asked.

"After the Melhados joined and brought their billions—"

"Billions?" Ott said, astonished.

"Well, maybe just a mere one billion. Anyway, Christian was kind of out of his league with all that money to handle. So that was why he got demoted. Plus, Crux was always making changes in the ... let's call it, 'hierarchy.' He liked us to be a little insecure, a little unsure of exactly where we stood. One congregant, who shall go nameless, came up with the perfect nickname."

"What was that?"

"Crux in flux."

SIX

TURNED out that Simon Petrie didn't want an undercover cop parked across the street after all. He didn't give a reason. Crawford said they'd check back in with him every day and make sure everything was all right. Best Crawford could tell, since leaving SOAR, Petrie had led a life of isolation.

Crawford had called Lucian Neville before the Petrie interview and asked him to set aside the afternoon for Ott and him to interview the other thirty-four members of SOAR who lived in the other four houses. Neville had been cooperative and told Crawford that he would instruct all of his members to come to his house at 1500 North Lake Way.

Ott and he were headed there now.

Ott had been silent for most of the ride, which was a bad sign. It usually meant he had been thinking, but not necessarily about the case. If he was focused on the case, he'd be talking about it. Theorizing, conjecturing, spitballing, and throwing stuff at the wall.

"You know, Charlie, I've been thinking."

"That's what I was afraid of."

"About *Bosch*. The TV show *Bosch* and the guy Bosch."

"Okay. What about 'em?"

"Well, for one thing, I think him liking jazz is kinda lame."

"Why do you say that?"

Ott scratched the side of his head. "'Cause it's like... old news. I've seen it before. A detective who likes jazz, I mean. Off the top of my head I can remember at least two others."

Crawford chuckled and shook his head. "I can't believe we're actually having a literary discussion."

"I wouldn't go that far," Ott said, gazing out the window. "Actually three, now that I think about it. Walter Mosely, Ian Rankin, and Lawrence Block."

"All wrote about detectives who liked jazz, you mean?"

"Yeah, Block's guy is Matt Scudder; Rankin's is Inspector Rebus; and Mosely's...ah, I forget."

"And Michael Connelly's the Bosch guy, right?"

"Duh."

"So, I guess the question is, who came first... the first detective who liked jazz?"

"Yes, that's the question," Ott said, pulling out his iPhone. "Google time."

Ott clicked and scrolled for a few moments. "Well, now, isn't that interesting. Rankin came out with Inspector Rebus in 1987 and..." He scrolled more "Mosely wrote his guy... Easy Rawlins in 1990. *Devil in the Blue Dress.*" More clicking and scrolling. "Michael Connelly came out with his first Bosch book in...1992."

"So, I'd call it a tie."

"I'd call it Ian Rankin, by a nose."

Crawford shrugged. "Okay, but what about Lawrence Block?"

"I already saw him when I was scrolling. He's actually the oldest of all of them but was the Johnny-come-lately with his jazz-loving cop. 2011, to be exact. The book I was thinking of is called *The Night and the Music.*"

"So, Ian Rankin it is, I guess."

Ott nodded as Crawford hit his blinker for the house at 1500 North Lake Way and drove in. "That was pretty good, huh?"

"Pretty good what?" Crawford asked.

"Pretty good way to kill a boring, ten-minute drive."

ONE OF THE other things Simon Petrie told them about was the SOAR hierarchy. Specifically, that people switched around between the five SOAR houses, the objective being to ultimately land a bedroom in Crux's house, which was known as Elysium. Petrie said Christian Lalley had lived in the same house as Crux until six months ago, when he was unceremoniously banished to 1450 North Lake Way, which seemed to be a house tenanted by those *least* favored by Crux.

Crawford pushed the doorbell at 1500 North Lake Way. A few moments later, a beautiful, short-haired blonde woman opened the door and smiled up at Ott and him. "Welcome to Elysium, gentlemen."

Crawford remembered seeing her a few times at Green's, his breakfast and lunch go-to.

"Thanks," Crawford said, "I'm Detective Crawford and this is my partner, Detective Ott."

"Nice to meet you both, I'm Capella."

Crawford felt reasonably certain that was the name of either a star or some celestial body in outer space.

She took a second look at Ott. "You're the guy who always has a mushroom omelet and those big squishy sausages at Green's."

"Breakfast of champions, ma'am," Ott said.

She glanced at Crawford. "And you…scrambled eggs?"

Crawford nodded. "And, occasionally, a stack."

She laughed. "Come on in, Crux is expecting you." She turned, walked into the foyer, and they followed.

She led them through a large, lavishly appointed living room, dominated by gold and silver furnishings, and into a room beyond. It was a library with floor to ceiling bookshelves on all four walls. Crux, with a book in hand, was sitting in a throne-like chair that faced two nondescript chairs. Crux's seat was made of hand-carved mahogany and had cherubic faces staring out from the heavy wooden arms and intricate carvings on the front legs as well as the upper back, which loomed high above his head. Crux was leaning against the chair's tufted, black leather back, which looked quite comfortable.

"Welcome, gentleman," Crux said, setting his book down on a side table and gesturing for them to sit facing him.

Crawford noticed the book was a Churchill biography. Crux's role model, maybe?

They sat and Crawford observed that his own chair was unusually low. He flashed to something he had once either read or heard about a king wanting his visitors or subjects to feel insignificant facing him. It was certainly an equalizer, as his own six-foot-three frame faced the five-foot-six Crux from below. Capella remained standing.

"Thanks for seeing us," Crawford began. "This will probably take most of the afternoon."

Crux nodded. "How do you want to do it? As I said, all the members you haven't spoken to are either here or on their way."

"Sounds good. What we'd first like to do is speak to all of your congregants as a group; then my partner and I can interview them one by one."

Crux glanced at Capella. "Would you usher them all into the living room. We'll do it there."

Capella nodded and walked out of the library.

"So, have you had any further thoughts," Crawford asked, "who might've killed Christian Lalley?"

"You call 'em *perps*, right?"

"Well, that's more a TV-movie thing."

Crux's right hand started to fidget on the head of the cherub carved into the arm of his chair. "I know you think it was someone in my congregation but, the reality is, no one here has any kind of a history of violence or hostility. If they did, they wouldn't be here."

"So, before your members are allowed to join SOAR, you vet them pretty thoroughly?" Ott asked.

"Absolutely. Like I'm sure the police department does before accepting new police officers," Crux said. "But I guess there are always bad apples. By the way, here's something I found out: the back door at fourteen-fifty was left unlocked."

"Oh, really," Crawford sad. "Why?"

"Because the congregants there felt there was no threat from the outside world. See, there's a twelve-foot wall on the property line on the sides. Pretty much impossible to get over that."

Crawford nodded as Capella walked back in. "All set," she told Crux.

Crux nodded at her. "Before we begin, I thought I'd give you gentlemen a tour of Elysium. Not that it's relevant to the case…just thought you might like to see it."

"Absolutely, we *would* like to see it," Crawford said.

"Yeah, sure," said Ott, "let's have a look."

Crawford figured the more he knew about Crux, SOAR, and their houses, the better.

The three stood and Crux reached for a black cane with a gold carved knob leaning against the side table. It definitely seemed like a scepter to Crawford. Pretty bogus, he thought.

Capella led them over to an elevator. She pushed the button and it opened. They walked inside and there was plenty of room to spare. It looked to be about eight feet high inside.

"You could fit half a football team in here," Ott said.

Crux chuckled. "Just about."

All four walls were sheathed in rich mahogany and an art nouveau chandelier hung from the lift's ceiling.

The elevator stopped at the third floor. They got out and walked down a corridor. The floors were a dark brown herringbone and three more art nouveau chandeliers hung from the ceilings at fifteen-foot intervals.

"Beautiful floors," Crawford said.

"Thank you," Crux said, opening a door and walking into a bedroom. It was massive, Crawford guessed about twenty by thirty, and dominated by an oversized canopy bed in the center. The canopy looked like a tapestry from a medieval European castle with four intricately carved wood columns supporting it.

"Wow," Ott said, "I'd need GPS to get around in that bed."

It occurred to Crawford how strange it was, being given a tour of Crux's bedroom. It felt way too personal.

He imagined Crux a mere speck in the bed.

Crux pointed at the bed. "I got it from a place in St. Petersburg,

Russia. The man who sold it to me said it was Catherine the Great's but… I'm not so sure I buy that."

Crawford turned and saw the Intracoastal waterway off in the distance and two boats going in opposite directions. "Quite a view," he said, noticing a telescope facing the Intracoastal.

"Yes, the other day I saw Tiger Wood's boat going north."

"Oh yeah," said Ott. "The *Privacy*. It's a hundred fifty-five feet long. He lives up on Jupiter Island. Little known fact… Greg Norman, who lives there too, has an even bigger one."

Crux turned to him. "Oh, yeah? How big?"

"I don't remember exactly but over two hundred feet."

Capella, who so far hadn't said a word, spoke. "How big's the one you're looking at, sir?"

This was the first time anyone had addressed Crux as "sir."

"A little over two-fifty…with a helicopter pad. But it's not a done deal yet, and I don't want to jinx it by talking about it."

As he led them out, Crawford noticed several doors on either side of the bedroom. He was glad Crux had skipped his bathroom. Again, there was something personal about a bathroom—even more so than a bedroom. Crawford didn't want to see Crux's toothbrush or razor. Nevertheless, he imagined a lot of Carrera marble, top-of-the-line fixtures and, no doubt about it, a bidet.

They made their way back toward the elevator.

"There are other bedrooms up here, right?" Crawford asked.

"Yes, one on either side of mine," Crux said.

As they walked down the hallway, Crawford looked to his left into one of the bedrooms. It was about half the size of Crux's and also had a lot of doors. One was open and looked to be a large walk-in closet with women's clothes in it.

They got back in the elevator and Crux pushed *B*. The elevator descended.

"I'm going to skip the second floor. Just a lot of smaller bedrooms there," Crux said.

"How many in all?" Ott asked.

Crux glanced at Capella. "How many?"

"Four," she said.

The elevator stopped at *B*.

"I figure you guys will like this," Crux said, then glanced at Crawford. "Looks like you work out?"

"Yeah, a little," Crawford said, "but my partner here's a total gym rat."

Crux turned to Ott. "Well, check this out."

The basement was one big open area with what was clearly a state-of-the-art gym dominating two-thirds of it. It consisted of about twenty shiny silver machines for every muscle in the human body, a mat area with medicine balls, heavy jump ropes and benches, a separate area for free weights, barbells, dumbbells, and kettlebells.

Ott shook his head. "I could live in this place... just bring me a sandwich every once in a while."

Crawford laughed, pointing. "A lap pool, huh?"

"Yes," Crux said as they approached the three-lane pool, which was separated from the gym by five fluted columns. "I use it a fair amount"—then pointing—"and the steam room and sauna over there."

"Can people from the other houses use this?" Ott asked.

Crux nodded. "Yes, I don't know if you noticed, but there's a separate parking lot for the gym, plus an outside door. Just park, walk down the steps, and start pumping iron."

"You need a key, right?" Ott asked.

"Yes, everyone in all the houses gets one."

"That reminds me," Crawford said. "I asked this before, but did other congregants have keys for fourteen-fifty?"

Crux turned to Capella. "Do you know?"

"I think some do," she said, "but I don't know exactly who."

Crawford nodded, again not satisfied with the answer, and making a mental note to pursue it later.

Ott was looking around, taking it all in. "This is my idea of paradise."

Crux chuckled. "In fact, Elysium's another word for paradise."

They took the elevator up to the first floor and got out.

"Well, thanks for the tour," Crawford said.

"Yeah, pretty amazing crib ya got here," Ott said.

Crux laughed. "Never heard it referred to as that, but glad you liked it."

He led them into the living room, where all the residents of the other houses had gathered. By Crawford's quick estimate they looked to be two-thirds women and one-third men.

"I'll let you take it from here," Crux said to Crawford. "I'll just observe."

Crawford and Ott walked in front of a tall white marble fireplace while Crux went and sat down in another high-backed chair that was clearly *his* chair. Crawford noticed that his feet did not reach the floor.

"Thank you all for coming here," Crawford said, then identified his partner and himself.

He expressed his condolences about the death of their fellow congregant, said they were eager to solve the Lalley homicide as quickly as possible and needed whatever information the congregants could provide in order to do so. He also assured them that everything they told him or Ott in their one-on-one interviews would remain totally confidential. He turned the floor over to Ott, who added that they were particularly interested in knowing about enemies Christian Lalley may have had. Or confrontations of any sort that they might have witnessed between Lalley and either another congregant or an outsider.

With that, they moved to the private interviews, with Crawford talking to a female congregant in a sunroom off the living room and Ott escorting another woman to the private dining room.

The woman who Crawford interviewed was emotional and, judging from her red eyes and smudged make-up, had been crying. It turned out she was Vega, who Simon Petrie had mentioned along with Cressida.

He was excited about picking her brain, particularly since Petrie had mentioned she knew SOAR and its congregants inside and out.

She was a brunette and, he guessed, in her late thirties. She was shapely and reminded him of Rose Clarke, but five inches shorter.

"Christian was a close personal friend of mine who I've known for a long time," she volunteered at the outset.

"I'm sorry for your loss and, of course, my partner and I would like to find his killer as soon as possible."

"I hope you do. He was a very productive member of our congregation and will be sorely missed."

Crawford then asked her why Lalley had moved from 1500 North Lake Way to the house where he had been killed.

She hesitated before answering the question. "It wasn't his idea."

"Whose was it?" Crawford asked.

"Crux's. He had to make way for the next treasurer."

"Treasurer? Could you explain that, please?"

Vega tapped the arm of her chair a few times. "I'll try, but it's not exactly my field of expertise. So, rumor has it that—are you ready for this—SOAR is worth over a billion dollars. That's billion...with a B."

"What?" Crawford said, pretending this was the first time he heard it.

"You promised you'd keep everything we say confidential, right?"

"Yes, absolutely."

"Okay, so Christian was in charge of buying the five houses with money donated by a member—"

"Who was that?"

"Her name was Marie-Claire Fournier. Plus, Christian maintained the stock portfolio, but that was back in the... *poor* old days, when SOAR had a mere twenty million in the bank."

Crawford did some quick math: twenty million plus the sixty-five million that Rose told him the houses had sold for was well shy of a hundred million. Where was the other nine hundred million? Oh yes, he remembered, that had to have been before the brother and sister entered the scene.

"Then along came"—she did the little quote thing with her fingers —"*the benefactors*."

"Benefactors? What do you mean?"

He knew she meant the Melhados but wanted to hear it from her. He had learned long ago that it was crucial to get multiple takes, even on so-called facts.

Vega nodded. "Well, as you can imagine, this little operation doesn't run on love. Someone—I forget who—told me once that the real-estate taxes alone on the five houses was over six hundred thousand dollars a year."

Crawford nodded. "So, you're not considered a philanthropic organization, I take it? Not tax-free?"

"Crux tried to be recognized as one, but it failed. Matter of fact, that was one of the reasons why Christian got demoted and ended up at 1450 North Lake Way."

"Why? I don't understand?"

"Because he struck out with the IRS. Crux gave him the job to get us tax-exempt and he failed. I don't know all the details."

From Elysium to ignominy. From a position of power and status to joblessness and... being stabbed to death in the middle of the night.

"I see. You're saying he was punished for not being able to get that done."

Vega nodded. "That's exactly what I'm saying. A major demotion. But if you ever mention anything I've told you to Crux, I'll vehemently deny saying a word."

Crawford put his hands up. "Please, in my business you have to be discreet. So, back to the benefactors you mentioned, who are they?"

Vega was silent for a few moments. Like she wasn't sure she wanted to answer the question. "Does the name Melhado mean anything to you?"

Crawford shook his head.

"It didn't to me either, but they're heirs to the Getty Oil fortune. As in the Getty Museum. As in multi-billionaires. As in that poor boy who got kidnapped and had his ear cut off."

Crawford nodded. "I remember. So, tell me about them."

"Brother and sister," Vega said. "His name is Freddie; her name is Fannie. I'd say he's about thirty, she's probably around thirty-three. He's nice and friendly, she can be kind of... well, bitchy."

Vega was Crawford's kind of interviewee. He could barely take notes fast enough. "And they live here? In Elysium?"

She nodded and smiled. "Oh, you bet they do. On either side of Crux, as a matter of fact."

Well, isn't that cozy? Crawford refrained from saying.

"I don't know if you noticed, but they were sitting next to each other in that white couch in the living room. She's a tall dark-haired woman, reminds me of Morticia; he's a nice-looking guy, wearing a red polo shirt, I think."

Crawford remembered them. He knew who his next interviews would be.

Out of the sunroom window, Crawford spotted Crux in the back yard. He was walking beside a dark-haired woman. She fit the description of Fannie Melhado.

"Let's go back to the billion dollars. So that money came from the Melhados?"

She nodded. "I read in the *Glossy* the other day that there are forty-three billionaires in Palm Beach. Did you know that?"

Thanks to Rose Clarke, he did know. But Crawford simply shrugged. "I figured there were a lot. So now I've got a lot more questions. First, did the Melhados donate that money to SOAR with no strings, or how'd it work?"

Vega sighed. "Sorry, I'm not really sure about that, not being well-versed in high finance. My understanding is that they pledged that money to the foundation. I guess, the SOAR Foundation."

Crawford nodded. "O-kay, but to do what with?"

"The simple answer is to spread the precepts of SOAR. So, it becomes a bona fide religion with real credibility."

"Right up there with Protestants, Catholics, and Buddhists?"

"You laugh, but Crux is a very ambitious man. Fannie Melhado, too. Woman, that is."

Crawford nodded. "I'll take your word for it."

Vega moved closer to him. "Did you ever hear about Bethesda?"

"The church, you mean?"

She nodded.

"What about it?"

Bethesda-by-the-Sea was the oldest house of worship in Palm Beach. It was where Donald and Melania Trump tied the knot back in 2005 and Michael Jordan and his second wife were married a few years later.

Vega leaned even closer. "Well, this is really hush-hush..."

"Okay."

"Crux tried to buy it last year."

"Whoa-whoa... *what*? That's crazy, you can't buy a church."

"Tell that to Crux. He offered 'em fifty million dollars for it."

"Okay. Same question as before: To do *what* with it?" Crawford was floored by the revelation. It seemed absolutely preposterous.

"What do you think? To preach the gospel of SOAR, give us instant credibility and respect. He figured that would be a highly visible pulpit."

"Wow. Can't argue with that," Crawford said, still dumbstruck. "But buying Bethesda seems kind of like trying to buy... I don't know, the Lincoln Memorial."

Vega shrugged. "This took place right after the Melhados joined. Word is, Fannie may have had a lot to do with it."

Crawford looked at his watch. He couldn't spend the whole afternoon with Vega. Others were waiting. But the woman was a goldmine.

"On another subject," Crawford said. "The impression I'm getting is there's a distinct hierarchy in SOAR. And that... how do I put it? Fourteen-fifty North Lake Way is where people who are out of favor end up. And that there's clearly an order of the most desirable houses down to least desirable ones?"

"Absolutely. Elysium is on top and fourteen-fifty is at the bottom."

"So, you must be pretty happy where you are? Here at Elysium?"

"I guess," Vega said with a shrug. "I mainly just like having the gym and pool in the basement. I'm not so concerned about all the politics."

"I get that," Crawford said. "So, let me ask you... Marie-Claire Fournier, I'm assuming she was also in Elysium when she was alive?"

Capella nodded. "You bet she was. But for two reasons. All the money she gave *and* being Crux's long-time girlfriend. Until she was *phased out*."

"'Phased out'... what exactly does that mean?"

Capella laughed. "It means sex. You see, Crux had a lot of women to choose from here."

Crawford was surprised and it showed.

"What did you think, people with high IQs don't like sex or something?"

"No, I just—"

"'Cause we all seem so serious, is that it? So damn purposeful or something?"

Crawford shook his head, wanting to stay on the subject of Marie-Claire Fournier. "Do you know how Marie-Claire died? What the cause might have been?"

"A brain aneurism."

"And how old was she?"

"Forty-nine."

"That's pretty young for something like that. Usually happens to much older people."

"Yes, I know."

"So, when she was *phased out*... I'm guessing, someone else was phased in."

"Good guess. Who do you think it was?"

"I'm going to take a wild guess: Fannie Melhado?"

"Bingo. Crux traded in the older, rich model for a younger, even richer one." Vega chuckled. "Longstanding Palm Beach tradition. Been going on forever in this town."

There was a knock on the door and Ott walked in. He held up a hand. "Sorry, to bother you. Just got done with my interview."

Crawford nodded. "We were just wrapping it up here." He put his hands on his knees to stand. "Well, thank you, Vega, I really appreciate your cooperation—"

She smiled, shot him an eyebrow wag, a thousand-megawatt smile, and reached for a pen in her purse. "Why don't I give you my phone number just in case you think of any other questions you might want to ask me?"

He stood as she wrote. "I was just about to give you my card."

"We can trade," she said, handing him the piece of paper she had just written her name and number on. "Even though I think you already got most of the good stuff out of me."

SEVEN

CRAWFORD AND OTT walked toward the living room.

"You rascal," Ott said, under his breath. "Chick was hittin' on you."

Crawford groaned. "She was just being cooperative," he said, "the way we like 'em."

"Bullshit. She was hittin' on you… the way *I* like 'em."

Crawford rolled his eyes as they entered the living room, which was packed with people who ranged in age from early 30s to mid-50s and wore expressions from anxious to bored. Some were reading magazines, others books. Some were on their computers, others on iPhones, and a few were simply staring off into space. One of the ones deep into a faraway stare, Crawford was pretty sure, was Freddie Melhado.

"Mr. Melhado?"

The man turned toward Crawford. "Yes," he said, standing up.

"Would you follow me, please?"

Melhado approached and they shook hands. "Freddie Melhado," he said with a smile.

"Detective Crawford."

They walked into the sunroom and sat down.

Melhado was a tall, handsome man with a tennis-pro tan and

longish hair combed straight back. He could have been a movie actor, though Crawford spotted a slight limp, which might have stunted the career of a leading man.

"I appreciate you meeting with me," Crawford said. "So how long have you been a congregant here?"

"A little over a year."

Melhado went on to explain he used to be a real-estate agent in Palm Beach. Something he did, "Not for the money, but just something to do." His sister, he volunteered, was an Olympic-caliber equestrian who had a thirty-two-acre horse farm with eighteen stalls in Wellington, a half-hour west of Palm Beach. He explained further—as if his biography were far less interesting than his sister's—that she "liked horses better than people" and felt a void in her life that even her huge inheritance couldn't fill. She was a contributor to many causes and had heard about SOAR through a fellow rider who had a friend who was a congregant. Fannie had gone for a visit and met with Crux but initially felt that he was "too slick" and resisted the leader's overtures to join SOAR.

Crawford was not dazzled by Freddie's Mensa intellect, having heard at least two grammatical errors in his speech, including "her and me" on several occasions. Plus, he sprinkled 'ya know' into practically every other sentence.

"I understand that one of SOAR's requirements is that all its congregants be members of Mensa."

Freddie laughed. "And you weren't picking up on that with me, is that it?"

"No, no, I wasn't saying that. I was just hoping you'd confirm that for me."

"Everyone except for me and Fannie," Freddie said. "And I heard, ya know, Marie-Claire Fournier wasn't Mensa either. Maybe a few others. Hell, man, I'd be lucky to crack a hundred," he joked, referring to his IQ.

It seemed clear that Crux was prepared to bend the rules for billionaires.

"Did you know Christian Lalley very well?"

"Not that well, but I liked him," Freddie said. "It's kind of like five fraternities here. Elysium is one, Runnymede, where Christian was, is another. The way it works is you kind of know people in your house really well, and you know 'em in the other houses, but not as well."

Crawford saw Crux and Fannie Melhado walk by the sunroom window again. They both looked dead serious.

"Do you know why Lalley moved out of Elysium?" Crawford asked.

Freddie raised his hands. "No clue."

"Were there... congregants he didn't get along with? Or did you ever see him having... maybe an argument or a fight with someone?"

Freddie shook his head. "Nah, Christian was a pussycat. At least that's what I saw."

"Is there anyone, either in Elysium or one of the other houses, who you might consider... capable of violence?"

"Oh, my God," Melhado said, shaking his head, "are you asking me if I think someone in SOAR is a murderer?"

Crawford didn't respond.

"I mean, Jesus, no. I've seen people get pissed off, raise their voices, stuff like that, but kill Christian... I can't think of anyone capable of that."

Crawford nodded. "You don't do real estate anymore, I take it?" he asked, making a mental note to ask Rose Clarke what she knew about Freddie.

"Nah, not anymore. Can't say I miss it much either."

Crawford had extracted some useful information from Freddie but guessed that was about all he was going to get.

"Well, I appreciate your cooperation. Is there anyone else you can think of who might be informative? I mean, in helping me on this whole thing?"

"My sister probably," Freddie said. "She's a lot more involved in the, ah, management of SOAR than me."

Crawford hoped that would be the case. Unless Crux—in their little stroll session behind Elysium—was telling her to clam up.

H E   M E T Ott in the living room. Ott had just wrapped up with a man named Sumner Harris. Fannie Melhado, it seemed, had just come back inside, and was talking to another woman.

Crawford walked over to the two women. "Ladies, if we could meet with you two in about ten minutes. My partner and I need to have a quick conversation first."

Fannie Melhado rolled her eyes, like she was being terribly inconvenienced, but the other woman smiled and nodded.

Crawford flicked his head, signaling Ott to follow him. They went into the sun-filled dining room and remained standing, facing each other.

"Whatcha got so far?" Crawford asked.

"Well, these people can call themselves a congregation or whatever the hell they want, but there's no doubt about it, it's a goddamn cult. And a cult leader can blow smoke up your ass and use fifty-cent words all day long, but when it comes right down to it, I think the dude's in it for sex and money."

Crawford smiled. "Okay, Mort, tell me what you really think."

"Isn't that the way you see it? I mean, this whole gang could be a rich man's Manson family… they're just about five murders short."

Crawford put up a hand. "Whoa, big fella, you're goin' a little overboard now. I'd say the jury's still out. My interview with the one in the black dress should be interesting. Fannie Melhado. Heard anything about her yet?"

"Yeah, she's the one bangin' the boss. Got a shitload of money, right?"

Crawford nodded. "Inimitable Ott-speak… never a man to mince words."

"*Inimitable*… shit, Charlie, you get around these people, you start talking like 'em."

"Did you notice on our little tour of the third floor, there was a door from Crux's bedroom to the bedroom on the right?"

Ott nodded. "The one that had women's clothes in the walk-in?"

"Yeah, you spotted it?"

"Hey bro, not much gets by ol' Morty."

Crawford chuckled. "That's Fannie Melhado's bedroom."

"Well, isn't that convenient," Ott echoed Crawford's reaction from earlier. "So, Fannie Melhado is just a door away from the boss."

Crawford chuckled. "Yup. You get anything else useful?"

Ott put his hand on his chin. "Well, for one thing, the death of Crux's old squeeze, Marie-Claire Fournier, sounds a little fishy after all."

"I agree with that. A lot fishy."

"For another, as you found out, we got a game of musical houses going on here."

Crawford nodded. "Yeah, people switching around from one to the other."

"Exactly. Everyone trying to get into Elysium," Ott said. "Shit, I would be, too, just to be a few steps away from that world-class gym."

Crawford nodded. "Yeah, but with these people Elysium's like a status thing."

"Like havin' a house on the ocean."

"Exactly. Or a power thing," Crawford said. "All right, let's see what we can get out of these two."

Ott nodded and they walked out of the sunroom back into the living room.

Crawford walked up to Fannie Melhado. "Ms. Melhado, if you would come with me, please."

She didn't say anything, just stood and followed him.

They went into the sunroom and sat down. "So, Ms. Melhado, I had a nice talk with your brother."

She shook her head and scowled. "He's quite the conversationalist, isn't he?"

Sounded like what she meant was that he was quite the gasbag. "Did you know Christian Lalley very well?"

"Not really. We spoke a few times, but that was about it," she said, tapping her hand on a side table.

"Ms. Melhado, I'm interested in what SOAR does. That hasn't really been explained in detail to me yet."

She smiled. "What? You want to join, Detective?"

Crawford smiled. "I'm a lapsed Unitarian who plays golf on the Sabbath."

"So, you mean, a heathen."

Crawford chuckled. "Pretty much."

"You're forgiven," Fannie said. "So, I'll give you an answer. For one thing, we're doing everything we can to end homelessness in this area. And it's a really big problem. You'd be surprised how much homelessness there is just across the Intracoastal in Lake Worth and West Palm and up in Riviera Beach," she said. "We also spend a ton of time teaching the indigent. Specifically, high-school dropouts and the mentally challenged. We believe that teaching kids about James Joyce and Ernest Hemingway or when the French and Indian War was fought is a complete waste of time... who gives a damn? That's not what these kids need, they need to be taught a profession. Robotics, computer science, or hell, how to be a plumber and make a hundred bucks an hour. We don't have any plumbers in SOAR, but we've got a lot of tech-savvy people—a few who used to have big jobs in Silicon Valley. Virtual jobs, in a lot of cases. If we at SOAR don't have the necessary teaching knowledge, we hire people who can teach these kids how to be dental assistants, electricians, cosmetologists, you name it. Fields where they can go out and get a job right away."

"So, in effect you're like a vocational school?"

"Kind of. But we go further. A lot further. Vocational schools, trade schools, whatever you want to call 'em, generally are government-run or for-profit. Government-run means all the usual government flaws and limitations and red tape; for-profit means—bottom-line—they're more interested in making a buck than teaching a kid what he needs to know."

"That seems very worthwhile."

"Thank you. I think it is."

She leaned back in her chair, quite satisfied with her explanation. Crawford's sense was that she seemed genuinely dedicated. Like she might have been an aimless dilettante for most of her life—riding horses, going to debutante parties and charity balls, jet-setting to fancy places—and had finally found a purpose. At least, that's how it came across. Or maybe she was just a good actress. Like Mensa-chick Geena Davis.

"Well, thank you," Crawford said. "Now I know. It all sounds pretty admirable... what you do, that is."

"Fuck admirable," Fannie said. "It's long, long overdue, what we do."

The f-bomb slid off her lips like it was nothing more than 'gosh' or 'golly gee.'

"I'm curious about something," Crawford said, "how you ended up in SOAR. Your brother told me a little."

She leaned back in her chair. "Why? You don't think I fit in or something?"

"No, actually I do. You seem very committed to the cause and making SOAR a success."

She looked amused. "And you seem like a very earnest young man."

To the best of his recollection, he had never been called *earnest* before. And *young*? Not in the last five years, at least. Besides, he was pretty sure she was younger than him.

"I wasn't trying to avoid the question," she said, "if there was a question there. See, here's the thing. You can either be rich and buy a lot of things and do whatever the hell you want, or you can be rich and make something of yourself and put your money to good use."

Crawford nodded.

"For the first thirty-two years of my life I bought whatever I wanted and did whatever the hell I wanted—" she laughed "—within reason of course. Then a while ago I decided I wanted to make something of myself. Make a difference somehow. Well, it wasn't going to be in business because I suck at business. And I wasn't going to suddenly become an actress and win an Oscar. And I sure as hell wasn't going to be a famous athlete because I'm not very coordinated—" she laughed again "—so it was pretty easy to rule out a lot of things."

"So, you decided to... do good?"

"Well, yes, I guess that's true, but I am not without ego. I wanted to be involved in something that will change the world. That will make it a better place. But I also must confess I want people to say, *Oh, yeah, SOAR... that's Fannie Melhado's brainchild.*"

That was a bit of a curveball. "But... isn't it Crux's brainchild?"

Fannie put her hand up. "Yeah, you are absolutely right… I meant to say, *Crux and Fannie Melhado's brainchild."*

Crawford made note of this, realizing that having a goal of being the next Joseph Smith, John Calvin or Jesus Christ was a lofty ambition. He wasn't sure what to say next and decided to go in a whole new direction. "So, I'm just going to come right out and ask, who do you think did it? Killed Christian Lalley? Or if you don't want to speculate on that, what do you think the killer's motive might have been?"

"I'm sorry, but I have absolutely no idea. It's not as though I saw someone walking around with a knife dripping blood—"

"No, of course not."

"Sorry, I didn't mean to be flip, it's just this whole thing makes us look so damn bad. It's a real set-back."

"I understand. I get that," Crawford said. "I have another question. Do you know how Marie-Claire Fournier died?"

"A brain aneurism, supposedly."

"Supposedly?"

"Why do you ask?"

"Because that's what I do."

"And seems like you're pretty good at it."

"Thank you, but I'm just asking basic questions," Crawford said. "Have you ever heard any other theories about what happened to Ms. Fournier?"

"Isn't a brain aneurism enough?"

"So, you never heard there might have been foul play?"

Fannie shook her head slowly. "You actually call it that? Foul play?"

Crawford shrugged. "Yeah, I agree, sounds a little dated. But that *is* what we call it."

Fannie shrugged back. "Okay."

"So, you never heard anything else about Ms. Fournier?" he persisted.

"You're a real dog with a bone," Fannie said. "Why would someone kill her?"

"I don't know, that's what I'm trying to figure out. Maybe it actually was an aneurism," Crawford said. "Let me go back to something from earlier."

"What's that?"

"Do you think Christian Lalley could have been killed by an outsider?"

She rubbed her chin. "I have absolutely no idea. But I hope so."

"Why?"

"Why do you think? 'Cause if it's someone in SOAR, the black eye will be even blacker."

Crawford nodded, then put his hand on his chin and thought for a second. "Why is it that you don't have the name of a star or something in the solar system? You know, like a lot of the others."

Fannie chuckled. "Fuck that. I gotta tell you, I think that whole star thing's kinda bogus. I mean, come on. Plus, I've got enough money to tell Crux I'll stick to Fannie, thank you very much."

She had refreshing honesty, in addition to her other attributes.

Crawford nodded and reached for his wallet. "Thank you, Ms. Melhado. Here are two cards"—he handed them to her—"in case you think of anything else."

"You think I might lose one?"

"No, the second one's for your brother. I forgot to give him one," Crawford said. "Oh, one final question."

"Yes?"

"Just curious, are you a Mensa?"

"No," she said, putting his cards in her leather handbag, and smiling, "but pretty damn close."

EIGHT

AFTER A LONG, exhausting afternoon of asking the same question to thirty-two different people, both detectives were weary and didn't know that much more than they had before. Whereas the Melhados were refreshingly candid, as was Vega to some degree, the others seemed like a bunch of highly intelligent eggheads bordering on sheep, who provided answers that were virtual carbon copies of everyone else's responses.

Crawford and Ott got back to the police station at just before five. They adjourned to their separate offices—well, office for Crawford and "executive cubicle," as Ott called his space—and jumped back onto the Lalley case. Crawford was convinced that there was more to the Marie-Claire Fournier death than he had heard so far. Ott had gotten phone numbers for Christian Lalley's ex-wife and brother and was eager to question them.

At just before eight o'clock, Ott called it a day. Twenty minutes later Crawford headed over to his apartment in West Palm.

SIMON PETRIE WAS WALKING his dog, Chief, along Washington Road in West Palm Beach on a loop they took every morning and night. It was exactly one point six miles. Petrie knew because it was one of the many functions his Apple Watch Series 5 performed. Petrie had researched all the functions his watch was capable of and figured he used at most two percent of them. Measuring his walk with Chief was his most commonly used function by far.

He walked late every night, after the eleven o'clock news. He liked to pick a story he had just heard on the news and memorize it word for word. Then he'd repeat it to Chief on their walk. Odd? Very possibly, but maybe it was just one of those things Mensa people did for amusement. If another pedestrian came along when he was reciting the news story to Chief, he'd stop, then continue on after the person was out of earshot.

Petrie was crossing a street when he heard footsteps approaching behind him. He stopped his recitation to Chief—it was about the armed robbery of a jewelry store up in Palm Beach Gardens—then felt a sharp pain in his right shoulder. It felt like someone had bashed him with a baseball bat, except the pain was more pinpointed. As he staggered under the attack, he felt another stab of intense pain in his neck and knew it was a knife. He tried to turn but couldn't. He heard Chief yelp and he released his grip on the leash. Then he felt the man behind him push up against his back and, this time, felt a sudden pain in his chest. He realized that the man had reached over his shoulder and plunged the knife into his upper chest. Petrie screamed out in pain and started to fall forward as he saw Chief bare his fangs and charge the man from the side.

Chief growled ferociously, a menacing sound Petrie had never heard in the four years he'd owned the dog. Then he heard a cry from his assailant and saw out of the corner of his eye the man slash his knife at Chief, missing by a few inches. As Petrie fell to the ground, he caught a glimpse of the man as he turned and ran. He tried to get a look at his face but all he saw was a dark gray hoodie. Chief didn't chase the man but just started whimpering. Petrie saw blood on one paw and didn't know if it was his own, the dog's, or the assailant's. Chief hunched into a crouch and licked Petrie's face.

"We're going to be okay, boy," Petrie said, but he wasn't so sure. He was losing a lot of blood.

Then a shape appeared on the sidewalk in front of him about twenty feet away.

"Are you all right?" a woman shouted. She was wearing a running outfit. "I heard a scream."

And that was when Simon Petrie lost consciousness.

CRAWFORD WAS in the middle of that dream that everyone has, the one where you wake up in a sweaty panic about not having done your homework. He had another recurring one in which he was walking with some faceless woman—not Dominica or Rose or anyone he knew—in a park. All of a sudden, he heard the shrill roar of a low flying airplane above him, then he watched in horror as it crashed into a stand of tall pine trees.

He woke up in a cold sweat and thought about both dreams for a moment. He wondered what a shrink would say about them. Did they symbolize something? Were they harbingers of something? Or, remembering the old Shakespeare quote from a course at Dartmouth, was it all *sound and fury, signifying nothing?* He always liked that quote—how it applied to so many things—and decided that's probably all it was.

Eyes open now, he heard a sharp noise somewhere and didn't know whether it was part of his dream or real life. He woke fully now and realized the noise was the ring of his cell phone beside the bed. He reached for it.

"H'lo."

"Charlie, it's me"—it was Ott— "that guy Simon Petrie got mugged. He's at Good Sam in pretty bad shape. I'm on my way."

Crawford slid one leg over the side of the bed. "All right, see you there," he said and clicked off.

Good Samaritan hospital was fifteen minutes from Crawford's condo in West Palm. He knew he could get dressed in three minutes—three and a half if he was tying a tie. He skipped the tie.

He and Ott pulled up to the emergency ward of the hospital at exactly the same time.

"These cult people are really cutting into my sleep time," Ott said, shaking his head as he approached Crawford.

Crawford chuckled. "Or in this case, a 'disgruntled former member.'"

They walked under an overhead light and Crawford noticed that one of Ott's shirt tails hadn't been tucked in, and it looked like he was wearing one blue sock and one black one. Crawford figured close enough and chose not to point it out as they moved quickly through the emergency ward door.

"You got any more details?" Crawford asked.

"He got attacked is all I know," Ott said, flagging down a man in scrubs. "Knife wounds on his neck and chest. Lost a shitload of blood."

"Guy with a knife seems to be getting around," Crawford said.

"Yeah, I wonder if there's a way to match it up with Christian Lalley?"

"That might be tough."

The man in scrubs came over.

"We're looking for the victim of a stabbing, took place a little while ago. Name's Petrie."

"Yes, sure," the man said, pointing, "go in this door here. Hang a right then you'll see him."

"Thanks," Crawford said.

Ott nodded and led the way through the door. Even though Ott's legs were considerably shorter than Crawford's, he could get them churning at a pretty good clip.

They followed the directions and stopped at a large room in which five or six doctors and nurses were bustling around, all apparently in the midst of saving the life of the man in the blood-spattered hospital bed. Amid it all, Crawford spotted Petrie's distinctive brush cut, his hair standing straight up but splotched with blood.

"Can't die with all those people taking care of you," Ott said.

"You wouldn't think so," said Crawford, noticing a West Palm Beach uniform walk into the room.

Crawford caught his attention and walked over to him. "Hey, you the first-on-scene?"

"Yeah."

"Detective Crawford, my partner, Detective Ott. Palm Beach homicide."

"I heard of you," the uniform said. "I'm Officer Green. Len Green."

"What can you tell us?" Crawford asked.

Green cocked his head. "Well, this woman jogger showed up right after it went down. Told me the guy was getting mugged. Put up some resistance, I guess, after the guy knifed him."

"How many knife wounds?"

"I'm not sure. Three, maybe four?"

"He missing anything?" Ott asked. "Wallet? Watch?"

"Think the guy got his wallet," Green said. "Jogger told me she heard the vic's dog growling and barking. Maybe saved his life."

"Jogger get a look at the perp?" Ott asked.

"Not really. The usual. Dark clothes, wearin' a hoodie."

"White? Black? Any description?"

"I got her name and number 'case you want to call her."

"Yeah, give it to me, please," Ott said.

The uniform handed Ott a card. "I need it back."

"Sure," Ott said, raising his old leather notebook. "I'll write it down."

"So, Len," Crawford said, "what's the area like where it happened. Pretty safe, right?"

"Yeah, every so often there'll be an incident," Green said. "Why you guys lookin' into it?"

"'Cause we interviewed the vic on something else yesterday."

"Was it that murder up on North Lake Way?"

"Yeah, it was... you know anything about it?"

"Nah, sorry. Just they're not all that common in Palm Beach."

"Yeah, don't happen much," Crawford said, giving Green a pat on the shoulder. "Well, thanks, for the info, Len." Looking over at the closed eyes of Simon Petrie on the hospital bed, he said, "Guess we're not going to talk to our guy tonight."

Green glanced over at Petrie. "Doesn't look it. Glad I could help."

Ott shook his hand. "Thanks."

"Sure, man."

Crawford and Ott walked away from Green. "You thinking what I'm thinking?" Ott asked.

"That it was an attempt to kill the guy made to look like a mugging?"

Ott nodded.

NINE

It was not a quality Crawford was particularly proud of. It first reared its head four months into his partnership with Ott, when Crawford took a woman out to lunch who he had absolutely no romantic interest in. He simply wanted to pick her brain about a case he was working. Then, Ott had gotten wind of it.

"And here I thought you were a complete saint. Charlie," Ott had said, shaking his head.

"You're right, I am. Why?"

Ott chuckled. "Using that woman you took out for lunch to get intel."

Crawford explained that since they had bupkis on the case, he felt it necessary to take a leave of absence from sainthood, at least temporarily. Until they came up with something. And, as it turned out, something his lunch date told him did jump-start the case and led to them clearing the murder two weeks later.

He was about to do it again: pick a woman's brain under the guise of taking her out to lunch. In this case it was Vega, a woman who clearly knew a lot about SOAR, and, he thought, knew more than she had revealed in their first interview. She also seemed pretty close to

Crux, having been a member of SOAR since back in the beginning, as well as being a current resident of Elysium.

He pulled the piece of paper out of his wallet that Vega had given him and dialed her number.

She answered after the third ring. "Hello?"

"Hi, Vega, it's Charlie Crawford. *Detective* Charlie Crawford."

"You didn't need to add that, Charlie. You're not that forgettable."

"I guess that's a good thing," Crawford said. "So, I just wondered, can I buy you lunch?"

"When?"

"Today, I was thinking."

"So you can pick my brain?"

Busted.

"Well, no, just because I'm sick of watching my partner eat. His table manners are atrocious."

Which was kind of true.

"I know. I've seen him wrestle with those big, greasy sausages at Greens."

"Not pretty, right?"

She laughed. "What time?"

"How's 12:30? At Greens? I'll pick you up."

"No need. I'll just take my bike. It's a pretty short ride down North Lake Way."

"Sounds good. See you then."

Talk about quick and easy.

WHEN VEGA WALKED into Green's she was wearing her dark brown hair up and looked quite attractive. She was dressed in a short beige skirt, which made Crawford wonder how that could have been compatible with pedaling a bicycle. Vega, possibly because she was a Mensa, seemed to anticipate his unasked question.

"I decided to walk after all," she said.

He nodded as he held her chair. "Welcome to Greens."

"Do all detectives have such good manners?"

"Every single one of 'em," Crawford said without hesitation. "Charm school's part of our training."

He walked around the table and sat facing her. "So, do you have a favorite thing here, since you seem like a... semi-regular?"

She picked up the menu, then put it down without looking at it. "I'm a vegetable-wrap gal."

Crawford smiled. "How's that ever going to put meat on your bones?"

"Because I have a side of tater tots."

Crawford nodded and chuckled. "Now you're talkin'. An excellent choice."

Vega nodded. "How about you?"

"The mouth-watering sardine platter with egg wedges and... tater tots"

Vega frowned. "Ew, gross. Sardines?"

He'd had to defend the oily little fish before and had his standard defense ready. "Little suckers are packed with nutrients and protein and an excellent source of omega-3 fatty acids."

"You sound like a commercial. Except I doubt they'd refer to them as *little suckers* in ads. I can't stand to even look at 'em—they're like oysters. *Ug-lee!*" she said with a shudder.

"Another one of my favorites. Oysters."

"Yuck," Vega said. "I guess we're just not very compatible in the culinary department."

"That's not true. The tater tots... can't live without 'em."

Crawford had learned to restrain himself whenever he was champing at the bit to question someone about a case. Dominica and Rose had called him out on it more than once. To the point where Rose had accused him of being virtually inept at conversational fore-play and Dominica had called him *All-Business Charlie* on several occasions.

Much as it was contrary to his nature, he figured he'd stick with non-dead guy questions for a bit longer. "So, I'm curious, where'd you grow up?" he asked her after they'd ordered.

"Why are you curious about that?"

"I just am. I'm going with the Midwest."

Vega shook her head. "Oxford, Mississippi."

"No kiddin'. Deep in the heart of Dixie."

"Yup. It doesn't get much deeper," Vega said, spearing a tater tot, then another.

"You don't have any accent."

"Yankee parents."

Crawford nodded. "So, where'd you go from there?"

"Yale University. Deep in the heart of beautiful downtown New Haven. How 'bout you?"

"Your Ivy League rival to the north...Dartmouth. Mensa scholarship."

Vega laughed. "Yeah, right,"

Not particularly funny, but a good transitional opportunity. "What's that about anyway, all you SOAR people being Mensas?"

"*Almost* all," Vega said, poking at her vegetable wrap. "I don't really know what it's all about, tell you the truth."

"It kind of limits the ability of SOAR to grow, doesn't it? I mean, it's a very small pool; there just aren't that many Mensas out there to recruit."

Vega put her fork down and wiped her mouth. "Let me explain a little because I'm sure you're just dying to know. Think of us—the forty-three members of SOAR—as kind of a Board of Directors. Crux calls us "the founders," meaning we collectively, in effect, came up with a constitution, then a game-plan for spreading the beliefs of SOAR across the country, and then, if all goes well, the world. And, just to be clear, we have no intention of requiring future SOAR converts to be Mensas. Or else it *would* be a very rarified religion. Hell, we'll take you if you got an IQ of eighty."

"Phew. I'd just make the cut-off."

"The modest detective," Vega said with a wide smile.

Crawford smiled. "So, you're in the early stages now, right?"

"Oh, yes, absolutely, the *early, early* stages. I don't expect to be around when it really ramps up and gets big," Vega said, picking up her fork again and taking a bite of her vegetable wrap.

"I've got so many questions I don't know where to start—so what exactly are the beliefs, or I guess you'd call it, the ideology of SOAR?"

Vega smiled. "We'd need fifty lunches for me to answer that question adequately. Suffice it to say that we share certain tenets of Zen Buddhism and Sikhism with certain elements of Crux-inspired ideology thrown in. That probably doesn't help much."

"Ah, I'm a little rusty on both Zen Buddhism and Sikhism. But I'm guessing you do a lot of meditation and reflection? Stuff like that? All I know about the Sikhs is they wear those turbans."

"Yes, and as you've seen, we don't."

"Why not?"

Vega thought for a moment. "Well, I'd say because we believe most Americans are suspicious, or maybe distrustful is the right word, of people who wear turbans."

"Really?"

"Oh, I'm sure you're aware of that. We've actually had long discussions about this," she said. "Not to mention, a turban's too damn hot in Florida."

"I hear you on that," Crawford said, nodding. "And so... how many members do you expect to end up with... say twenty years from now?"

"Crux's prognostication is that in ten years, a million members. In twenty years, five million. In fifty years twenty-five million."

Crawford whistled.

"If you think *that's* a lot, you should read the projections on the growth of Islam. I remember the figures: 1.6 billion ten years ago, to 2.76 billion in 2050."

"Not sure I want to be around then. We're gonna have a pretty packed universe."

Vega smiled. "I'm guessing you'll be a spry ninety-year-old then."

The magnitude of what Crawford was hearing was mind-boggling. A religion from out of nowhere, born in the unlikely and rarified air of Palm Beach, with twenty-five million members in fifty years.

"Do you call it a religion, a sect, or what?"

It was like Vega had been asked the question before. "We just call it SOAR."

Crawford nodded. "So, change of subject: Christian Lalley, you've had time to think about it, who do you think might have killed your friend? Of the forty-three members of SOAR, would anyone have had a motive, or was there anyone you can think of who just plain didn't like the man? I mean, *really* didn't like the man."

This time Vega speared a threesome of tater tots, then put the fork down, saving them. "I honestly don't know. I mean, there're politics in SOAR and definitely a hierarchy, but Christian was on the descent, not the ascent. The power he had was in the past. Crux, I'm sure, deemed him not enough of a heavyweight to handle SOAR's finances when their assets went from a hundred million to a billion. Which is why he brought in Guy Bemmert."

Crawford had a fleeting memory of Bemmert from one of his first interviews the day before.

Vega thought for a moment, then. "You seem like a nice guy and a good detective—I read about a case of yours, by the way, in the *Post*—so I'm going to give you a tip. Look into Leo Peavy. Look deep into Leo Peavy." Crawford clearly remembered Leo Peavy—one of the men he'd also interviewed the day before. He had rheumy, watery eyes closest in color to a washed-out, faded yellow; thick, mutton-chop sideburns (think Neil Young circa 1985), and thin brown hair combed straight forward

"Look into him... how do you mean?"

"He's just one of those guys who bears examination. That's all I'm going to say on that subject," Vega said. "But I'll give you another scoop while I'm gossiping."

"Please do."

Vega leaned closer to Crawford and lowered her voice. "Do you know what blabbermouth soup is?"

He smiled. "No, can't say I do."

Vega smiled. "It's another name for a martini," she said. "So, every couple of weeks or so, Christian and I would go to Ta-boo for Happy Hour and get...well, happy."

Crawford laughed. "Martinis will do that."

"No kidding. And as the name implies, Christian sometimes would get pretty talkative."

Crawford was eager to know where the story was going but didn't want to push it.

Vega read him. "I know, I know, 'Get on with the story, Vega,'" she said. "So, do you remember that scandal a year or so ago when the bank president here was accused of having young boys come to his house for… whatever?"

"Yeah, like that guy Epstein, but boys instead of girls."

Vega nodded. "Except it was all… you'll excuse the expression, bullshit."

Crawford couldn't remember all the details except it ran under big lurid headlines in the *Palm Beach Post*. He wasn't seeing the connection to Christian Lalley but guessed he soon would. "So, go on, tell me about it."

She lowered her voice to a whisper. "Do you know anything about Crux's father?"

Crawford shrugged. "Nothing except he was recruited from a bank in New Zealand to head a British bank in New York. Got fired, as I remember it."

"Okay, here's the whole story: so, the banker who took over after Crux's father got fired was that same guy who got accused of pedophilia with those boys here."

"You're kidding."

"No, and it gets worse. That same man who got accused—Whitmore's his name—supposedly had an affair with Crux's mother when Crux's father was off on some gambling junket somewhere"

Crawford shook his head slowly. "Jesus, this is a lot to comprehend. And when did all this take place?"

"Long time back. Like twenty, maybe twenty-five years ago. So according to Christian, who knew Crux way back then, Crux always had it in for this guy Whitmore… I forget his first name. Crux apparently has a very long memory."

"Boy, I'll say," Crawford said putting up a hand. "So now, I've got a ton of questions."

"I figured you would. I'll try to answer them as best as I can, but here's a little bit more," Vega said. "According to Christian, Crux and Peavy came up with a plan to, excuse my mouth"—she looked around to make sure the waitress wasn't nearby—"fuck over Whitmore." Suddenly, she snapped her fingers. "*Now* I remember: his first name is

Holmes. Holmes Whitmore. Anyway, Christian figured that it was probably Peavy's plan, but Crux approved it. Approved it with gusto, no doubt. So, what Peavy did was hire these boys to go—one by one, over a period of a few days— to the rear door of Whitmore's house, then just stand there. In the meantime, they were caught on surveillance cameras from the street."

Crawford was staggered. "That was it? So, you mean, they never went inside?"

Vega nodded.

Wow, thought Crawford, the plan was perfect in its simplicity. He remembered seeing one of the tapes on WPEC news, the CBS affiliate. A grainy photo of a boy, maybe twelve or thirteen, casting his eyes around furtively in what was clearly the back door of a recognizable house. Holmes Whitmore's house, it turned out. That was the only one he saw, but he remembered hearing there were also tapes of two other boys as well. What was amazing was that Holmes Whitmore was tried and convicted in the court of public opinion by three tapes that didn't even show any of the boys going into his house.

As Crawford recalled, Whitmore was never tried; he moved away from Palm Beach after vehemently denying any guilt. But no one, it seemed, not a soul, was buying his innocence.

"So that was Crux's revenge, huh, for something that happened twenty years ago?"

"Yeah, apparently his father and mother got divorced after her affair with Whitmore. And I forgot which—either the mother or the father—turned into a raging alcoholic." Vega shrugged. "Maybe both of 'em"

"So—"

"I know. Now you have a gazillion questions," Vega said. "So, how'd Christian find out about all this is one question, right?"

Crawford nodded.

"Christian, who was treasurer of SOAR at the time, had the job of being... well, the unflattering word for it is *bagman.* Meaning he paid off each of those boys. Two hundred dollars apiece to go up to the back door of Whitmore's house and be caught by the cameras. He was also told to pay them a thousand apiece to claim they had sex with Whitmore. But it never got that far."

"He was told. By who?"

"By Peavy."

"Not Crux."

"No, but Christian figured the order came from Crux," Vega said. "Anyway, turned out the boys were never called on to testify or anything. They never were even interviewed by the cops. The damage done just by those tapes alone was plenty."

Crawford shook his head. "Unbelievable."

"In defense of Christian, he had a lot of guilt about that whole incident."

"But he did it anyway."

Vega nodded solemnly. "And there's another chapter."

Crawford tried not to look too eager.

"Fast-forward a year. A reporter named Jerry Kopinski, who somehow got word that the whole thing was trumped up, contacted Christian. He told Christian he had some hard evidence about the set-up and wanted to interview him."

"And?"

Vega looked down and tapped her fingers on the tabletop. "And two days later… Christian was dead."

TEN

"HO-LY SHIT," Ott said.

He was in Crawford's office, facing his partner, who had just laid out the entire Holmes Whitmore story that Vega had recounted at lunch.

"Pretty incredible, huh?" Crawford said, shaking his head.

"How to ruin someone's life and only spend six hundred bucks doing it."

Crawford put his leg up on his desk. "What do you think of the timing?"

"You mean, Lalley getting offed right before the reporter could question him?"

Crawford nodded.

"I think we should go see our friend Crux again," Ott said. "Along with this guy Peavy."

"I agree," Crawford said. "I also want to check into Vega."

"Why?"

"I don't know. Just... anybody as forthcoming as she was with all that information... I just wonder why."

"I know what you mean. So, want me to call Crux?" Ott asked. "Set up another meet."

"Yeah. I'll call the newspaper reporter," Crawford said.

WHILE CRAWFORD WAS HAVING lunch with Vega, Ott had had a guest at the station. Her name was Kelly Wick, and she was the woman jogger who might just have saved Simon Petrie's life by showing up when she did. She had volunteered to come into the police station when Ott called her. Ott interviewed her in a corner of the reception area.

Ott had his old leather notebook out and was facing her. "So, what was the first thing you saw or heard, Ms. Wick?"

"I heard something that was like a half-scream and half-groan," Wick said. "Then right after that I heard a dog barking. To be honest with you, my first reaction was to run."

"Can't say I blame you," Ott said, "but you didn't. So, what happened next?"

"I walked toward the noises, then I saw movement. One man was in back of another man and I saw his arm go forward fast."

"The man who was behind the other man?"

"Yes, which was when I saw the knife in his hand."

"And the dog?"

"The dog was barking really loud a few feet away," she said. "Then it charged the man holding the knife. And he tried to stab the dog. As he did, he let go of the man he stabbed."

"And the man who had been stabbed... fell to the ground?"

Wick nodded. "And the one with the knife started running."

"Did you get any kind of a look at him?"

"Not really. Obviously, it was dark, plus he was wearing a hoodie."

"How tall would you say he was?"

She sighed. "It was really hard to tell. I mean, taller than the man who got stabbed, but he was kind of bent over."

"Rough guess, how tall?"

"Um, maybe six feet."

"White or black man?"

"White?"

"And did you get a look at the knife?"

"Just for a split second. There was kind of a glint off of it. I don't know whether it was from the moon or the streetlamp. But the streetlamp was pretty far away."

"When you say a glint, what exactly do you mean?"

"I mean, the blade was silver, so it kinda caught the light."

"Gotcha. And how long would you say the knife was?"

"Really long. The blade especially."

"So definitely not like a pocketknife or something?"

"Oh God no, it looked like it was close to a foot long. Maybe longer."

"And when the man ran, which way did he go?"

"I'm not sure. I was more interested in helping the man who got stabbed."

"That was good of you. But the man, the attacker—"

"I never saw him after that."

Ott closed his notebook. "Well, thank you very much, Ms. Wick. I appreciate you coming in."

"No problem. Happy to help."

Ott stood, then reached into his wallet and pulled out a card. "Here you go," he said, giving her a card, "in case you remember anything else that might be helpful, please give me a call."

She took it. "I sure will."

ELEVEN

IT WAS three in the afternoon. Crawford and Ott had a busy remainder of the day scheduled. Crux had agreed to meet them at 3:30, and they expected things might get a little heated when he found out what the topic of conversation was.

After meeting with him, they would drop by the hospital to see Simon Petrie. And at six, they were scheduled to meet the reporter, Jerry Kopinski, from the *Palm Beach Post*, at Mookie's Tap-a-Keg, their unabashedly downscale cop bar on the shaky side of West Palm Beach.

Five minutes after pulling into the driveway of 1500 North Lake Way, they were facing Crux in his throne-like chair. Crawford half-expected him to be wearing a crown.

Crux greeted them cordially. "So, fellas, are you getting anywhere on Christian's murder? Any progress, I hope?"

Crawford gave him Standard Answer Number Three, Variation Two. "We're pursuing a lot of different angles at this point. Talking to as many people as we can. People who might be helpful in solving it."

"So… that's a no," Crux said, bluntly.

Exactly what Chief Norm Rutledge would have said.

"We want to ask you about an incident that recently came to light," Crawford said.

"Okay," said Crux with a smile. "What's that?"

"An incident involving Holmes Whitmore"—Crux's smile morphed into a wrinkled frown—"that took place a year ago or so."

"You do know Whitmore, right?" Ott asked.

Crux sighed painfully, like he'd been ambushed. "Yeah, I know him."

Crawford nodded. "So, we don't need to rehash everything involving your father and mother—"

"Get on with it," Crux cut in. "What's this got to do with anything?"

"We think maybe a lot," Crawford said. "We heard there's someone in the media"—he didn't want to give away Kopinski's identity by calling him a newspaper reporter—"who believes Whitmore may have been set up."

"What are you talking about? The guy was a pedophile."

Crawford nodded. "Yeah, well, so it seemed, but let me ask you a question."

Crux's frown got deeper. "What?"

Crawford looked over at Ott. "You want to frame it, Mort?"

"Sure," Ott said. "Okay, let's just say you lived in a house. Not this one, but a house where you lived all alone—" Ott paused "—and you saw three photos on the news of three different young boys standing outside your back door. And you knew for a fact—there was absolutely no question about it—that none of those boys ever stepped foot inside your house… would you think it fair that everyone had jumped to the conclusion that you were a pedophile?"

Crux groaned. "Come on, that's ridiculous, the guy was clearly guilty."

"Is that right?" Ott said. "What *real* proof is there?"

"Is it possible that your right-hand man, Leo Peavy, came up with the whole thing?" Crawford asked.

"Yeah, we heard he's got a rep for being kind of a dirty trickster," Ott chimed in.

Crawford nodded. "Maybe he planted evidence. Sent photos of the three boys to a few TV stations and newspapers?"

"What's Leo Peavy got to do with this whole bullshit scenario?"

"That's exactly what we're going to be talking to the media person about."

"What the hell's the point of all this?" Crux said, shaking his head with all the disdain he could muster.

"Point is, Christian Lalley might have been killed because of something he was about to reveal."

"And point number two is, you might have been behind what happened to Holmes Whitmore," Ott added.

Crux laughed derisively. "I'm hearing the word *might* a lot here... Now just imagine if a prosecutor in a court of law were to say, 'this defendant *might* have done this, this *might* have happened.'" He added a head-shake to his derisive laugh. "I mean, come on, you guys really are desperate, aren't you? You come here and try to connect me and one of my congregants to a guy who committed a bunch of sex crimes. Maybe you ought to be reminded of your mission: to find who killed a beloved member of my congregation, Christian Lalley. Now... I've got better things to do with my time."

He motioned with his hand as if he was shooing away a pair of annoying fleas.

TWELVE

"WELL, it's not like we expected him to say, *Hell, yeah, I did it, boys, slap the cuffs on me,*" Ott said, as they walked down the steps of the house at 1500 North Lake Way. "Fact is, even if he was behind the Whitmore thing, it's not a crime of any great consequence anyway."

"I know, but I'll bet you he'll still be having a nice long conversation with Leo Peavy before we're halfway to Good Sam."

Good Samaritan Hospital in West Palm Beach was only five minutes away. Aside from their late-night visit to see Simon Petrie in the emergency room, the last time they'd been there was when Rose Clarke had been struck by a hit-and-run driver six months before. Rose was, of course, back on her feet now, as good as new, almost like it had never happened.

It turned out that Simon Petrie was in a room on the fourth floor at Good Sam, right next to the one Rose had been in. As with Rose, Crawford had assigned a pair of uniformed cops to remain stationed outside of Petrie's door around the clock. He wasn't sure that it was necessary but didn't want to take any chances.

Petrie was conscious and hooked up to an IV as Crawford and Ott walked into his room.

"Oh, Jesus," Petrie groaned. "You two. Is this what happens when I talk to you? Someone tries to kill me?"

"We're very sorry about what happened, Mr. Petrie," Crawford said. "As I'm sure you know, there are two police officers guarding you and we'll provide round-the-clock protection until you leave the hospital."

"And, if you like, we'll have them watch your house, too," Ott said.

"So, I guess you've come to the conclusion the guy wasn't a mugger," Petrie said.

"What do you think?" Crawford asked.

"That whoever it was wanted to take my life, not my wallet."

Crawford nodded. "Do you have any idea who might have done it?"

Petrie thought for a few moments. "I'm thinking it might not be such a good idea talking to you about it."

Crawford had run across resistance like this many times before. "I hear what you're saying, but look at it this way, you help us find the guy who did it and you're out of harm's way."

"I look at it *this* way," Petrie countered: "If you *don't* catch him and he finds out I've been talking to you, he's even more motivated to kill me."

"Whoever it is, isn't getting past those men at the door," Ott said.

Petrie fell silent for a few moments.

"Is the name Holmes Whitmore familiar to you, Mr. Petrie?" Crawford asked.

Petrie winced at the name.

"I can see he is," Crawford said. "How about Jerry Kopinski?"

Petrie nodded. "He contacted me."

"And I'm assuming he asked you what you knew about Whitmore's connection to Crux?"

"He did."

"That Crux and Leo Peavy set up Whitmore with those three boys?"

Petrie hesitated, then managed a half-nod.

"So, he was looking for corroboration of the story he got from Christian Lalley. And the reason he contacted you was because Lalley probably told him you knew about the affair between Crux's mother and Whitmore because you knew Crux way back in college."

Petrie shrugged. "What do you need me for? You've got the whole thing sussed out."

Crawford smiled. "Not entirely. So, if the reporter publishes that story, it could lead to the downfall of Crux and Peavy and maybe others."

"So, the question is, is anyone else involved?" asked Ott.

A nurse walked into the room. She ignored Crawford and Ott. "How you doing, Simon?"

"I'm okay," he said. "Is dinner soon?"

"In about twenty minutes... meatloaf."

He frowned. "Yummy."

"Beats that delicious Salisbury steak last night," she said, and walked out of the room.

"Not great food, huh?" Ott asked.

"Reminds me of British swill," the Englishman said.

"Who else might have been involved in trying to kill you, Mr. Petrie?" Crawford repeated Ott's question.

"I don't know," Petrie said. "This is just speculation. I reckon maybe the chink... or the new CFO and his boy toy or maybe Fannie Melhado or that jackass Peavy—"

"Wait a minute, slow down," Ott said, "how many people do you have on your list?"

"Umm, that's about it."

"Okay, of those people you just said—four, I think—tell us about them."

"Actually five. So, the chink—I know that's not politically correct —is a man named Xi Kiang. Crux recruited him, I think anyway, to build up the membership of SOAR. That's what he did in China, apparently, though I don't know all the details."

"I remember him from the interviews," Ott said to Crawford. "Not real chatty. A lot of 'yes/ no' answers."

"Coulda just been conveniently blanking out on the English language."

"That occurred to me," Ott said with a nod. "So, after the, ah, Chinaman you mentioned the new CFO and his... *boy toy?*"

"Yeah, they're married and live down in Boca."

Ott glanced over at Crawford. "Really? And what are their names?"

They hadn't interrogated these two, presumably because they lived down in Boca and hadn't taken part at the Elysium interviews.

Petrie scratched his forehead. "Let's see, the CFO is named Guy Bemmert and the boy toy is Larry Swain."

"And then, I believe," Ott said, "you said Fannie Melhado and Leo Peavy."

"No, I said, that 'jackass Peavy.'"

"Right," Ott said. "So why those five?"

"Xi Kiang because he's just an all-around mysterious, inscrutable Asian guy and hardly ever speaks. Bemmert and Swain because, I don't know, there's just something about them that I don't trust. Fannie because she's so damn ambitious, despite her billions. Leo Peavy just because he's an arrogant jackass and I just get the sense that he's got a murky past that he doesn't want anybody to know about."

"O-kay," Crawford said. "That's all pretty general, do you have anything a little more specific?"

Petrie cocked his head and thought for a few moments. "You know, you have to bear in mind I haven't been around SOAR in a while, so I've forgotten things."

"Understood," Crawford said. "Do us a favor, and give it a little more thought, will you. And if there's anything you remember that might be helpful to us, please give us a call right away."

"Indeed, I will."

"So, Guy Bemmert took over from Christian Lalley, right?" Ott asked.

"Yes, exactly," Petrie said, raising his hand. "Oh, wait, I just remembered something that might help you, Larry Swain punched Christian once. Knocked him out, actually."

"Really?" Ott asked. "Why?"

"Because one time after a few drinks, Christian called him a poofter."

Ott, bewildered, glanced at Crawford for clarification.

"A British slur for someone who's gay," Crawford explained.

Petrie nodded and smiled at Ott. "It gets confusing...for us, a fag means a cigarette."

"When was this?" Crawford asked. "When Swain knocked out Lalley?"

"Right before I left SOAR."

"Anyone else, Mr. Petrie?" Ott asked.

Petrie raised his arms. "Nobody I can think of. I mean, I guess it could have been a mugger."

"I don't think so," Crawford said.

"Neither do I," Petrie said.

"What else, Mort?" Crawford asked his partner.

Ott scratched his head. "What about a guy named Pollux? He lives at Fourteen Fifty North Way, what do you know about him?"

"Man's afraid of his own shadow," Petrie said. "Used to be a librarian. Need I say more."

"Thank you," Crawford said. "If you're good with it, we're going to guard you until we solve the case."

Petrie nodded. "What if you never solve it?"

"We will. You've given us some good information to work with."

"Right...well, good luck," Petrie said.

"Thanks," said Crawford. "And good luck with that meatloaf."

THIRTEEN

CRAWFORD AND OTT had spent more time than they expected at Good Sam with Simon Petrie, which meant they were going to be late for their appointment with reporter Jerry Kopinski.

On their way to Mookie's Tap-a-Keg, Crawford called Kopinski to tell him they were on their way, but the call went straight to voicemail.

———————

JERRY KOPINSKI WALKED into Mookie's ahead of schedule and found the Palm Beach detectives hadn't arrived yet.

He sat in a bar stool and Jack Scarsiola came over to him.

"Yes, sir, what can I get ya?" Scarsiola asked.

"Gimme a shot of Jack and a Yuengling. Put it on Charlie Crawford's tab."

"Charlie a friend of yours?" Scarsiola asked.

"Never met the man. But he called and asked for a meet."

Scarsiola nodded and got him his drinks.

Kopinski knocked back the shot of Jack Daniels in one pull and the beer in three.

"Re-load," he told Scarsiola.

Scarsiola looked at him skeptically. "Charlie good with you runnin' up a tab?"

He nodded at the owner. "Hey, man, I don't come cheap."

From behind Kopinski a voice rang out. "Is that you, Kopinski, you lowlife motherfucker?"

Kopinski turned to see a bald undercover cop with a bushy mustache eyeing him with something decidedly less than love.

"Who the hell are you?"

"Buddy Bridges," the man said. "You accused me and my partner of police brutality in that ass-wipe birdcage liner of yours."

Kopinski had to think for a second what Bridges meant by "ass-wipe birdcage liner." Then he got it, a reference to his newspaper, the august *Palm Beach Post*.

He got to his feet, using his above-average height to fend off the angry cop. "Speaking of ass-wipes," he started, but before he could get anything more out, Bridges reared back and threw a round house right to his head.

Kopinski pulled back a few inches and the punch grazed his chin. "That's all you got?" he said, putting his fists up.

"I got this too," Bridges said, and his knee came out of nowhere and smashed Kopinski squarely in the nuts.

As Kopinski lurched forward, Bridges took a hard uppercut swing, catching the much bigger man directly on the nose. Kopinski crashed sideways, breaking a barstool on his way down to the sticky oak floor.

He was out cold.

"What the fuck, Bridges?" growled Scarsiola from behind the bar.

Bridges shrugged. "Big assholes like him can't take a punch," he said. He took a long victory sip of his beer and poured the rest of it on Kopinski's face. "Well, say good-bye to him for me," Bridges said and put twenty bucks down on the bar. "For that piece-of-shit bar stool."

———

CRAWFORD AND OTT had just arrived and were walking in as Bridges strolled out of Mookie's.

"Hey, boys," he greeted Crawford and Ott.

"Hey, Buddy, what's goin' on?" Ott said.

Bridges stopped. "Gotta warn ya, you're gonna need to step over a big mook lyin' on the floor."

"He have one too many?" Ott asked.

"*I* gave him one too many," Bridges said with a proud smile and headed to his car as Crawford and Ott stepped inside Mookie's.

Kopinski was, in fact, on his feet. He was standing shakily, supported by a bar stool, with blood trickling out of his nose.

He matched the description Vega had given Crawford: he stood at least six-five and had a paunch that made Ott look like a beanpole. He was in his late 40s and sported a comb-over that was more like a comb-around. Meaning it started on the right side of his head and went around in almost a full three-hundred-sixty-degree circle.

"Jerry?" Crawford asked.

"Yup?" he said with a slow nod. "Crawford?"

Crawford nodded back, then flicked his head in Ott's direction. "And my partner, Mort Ott."

Ott nodded a hello and handed the reporter a napkin for his nose. "What happened to you?"

"Got sucker-punched," Kopinski said. "I'll get that scumbag. The pen's mightier than the sword."

"So they say," Crawford said.

"How 'bout getting me another drink?" Kopinski asked Scarsiola.

"Another?" Crawford inquired.

Scarsiola shrugged. "He's already had four… on you."

Aw, what the hell, Crawford thought, *it's Chief Rutledge's money.*

Crawford, Ott, and Kopinski got drinks and went over to a table.

"So, what the hell happened?" Crawford asked.

"One of your… cop buddies didn't like a story I wrote."

Ott shrugged. "Guess he doesn't know about freedom of the press."

"Yeah, guy's a douchebag."

"Just for the record, you're not the first to mix it up at Mookie's," Ott said.

Crawford knew what he was referring to. Shortly after he and Ott hooked up as partners, they'd had a real donnybrook with two West Palm cops who were drunk and obnoxious. Ott had proven himself to be a man not to be messed with. Crawford had ended up with not one but two goose eggs, one on either side of his head.

"So, what can I do for you guys, besides drink your booze?" Kopinski asked.

"You can tell us what you know about Holmes Whitmore, Christian Lalley, Leo Peavy, and 'Crux,' the head of SOAR," Crawford said, then took a sip of his beer.

"Who?"

That was not the response Crawford had hoped for. "You don't know those names?"

"One of 'em," he said. "Christian Lalley. He was the guy who got killed a few days ago? In Palm Beach?"

"Yeah," Crawford said. "And we have reason to believe he contacted you."

Kopinski scratched his cheek and went into a thousand-yard stare. "Nah, never happened. Who told you that?"

"A source of ours. Said Lalley spoke to you."

"He's misinformed."

"Told us Lalley talked to you about Holmes Whitmore," Ott said.

"Hang on a second," Kopinski said. "Holmes Whitmore? Wasn't he that pedophile… with the three boys? Like from a year ago?"

"Yeah, that's him."

"Story broke when I was on vacation. Bad timing for me… that's the kind of story that's right up my alley."

Ott was staring so hard at Kopinski, it was like he was trying to get a peek into his soul. "You saying you never spoke to Christian Lalley?"

Kopinski shook his head. "I don't forget people who get murdered."

"Did you ever hear the name Leo Peavy or Crux?"

"Crux? What the hell kinda name is that?"

"He's a guy who's the leader of a certain… religious group." Crawford came close to saying cult but didn't want to open up that can of worms.

Kopinski shook his head. "Can't help you, man."

Crawford sat back and pointed at his own empty glass. "If we bought you a couple more drinks, would it shake loose anything in that memory of yours?"

"You don't want me making stuff up, do you?"

"No, but we sure as hell don't want you conveniently forgetting stuff either."

FOURTEEN

"Son-of-a-bitch was lying through his teeth," Ott said as they got into their Crown Vic.

"Yeah, but it was more what he was choosing to forget than lying about."

Ott shut his car door. "You thinkin' someone at SOAR got to him?"

Crawford nodded. "Yup. That's exactly what I'm thinking. With an envelope full of cash."

"So he wouldn't write the story?"

"Exactly."

"I agree," Ott said. "So, what do we do now?"

Crawford looked at his watch. 7:50 p.m. "Me. I'm going to the movies. Been a long day."

"Kind of late for that, isn't it?"

"8:25 show," Crawford said. "Tomorrow we need to go see some of the other guys from SOAR. The ones Petrie mentioned. Xi Kiang, Guy Bemmert and Larry Swain in Boca and Leo Peavy up at Elysium. I'll call 'em after you drop me at the station. Get their numbers from Vega, hopefully."

"Think they might have memory lapses like Kopinski?" Ott asked.

"Oh, I guarantee you they will," Crawford said with a nod. "But we gotta see what we can get out of 'em anyway."

Ott, behind the wheel of the Vic, turned the key in the ignition. "You know, I was just thinking… that's the first time I've ever been to Mookie's and had less than three drinks."

Crawford smiled and shook his head.

"What?" Ott asked.

"Got news for you Mort. That's the first time you've ever been to Mookie's and had less than *five*."

BEFORE CHRISTIAN LALLEY'S MURDER, Dominica McCarthy, crime-scene tech extraordinaire and Crawford's FWB, had asked him to go to a movie at the Mandel Library in West Palm Beach. His antennae went up when she said it was a library—his biggest concern being the unlikelihood of popcorn being served amidst stacks of musty books. Then, after he said *yes*, she told him the name of the movie. It had the world *Le* in it and, he thought, *chien*, which he was pretty sure meant either dog or cat in French. One thing was certain, it was a foreign film, but by then it was too late to back out. What he really wanted to see was a race-car movie that had just come out. Ott, a lifelong wannabe Formula One driver, had already seen it three times and raved about it. Dominica had mentioned that Salvador Dali had something to do with the film and Crawford immediately flashed to pocket watches that looked like they were hanging on clotheslines and a lobster claw telephone handset that he remembered from a gut course in art back at Dartmouth.

He offered to pick Dominica up for the movie— *film*, as she called it—but she said she was going to be near the library beforehand and would meet him there.

At 8:23 he walked into the library and immediately saw Dominica across the room in a clingy black skirt waving at him—not quite frantically, but more than eagerly. He recognized it from past dates as her, *Where the hell have you been?* look. On more than one occasion she had referred to him as *Last-minute Charlie*. She and Rose had lots of nicknames for him.

He picked up the pace and hoofed it up to her. She grabbed his hand and tugged him toward a door. "Jeez, where you been?"

"Sorry, I was at Mookie's."

She rolled her eyes. "Oh, great."

"On business."

"Yeah, I know… monkey business."

"Hey, I figured they'd have previews first."

"Come on, Charlie, this isn't AMC."

They walked into the darkened room, sat on metal chairs, and a few minutes later the film started rolling. It was bizarre from the get-go, with actors playing around with razors, a woman lying on a beach with abundant armpit hair, and a disembodied hand covered with a swarm of ants, but, Crawford was happy to find out, it was a mercifully short film. Like twenty minutes or so.

At the end, he started to stand, but Dominica grabbed his hand and pulled him back down. "There are two more."

Swell, he thought, but smiled dutifully.

The next one at least seemed to have something of a plot, but far from an interesting one. It was about double the length of the dog movie (Dominica confirmed that *chien* did, in fact, mean dog in French.) The third flick could best be described as violently surrealistic, with macho Crawford averting his eyes from the screen several times to look down at the top of his shoes. After a while, the violence died down and it became flat-out boring. To the point where Crawford's eyes got heavy several times until, finally, he nodded off. He was in the first few frames of a nice dream when he felt a sudden pain in his side. It was the sharp elbow of Dominica. "You were snoring," she hissed. (Movies… *er*, films, were about the only places where Dominica hissed.)

Fifteen minutes later, the third "short" ended. With the exception of the first one, the *shorts* had been way too long for Crawford.

Dominica nodded at a few people she knew on the way out and thanked a man who Crawford thought looked French. The man had long hair in a ponytail with glasses that had a slight dark tint to them and sandals with a lot of mileage.

"Was he the guy who put the thing together?" Crawford asked when they were out of earshot of the pony-tailed man.

"Yes, his name is Jean-Paul"—*of course, it was*—"a very nice guy."

Crawford was tempted to show off his knowledge of famous French men and ask, "Belmondo or Sartre?" but held his tongue.

"Can you explain something about the dog movie?" Crawford asked Dominica as they walked out of the library.

Dominica laughed. "Dog movie? You're so cultured, Charlie."

"Thank you," he said. "So, when the cop places the severed hand in the box and gives it to the woman, who then gets run over by a car as the couple watches from the apartment window… what does that all mean?"

Dominica laughed again. "For God's sake, Charlie, they're all a bunch of dreams," she explained. "They mean whatever you want them to."

"I think I liked my own dream better," Crawford said.

"Your own dream?"

"Yeah, when I nodded off halfway through the third one and you jabbed me in the ribs."

"You're terrible."

"I'll take that as a compliment," he said as he held the library door for her. "Hey, how 'bout I come over to your place?"

She grabbed his hand as they went down the library steps. "Didn't I tell you, my mother's staying with me for a few days."

That wasn't part of the plan that he had drawn up in his head earlier that night. "Then… why don't you come over to my place?"

"Come on, Charlie. I don't want my mother thinking I'm a tramp."

Crawford thought for a second. "Well, how 'bout just staying for a little while then?"

Dominica shook her head. "You mean, for as long as it takes us to make love."

"I was thinking as long as it takes us to make love *twice*."

He spotted Dominica's car, walked toward it, and went around to open its door. "Or we could always have a quickie in the car." He held up his hands. "Just kidding."

"Yeah, but if I said yes, you probably would."

"Probably."

She shot him both the eyeroll *and* the headshake. "So that's all I am to you… a sex object?"

"No, you're a woman who introduces me to culture—you know, like women with hairy armpits and hands covered with ants—*and* a sex object." He leaned forward and kissed her on the mouth. "Good night."

"You're not as funny as you think."

"I'm not trying to be funny," he said. "I'm just trying to wrap my head around all that symbolism and dream interpretation."

FIFTEEN

THE ONE-TWO PUNCH. First, Dominica, then Rose.

He called Rose first thing in the morning, aware that he'd already tapped her knowledge of the Lalley case and didn't want to overdo it.

She said she had a nine o'clock croquet lesson at the Palm Beach Country Club at the S turn on North Ocean Boulevard. He didn't realize you needed a lesson on something as basic as how to hammer a wooden ball through a bunch of wickets.

Rose was dressed in white pants, white Nikes with orange soles, and a snug-fitting Lacoste shirt. The instructor, a skinny man in his fifties, was wearing the exact same thing, except his collar was popped. Not one of Crawford's favorite looks. The man introduced himself as Edmundo-Ernesto something, and Rose added that he was a former runner-up in the World Croquet Championship in Cairo and number three ranked player in the U.S.

Nothing but the best for Rose.

She hit the ball while Edmundo-Ernesto critiqued her technique, although Crawford noticed her instructor paid particularly close attention to her cleavage when she bent over to line up a shot.

Crawford admired the manicured croquet court. "This looks better groomed than the greens at Augusta," he commented, referring to the course where the Masters was played.

Edmundo-Ernesto just nodded. He seemed to have decided a Palm Beach detective was an irritating intrusion on his one-on-one with Rose. But at 9:30 the lesson ended with Edmundo-Ernesto assuring Rose that she surely had championship potential. He walked toward his car with two—no doubt battle-tested and incredibly expensive—croquet mallets slung over his narrow shoulder.

"Thanks for being so patient, Charlie," Rose said.

"No problem. Back in my croquet days, the object was to just whack the other guys balls as far as you could into the pucker brush."

Rose laughed. "What in God's name is pucker brush?"

"Something we had up in Connecticut," he said as they walked over and sat down in two Adirondack chairs facing the croquet court.

"So, I need your help again," he said. "Have you ever run across Leo Peavy, Guy Bemmert, Larry Swain, or Xi Kiang?"

Crawford had called and spoken to Guy Bemmert the night before. The man was not the most cooperative person Crawford had ever come across, but he'd managed to talk Bemmert into meeting with Ott and him at his Boca house at 11:30.

Rose thought for a few seconds before answering. "Guy Bemmert is the only one. He was head of one of the largest mortgage companies a while back. I heard he was making really big money back then." She tapped at her lips as she plumbed her memory. "As I remember it, there were charges he defrauded Fannie Mae or Freddie Mac—or maybe both. He got off but from what I heard that was the end of his corporate career. He was the man who I dealt with on the purchase of the last house SOAR bought."

That made sense to Crawford, as Bemmert had become the cult's new treasurer, replacing Lalley. What didn't make sense was that Crux would hire a man with his history.

"What was your impression of him?"

Rose thought for a second. "Slick, with a distinct tinge of slippery," she said. "Remember how I told you that the Christian Lalley was kind of humorless but at least straightforward?"

Crawford nodded.

"Well, Bemmert was the opposite. There was an inspection of the house, then he used the report to try to knock down the price by half a million bucks. But the report only had a few minor things on it. Like the fact that there was a little wood rot. I remember thinking, 'You're quibbling over a tiny patch of wood rot and you just got someone to donate a billion dollars to SOAR.'"

"The Melhados, you mean?"

"Yes, exactly."

"I also wanted to ask you about them. But you've never come across the names Leo Peavy, Larry Swain or Xi Kiang?

Rose shook her head. "I think I've heard Peavy's name but that's all. Larry Swain or Xi Kiang, sorry, never heard of them."

"Okay, then, the Melhados… what can you tell me about them?"

Rose leaned back in her Adirondack chair. "Well, I know that Fannie had like a five-minute marriage to one of the Hearsts. You know, the newspaper Hearsts."

Crawford nodded.

"And Freddie… he's a classic hail-fellow-well-met guy."

Crawford nodded. "Gotcha. That was my impression, too."

"Hey, by the way, how's Dominica? I haven't seen her in a while."

"She's good," he said. "Well, Rose, I appreciate your help, as always —" he got to his feet "—I gotta get going, catch me some bad guys."

"You're welcome, as always…. If you ever want to get into a high-stakes game of croquet, let me know."

"Thanks, but I don't own any white shirts where the collar defies gravity."

"What do you mean?"

"Stays in the up position."

Rose laughed. "Oh, right."

"So, I think I'll just stick to being a barely-adequate golfer."

IT WAS JUST BEFORE ten when he walked into his office. Ott was waiting for him in a chair facing his desk, banging away on his laptop.

"Hey," Ott said. "What are you doing, putting in Rutledge hours?"

Their chief was well-known for never getting to work before nine or leaving past five.

"I had an early morning croquet lesson."

"*What?*"

"My secret life," Crawford joked. "So, got anything new?"

"Not really, how 'bout you?"

"I got a little backstory from Rose about Guy Bemmert," Crawford said and filled Ott in on what Rose had told him. "We got a date with him and Swain in Boca."

"Yeah, I dug into Bemmert, along with a few others. Spent a couple hours on 'em," Ott said. "Didn't really find much on Bemmert, though. Just some reference to him heading a mortgage company."

"Nothing about him defrauding Fannie Mae or Freddie Mac?"

"No, just that he was CEO of… I forget the name."

"Well, we'll see what he has to say about it," Crawford said. "I've also got a bunch of calls into Leo Peavy, but he's clearly in no hurry to call me back."

Ott smiled at that. "We'll track him down."

Crawford nodded. "Yes, we will. But first, the boys in Boca."

"WHAT'S THE ADDRESS?" Ott asked as they got into their aging but still game Crown Vic.

"702 Coquina Drive B," Crawford said.

"B?" Ott looked over at him. "What kind of address is that?"

Crawford shrugged. "I don't know, a condo maybe."

Ott dialed it in on his GPS.

The morning sky had darkened, and it looked like a storm was coming in, so Ott flicked on his headlights.

They had just merged onto I-95 south when Ott's phone rang. Ott looked down at the number and seemed to ponder whether to answer it or not.

"Hey," he said finally, clicking his iPhone.

Crawford could hear a woman's voice.

"Ah, sure," Ott said after a few moments, then in an apprehensive tone. "In a library?"

More listening.

"Okay," he said, frowning. "Really, subtitles?"

Crawford heard the woman's voice say, 'Yes.'

"Okay, honey, I'll pick you up," Ott said, clicking off.

Crawford had heard just enough to dope out the gist of the conversation. "They really suck."

Ott frowned. "What does?"

"The three French 'shorts' you're going to see at the West Palm library."

"How the hell—"

"The clues were 'library' and 'subtitles,'" Crawford said. "But the big question is, who's *honey*?"

Ott's face turned ripe-tomato red. "Oh, just... this woman."

"Come on, Mort, details."

Ott sighed. "That's enough."

"No, no, no. You're always wearing me out with questions about women. Now it's my turn. Who *is* she?"

An even deeper sigh. "Just this woman I met."

"How'd you meet her?"

Ott started tapping the steering wheel like he was going to break it. "Just, you know, around."

"Cut the shit, Mort. How'd you meet her?"

The tapping got more intense. "On one of those sites."

Crawford's head went up and down. "Hey, that's nothing to be ashamed of. Which one? *Match*?"

Ott shook his head. "No, it's called Elite."

"Well, hell, man," Crawford said with a big smile, "that you are."

"Douchebag."

"So... more questions. How many dates have you had?"

Reluctantly. "Three."

"So, you did the coffee date ice breaker. Then the drinks date. Then the dinner one. Now it's the foreign-film date. Watch it: she's testing to see if you've got any culture."

Ott laughed. "We both know the answer to that."

"Hey, you got more than I do."

---

702 COQUINA WAY B turned out to be a modest two-story garage apartment behind 702 Coquina Way, which itself was anything but modest.

They had to go through a barrier gate to get there. First, Ott pressed a button, then a few seconds later a voice asked, "The detectives?"

"Yup," said Ott and the mechanical arm went up and Ott drove in.

702 Coquina Way, the large house they went past, was close to ten thousand square feet, Crawford estimated. It was a grey steel modern house with more windows than he remembered ever seeing in any place before. As Ott drove past it to the adjacent garage apartment, Crawford imagined an exorbitant monthly bill for window-washing. More than his monthly rent, no doubt. He could picture the crew finishing the massive window-cleaning job, only to have to start all over again.

Ott parked in front of the four-car garage, which was underneath Bemmert and Swain's garage apartment. A blue Nissan Sentra was also parked there.

"Not much of a car for the treasurer of SOAR," Ott said.

Crawford nodded as they walked up the outside stairway.

Crawford pushed the doorbell. Nobody came to the door right away, so he hit it again. This time the door opened and a man who looked to be in his mid-thirties gave them a big smile. "Welcome, fellas."

Crawford put out his hand. "Hi, Detective Crawford and my partner, Detective Ott."

"Larry Swain," the man said. He had close-cropped hair, bright emerald-green eyes, a three-day growth, and muscles that would have made Schwarzenegger in his prime envious.

His handshake was predictably bone-crushing.

"Get you fellas something to drink?"

"Water would be great," Crawford said.

"Me, too," said Ott.

They followed him into the kitchen, and he opened the refrigerator door.

"How 'bout a Perrier?"

"Sure," said Crawford and Ott nodded.

Swain pulled out two bottles of Perrier and a black can of something called Monster, which Crawford was pretty sure was an energy drink. They followed him through the living room to a terrace that looked out over a back lawn to a tall ficus hedge beyond. Crawford was struck by how little furniture there was and, with the exception of one lone travel poster that said *Amalfi Coast*, how bare the walls appeared.

Swain introduced them to Bemmert, who was reading *The Economist* as they sat and joined him. Bemmert was the diametric opposite of Swain: short and pudgy with scraggly blond hair and clumps of grey on the side. Crawford's first impression was that he actually looked like a man who had an IQ of 150.

He welcomed Crawford and Ott, then fell silent.

"So," Crawford said, picking up the slack, "as I said on the phone, we're the lead detectives on the Christian Lalley murder case and would like to ask you some questions."

Bemmert nodded. "Sure, ask away."

Crawford didn't sense that he should start with his standard alibi question: *Where were you the night Christian Lalley was killed?* So, he took a softer tack.

"How long you guys been living here?" he said.

"'Bout six months."

"And how long have you been with SOAR?"

"A little longer. Around nine months or so."

"What exactly do you do for SOAR?"

"Well, actually, I'm the Chief Financial Officer of SOAR," Bemmert said. "And Larry's my assistant."

"So," Ott said with an innocent smile, "I guess that means you're in charge of the money?"

"Yeah, I guess that's one way to put it," Bemmert said as Swain nodded.

"And, as I understand it," Crawford said, "you just had a major windfall a while back?"

"What do you mean?" Bemmert asked.

"A brother and sister named Melhado committed to donating a lot of money to SOAR."

"Well," Bemmert said. "I wouldn't say donate is quite accurate."

"Okay, well then, what would you call it?"

"I'd call it more like ... providing working capital."

"Fair enough," Crawford said. "So, let's call it that. But, if I'm not mistaken, SOAR's not regarded by the government as a philanthropy, correct?"

"We're working on that," Bemmert said.

"Good luck with it," Crawford said. "Mind me asking, what did you do before SOAR?"

"I worked for a financial company. Kind of similar to what I'm doing now at SOAR."

"Understand. And what was the name of that company?"

"Martell Mortgage Capital," Bemmert said. "It's not around anymore. Principals sold it to a competitor last year."

Crawford nodded. "How 'bout you, Mr. Swain?"

"My prior job, you mean?"

"Yes."

"I worked in construction."

"Oh, yeah, where?"

"Columbus, Ohio."

Crawford flicked his head at Ott. "He's from Cleveland."

Swain nodded. "Just down the road."

"So, let me change the subject a little," Ott began, turning to Swain. "Mr. Swain, as we understand it, you once had an... altercation with the murder victim, Christian Lalley?"

Swain waved his hand, "Oh my God, that was nothing. Christian had one too many and said something that was offensive. So, we had a little... shoving match."

"And that was it?"

"That was pretty much it."

Ott nodded and glanced back at Crawford.

"Okay, as we ask everybody we interview," Crawford said, "including all the SOAR members in the various houses, where you were at the time Christian Lalley was killed. Meaning last Wednesday night at about one in the morning. First you, Mr. Bemmert."

"Sound asleep," Bemmert said. "Right here."

"And you, Mr. Swain?"

"Same."

Ott nodded, then turned to Bemmert. "And what about the night before last?"

"The night before last?" Bemmert asked.

Ott nodded.

"What time?"

"Just after eleven p.m."

"Reading a book," Bemmert said, "or probably by that time, I had fallen asleep."

"What about you, Mr. Swain?"

"I was here," Swain said. "Watching something on Netflix."

"Oh, yeah, what?" Ott asked.

"This documentary on high-school quarterbacks," Swain said.

"*QB1*," Ott said. "Good show."

"I agree."

Crawford turned to Bemmert. "Does the name Holmes Whitmore mean anything to you?"

"No," Bemmert replied quickly.

Crawford shot a look at Ott. "That's a little surprising because the man was a big story about a year ago."

Bemmert shrugged. "We was just getting here then. Guess we missed it."

"He was the man who took over for Crux's father when he had all that trouble up in New York. Back about twenty years ago. You know what I'm talking about?"

"Not really," Bemmert said. "That's a long time ago. Crux never told me his life story."

"Okay, then I'll just give you a few chapters." Crawford said.

And for the next five minutes, Crawford recounted how Crux's father lost his job during the time Holmes Whitmore was having an affair with Crux's mother. Then he went over the accusation—false, he was now sure—that Whitmore was a pedophile, based on the photos of the boys at Whitmore's back door. Then he put forward the scenario that Crux might have been behind the whole thing and charged Christian Lalley with the job of paying the boys for their service. Crawford said he and Ott suspected that there were probably others involved but didn't have proof who they were.

"That's all very interesting, but what's it got to do with us?" Bemmert asked.

Crawford shrugged. "I just wondered if you knew anything about it."

Bemmert shook his head. "Now you know. And, by the way, if I ever knew that Christian Lalley had been involved in something like that, I would have urged Crux to toss him out of SOAR immediately."

"That's commendable, but what if Crux ordered him to do it?"

Bemmert exhaled deeply. "You seem to think Crux is an evil, scheming sociopath or something, detective."

"No, I just—"

Bemmert held up a hand. "I'm not buying for a second that Crux was involved, and as for Larry and me... we've got nothing to hide. Me and Larry are law-abiding men."

"Religious, law-abiding men," Swain added earnestly.

Bemmert nodded and smiled.

"Good to hear. Well, I guess that'll do it, then," he glanced at Ott. "You got anything else, Mort?"

Ott shook his head. "Nope. Not that I can think of."

Crawford stood. The other three followed suit. "Oh, one last thing. Just curious, do you rent this place from the owner of the big house in front."

"Yes, we do. We have a one-year lease."

"And you've been here six months?"

Bemmert nodded.

Crawford looked out the window at the stretch of lawn and perfectly maintained ficus hedge. "Nice view."

"Yeah, we like it," Bemmert said.

"Well, thanks for your time."

"You bet."

All four shook hands. Then Crawford and Ott went out the door, down the steps and got into the Crown Vic.

"Pretty sparsely furnished for them having been there half a year," Crawford said.

"Yeah, sure is," Ott said, driving away from the garage apartment.

SIXTEEN

"OKAY, but what do you think most of 'em have in common?" Ott asked as he drove up the on-ramp onto 1-95.

They were talking about cults or NRMs, as Ott, who had delved into them extensively on-line, pointed out they were called by experts. NRM stood for New Religious Movements and, indeed, a new one seemed to pop up every few years somewhere.

"Most of 'em end badly, in answer to your question," Crawford said.

Ott nodded. "Yeah, fact is, a lot of 'em end in mass suicides. Jonestown being the best known. There was also that one called Heaven's Gate in California, remember? Another one called the Order of the Solar Temple, where a bunch of their members committed suicide in Canada and Switzerland. Then this other one—this is a mouthful— the Movement for the Restoration of the Ten Commandments of God."

"I don't remember that one."

"Supposedly started by a couple of ex-Catholic priests, some nuns, and a former prostitute."

"Hell of a combination."

"Yeah, back in 2000 or so. Hundreds of 'em either committed suicide or were murdered; they're not sure which."

Crawford shook his head slowly. "And Heaven's Gate, what happened to them; I forget?"

Ott shook his head and sighed. "Talk about whack jobs," he said. "So, do you remember the Hale-Bopp comet back in the late 1990s, I think it was? It was supposed to come close to earth?"

"Sort of."

"Well, these Heaven's Gate people were convinced there was a UFO following it."

"Following the comet, you mean?"

"Yeah, so a bunch of 'em thought it was a good idea to commit suicide, thinking the UFO was going to transport them off to heaven. Not quite sure how that was supposed to work. Know what else a lot of them had in common?"

"What?"

"'Free love' was what they used to call it. But it was worse than that. Sex abuse of kids was more like it. In this other cult called Children of God, the leader, a guy named David Berg, boasted how his toddler son, or maybe stepson, had engaged in sex with adult women. Turns out the kid ended up murdering his former nanny, then shot himself."

"Jesus, man, bunch of very sick people."

"You ain't kiddin'."

"One good thing about SOAR…"

"What's that?"

"They don't have any kids."

Crawford nodded.

Later, as they were driving across the bridge to Palm Beach, Crawford turned to Ott. "You forgot a more recent one."

"Which one?"

"That guy who had the cult somewhere in upstate New York. Stole a ton of money from the Bronfman sisters. Remember?"

"Oh, yeah, right," said Ott. "Nexus or something. Up in Albany, I think it was. Took the Bronfman babes for a hundred mil or so. Can't remember the guy's name."

"Neither can I. Just that he had something going with underage girls too."

"So, as usual, all roads lead to sex and money."

When they walked into the station, Bettina (don't call me Betty), one of the receptionists, told them the chief wanted to talk to them.

"What do you suppose that's about?" Ott asked as they walked back to Rutledge's office.

"Probably got it all figured out. Who did Lalley."

Ott laughed. "No doubt."

Rutledge was in his office on the phone. "Got a bunch of redfish and tarpon—" pause "—Yeah, pompano, too. Hey, man, I gotta jump. Got a couple of my men here I gotta straighten out… yeah, later."

Rutledge clicked off and turned to Crawford and Ott.

"Fishing the Intracoastal?" Ott asked.

"How'd you know?" Rutledge asked.

"Cause redfish, tarpon, and pompano are what you catch there."

"Very good," Rutledge said. "If you're such a good figurer-outer-of-shit, Ott, how come you haven't figured out who did Lalley?"

"Come on, Norm," Crawford said. "Next you're going to tell us murder's not good for the Palm Beach ecosystem."

"Ecosystem?"

Crawford glanced at Ott. "Maybe I've been hanging around Mensas too much."

"What?"

"Never mind. This is the point we usually get the speech," Crawford said. "When a case is less than a week old and we haven't solved it."

"Yeah, well, you wouldn't have to hear it if you caught the guy in the first forty-eight, like some guys."

"The first forty-eight's overrated," Ott said. "And do we need to remind you what our clearance is?"

"I know. I know. So, make you a deal, and we'll skip all the bull-shit. Just catch me up on what you got."

For the next fifty minutes, Crawford and Ott filled him in.

"So, you've basically zeroed in on it being someone in this outfit SOAR?" Rutledge asked.

"Not sure I'd call it an outfit, but yeah," Crawford said. "Take your pick: Crux, Peavy, Swain, Bemmert, a Chinese national named Xi Kiang, a billionaire brother-sister duo—for one thing, a lot of 'em had a lot to lose if Lalley went public on that bogus Whitmore thing. Which was Crux's revenge on what happened to his old man... and some of 'em wanting to please Crux."

"Yeah, please the boss, something we always try to do," Ott said with a grin.

"I hadn't noticed," Rutledge said stone-faced. "Okay, so I get that, and it makes sense, but what about something more basic?"

"Basic?" Crawford said. "Like what?"

"I mean, what if Christian Lalley was screwing someone's wife. Or, I don't know, he owed someone a bunch of money and wouldn't pay. Guys get killed for shit like that every day of the week. Doesn't have to be a SOAR thing, ya know."

Crawford did know and damned if Rutledge didn't have a point—as hard as that was to admit.

He looked at Ott, who nodded.

"You know what, Norm? You're absolutely right," Crawford said, then to Ott, "We've been investigating everything but Lalley's personal life. Time to dig down into the man's past."

"Yeah, there's gotta be something there," Rutledge said

"I agree," Ott said, then turning to Crawford. "Maybe you talk to your friend Vega again. She seemed to know him pretty well."

Crawford nodded. "Anything else, Norm, while you're on a roll?"

"Nah, that's all I got," Rutledge said. "I'm just glad I could set you boys straight."

The man couldn't leave well enough alone.

A few minutes later they left his office. Crawford turned to Ott and smiled. "How's that expression go? 'Even blind squirrels—'"

"'—find a nut every once in a while.'"

The first thing Crawford did when he got back to this office was call Vega and ask to buy her a drink that night.

"Stalled out on Christian's murder, huh?" she said. "Need to pick my brain again."

"How'd you guess?" It was better than bullshitting her and saying he really missed her company.

"Okay, sure…where and when?"

"How 'bout I buy you a Grease Burger. Bet you've never had one before."

"A grease burger? That doesn't sound too appetizing."

Crawford laughed. "It is, though. The Grease Burger on Clematis. You're just gonna have to trust me on this. Best burger around. Beats your veggie wrap any day. I'll pick you up. Seven good?"

"Okay, I trust you… I guess. Even though you are the man who likes sardines."

"You won't be disappointed," he said. "Hey, I have a quick question. My partner's been trying to get in touch with Lorinda Lalley, Christian's ex, but having no luck. You wouldn't know how to reach her, would you?"

"Hang on a sec, I used to have her cell."

Crawford waited as her heard her clicking on her iPhone.

"Here you go…" and she gave him her number.

"Thanks. Do you know where she lives?"

"Palm Beach Gardens. I think she might be remarried. Wait, come to think of it, no, that fell through."

"Did Christian tell you that?"

"Mm-hm."

"Okay, see you at seven."

Crawford clicked off and dialed Lorinda Lalley's number. A woman answered.

"Hi, Mrs. Lalley, my name is Detective Crawford, the lead detective on the murder case of your former husband. I'm sorry about what happened to Mr. Lalley but wondered if I could ask you some questions."

"Sure, go ahead."

"I was hoping I could meet you in person."

"That's fine. How 'bout right now?"

It was extremely rare when he found someone so readily available. Was she lonely or bored? "I can be there in about twenty minutes."

"Okay, I'll leave your name at the gate. They'll let you in. Crawford, you said?"

"Yes."

"Okay, see you in a little while." And she gave him her address.

———

IT WAS a typical Florida housing complex and a typical Florida house. First thing you saw was the two-car garage, then a sidewalk to a cramped front entrance that tried to jam together too many architectural elements: two skinny Corinthian columns, scrawny acanthus leaves, a triangular pediment with an undersized dentil, and an oversized front door. Palm Beach Gardens had tons of high-end houses and condominiums; this was mid-level. Nice enough but basically plain vanilla, with a view of a skinny, black lagoon in back.

Lorinda Lalley, tall, broad-shouldered and a bottle blonde, offered Crawford the requisite bottle of water. He smiled, said no thanks, and they sat down in a low-ceilinged living room that had Fox News muted on a big Samsung screen behind Lorinda.

He didn't know how Lorinda felt about the death of her ex, so he led off with the usual. "As I said, I'm sorry about what happened to your ex-husband, Mrs. Lalley, and assure you my partner and I are doing everything we can to find his killer."

"Thank you, detective. I appreciate it," she said, like it wasn't all that high on her list of priorities. "Do you have any suspects at this point?"

"We have a lot of people we're talking to and I'd appreciate any thoughts you might have on that subject. You know, people you think we should speak to. People that Mr. Lalley may have mentioned who might have threatened him or whom he may have had a disagreement or dispute with. Anybody come to mind?"

Lorinda shifted in her chair. "Well, of course, I've given it some thought since it happened and there's only one person I can think of. A man named Ray Gerster."

Crawford nodded. "Tell me about him, please."

"Well, as I'm sure you know by now, before SOAR, Chris was a CPA. A good one, too. Ray Gerster was one of his clients. I remember Chris telling me that Gerster played fast and loose with the IRS. He apparently ran some sort of a fund which turned out to essentially be a Ponzi scheme. Tell you the truth, I don't exactly know what a Ponzi scheme is except he wanted Chris to sign his tax return and when Chris saw a bunch of phony numbers on it, he refused."

"How long ago was this, Mrs. Lalley? Approximately."

"Ah, I'm guessing about three years ago."

"Okay, so what happened next?"

"A few months later, maybe like six months, Gerster was arrested for fraud, income tax evasion, and a bunch of other stuff. And Chris testified against him. He didn't really want to but the government put heavy pressure on him. Threatened to turn his life upside down if he didn't." Lorinda ran her hand across her mouth, then took a deep breath. "So anyway, when the case began, Gerster called Chris and threatened to kill him if he testified."

"Really? To kill him?"

"Yes, but I'm not sure how seriously Chris took it, 'cause he told me he didn't think Gerster was really the violent type or, you know, a mafia kind of person."

"But he *did* threaten to kill him?"

"He sure did, according to Chris anyway," Lorinda said. "But Chris went ahead and testified anyway."

"Against Gerster?"

She nodded.

"What happened?"

"Gerster got convicted and went to jail."

"Do you know for how long?"

"Sorry, I don't," Lorinda said. "I just know Chris felt kind of bad about it."

"Why? It wasn't his fault if his client was a crook."

"Yeah, I know. But he just... did."

"As far as you know, did Gerster just threaten him the one time?"

"That I couldn't tell you," Lorinda said earnestly. "Isn't once enough?"

Crawford nodded. Now, he wanted to dig up everything he possibly could on Gerster. "Do you remember the name of Gerster's company? Or his fund?"

"I do, 'cause it was really simple: Go Fund!—with an exclamation point."

Crawford wrote Go Fund! down on his iPhone. "And do you have any idea who his lawyer was, or who the prosecutor in the case was, by any chance?"

"Sorry, I don't."

"Or where the trial took place?"

"Sorry." She shrugged. "Around here somewhere, I assume."

"Thank you, Mrs. Lalley, that's very helpful. Now on the subject of SOAR—"

She quickly held up her hands. "That's a subject I don't talk about. Never. Period. End of story."

He could see there was no way in hell he'd be able to talk her into answering any questions even remotely SOAR-related.

He got to his feet and reached for his wallet and a card. "Well, thank you very much, Mrs. Lalley, you've been very helpful." He handed her a card. "If you think of anything else that might help me find your ex-husband's killer, please give me a call."

"I sure will."

Crawford walked to the door, opened it, and walked down the steps to his car.

Ray Gerster might just be the man he was looking for and he had to give Norm Rutledge full credit for steering him in this direction.

Jesus, would wonders never cease.

SEVENTEEN

CRAWFORD GOT a call on his cell phone on his way back to the station.

"Hello?"

"Detective Crawford. It's Leo Peavy. You've left me a few messages."

Like five. Maybe six.

"Yes, Mr. Peavy, we met the other day at Elysium, and as you know I'm the lead detective on the Christian Lall—"

"I know, and you want to pick my brain."

"Well, yes. Ask you a few questions."

"Come on by."

"Right now?"

"No time like the present."

"You're up at Elysium?"

"Yup."

"See you in fifteen minutes."

"Okay."

Wow, two in a row, Crawford thought. People who actually wanted to be questioned by him right away. He was accustomed to being the least popular man in town who no one wanted to talk to. This was a nice change. He felt like Sally Field...*they like me, they actually like me...* or whatever it was she had said.

He dialed Ott, who picked up right away.

"You doin' anything right now?" Crawford asked.

"Nah, whatcha got?"

"Leo Peavy in fifteen. At Elysium."

"Can't wait."

CRAWFORD WAS EVEN MORE aware the second time around that Leo Peavy was one of the oddest-looking ducks he had ever laid eyes on. The same rheumy, yellow-tinged eyes, the same thick Neil Young muttonchops sideburns...and something he hadn't noticed last time: the man had about the skinniest legs Crawford had ever seen. He knew that because Peavy was wearing madras shorts that he had probably bought on the three-dollar rack at Salvation Army twenty years ago. Peavy also had the largest, bulkiest, ugliest watch in creation. As thick as a hamburger, the sucker had to weigh close to three pounds.

Crawford, Ott, and Peavy were sitting in the library at Elysium. Crawford was in the same comfortable club chair from which he'd interviewed half of SOAR's congregants two days before.

Peavy beat Crawford to the punch in the interrogation. "So, you must be about the first Ivy Leaguer to end up a homicide cop. How in God's name did that happen?"

"It's a long story."

"So All-American in lacrosse at Dartmouth, not too shabby a running back on the football team."

The guy was a Mensa, what did Crawford expect?

"And then after Dartmouth, Charlie, you ended up in the Apple. Went out with that foxy actress, Gwendolyn Hyde, as I recall?"

"Briefly," Crawford said, barely audibly.

Ott glanced at Crawford and smiled. He had razzed Crawford about that on more than one occasion. He had always been more than a little envious.

"Mr. Peavy, you mind if we ask the questions here?" Crawford asked.

"Not at all, just making a little small talk," Peavy said. "I also heard something about you and Dominica McCarthy. Gorgeous specimen, that one. And Rose—"

"Okay, okay. Maybe you should write my biography."

"Maybe I should," he said. "I have a feeling it'd be pretty colorful." He turned to Ott "And you, Mort: Cuyahoga Community College, if I'm not mistaken."

Ott nodded. "Go Muskrats."

"Was that your mascot?"

Ott thought for a moment. "Either that or a gerbil. Mr. Peavy, we really need to move on and—"

Peavy smiled. "Laura Shearer, right?"

"What?" Ott said, his eyes narrowing.

"The woman you've been seeing."

Ott sighed. "Hey, listen…. we've got a lot of questions to get to."

Peavy patted the arm of his chair. "Okay. So, ask away."

Crawford glanced over at Ott, who looked somewhere between bemused and agitated. "How well did you know Christian Lalley?"

"Pretty well," Peavy said. "Christian used to live here in Elysium. We'd talk a fair amount."

"Talk about what," Crawford asked, "if you don't mind me asking?"

"Quantum physics, Sudoku, the New York Yankees, to name three. We both grew up in New York and were Yankee fans. You were a Red Sox fan, right, Charlie? Growing up in Connecticut and all? Even though I guess half the state are Yankee fans."

Crawford nodded and cut to it. "Who do you think killed Lalley?"

"Wow. Talk about direct questions." Peavy shrugged. "I have absolutely no idea. Who do you think did?"

"You're making this shit up," Crawford said.

"Here's the thing," Peavy said. "As I'm sure you've heard, Christian allegedly paid off those boys to implicate that guy Holmes Whitmore, so you're probably thinking Crux is behind it. Because of his father and mother's history with Whitmore. In reality, Christian paid them that money for a totally different reason."

"Oh yeah, what was that?" Crawford asked.

Peavy glanced away from Crawford, then his rheumy yellow eyes slowly wandered back to him. "See, I don't know if you know much about what we do here, but a big part of it is mentoring kids. Trying to help young people out, ones who aren't going anywhere, get 'em into professions where they can make a go of it." Crawford remembered what Fannie Melhado had told him; this seemed to echo that. "One of our members used to be, basically, a high-end electrician. 'High-end' meaning he used to do lots of jobs for corporate headquarters, mainly in the Atlanta area. Well, he sold the company for pretty big money and joined SOAR. What he does now is hire out as an electrician, mainly small jobs, the purpose being to take kids along with him on those jobs to be his apprentices, teach them the ropes. Well, I guess, in this case, it would be, the wires."

Despite his looks, Peavy had an engaging way about him.

"So, let me make sure I got this straight," Crawford said. "He'd get paid for the jobs, then Christian Lalley would pay the kids for their share of the work?"

Peavy smiled and pointed a finger at Crawford. "Very good, Charlie," he said. "You're just as advertised. But then, I'd expect nothing less from a Dartmouth man."

"But, as you mentioned, you're aware of the other story going around," said Ott. "Which seems pretty credible, too."

"Yes, that those boys were being photographed at Holmes Whitmore's house so it would look like he was a pedophile. And Crux being behind the whole thing. That would mean that Crux was a very vengeful man. Which, I can guarantee you, he isn't. And besides, can you imagine carrying around a grudge like that for—whatever it was— twenty or thirty years, then finally delivering on it?" He paused. "Because I sure as hell can't."

"You know him better than we do," Crawford said. "One thing I've noticed is you're very adept at changing the subject, taking the focus off you."

"Thank you, Charlie."

"It wasn't exactly a compliment," Crawford said. "Where were you when Christian Lalley was murdered? Meaning last Wednesday at one in the morning?"

"Sound asleep here at Elysium."

"Do you have a key to Lalley's house at 1450 North Lake Way?"

"No, only one for here."

Crawford nodded. "How well did you know Simon Petrie?"

"Simon…? Ah, not that well. He kept to himself most of the time."

Ott jumped in. "And where were you on the night of Thursday the 8th at 11:30?"

"Jesus, do you guys really think I skulk around at night with a knife in my hand? I mean, look at me. Do I look like a killer?" He pointed a finger at himself. "I'm in bed every night at ten with a book in my hands, not a goddamn knife."

"Okay, so back to Lalley," Ott said. "As my partner asked, you must have speculated about who might have had a reason to kill him?"

Peavy tapped on the arm of his chair for a full ten seconds. "You ever talk to his wife?"

"Matter of fact, I did," said Crawford. "Pretty recently."

Peavy, his eyes lowered, patted the arm of the chair again. Then he looked up. "And, my guess is, she didn't tell you why they got divorced."

EIGHTEEN

CRAWFORD SHOOK HIS HEAD. "No, she didn't."

"Well, put your seatbelt on," Peavy said. "In your investigation of this whole thing, you never heard about him and Marie-Claire Fournier?"

Both Crawford and Ott shook their heads.

"Do you know anything about Ted Turner?" The question not only came out of left field, but *deep, deep, deep* left field.

"What?" Crawford said. "Where are you going with this?"

"Bear with me, I'll explain: Ted Turner, according to a reliable source, has four girlfriends…"

Crawford nodded. "Okay, I'll take your word for it."

He had sort of lost track of Turner since Jane Fonda cut him loose. Or maybe it was the other way around.

"He spends a week with one, a week with another, a week with a third, then a week with the fourth, then does the same thing all over again the next month."

Ott laughed and shook his head. "You're making this shit up."

Peavy held up his hands. "It's a fact. Now, does he occasionally spend two weeks with one and no time with another? I don't know. Probably."

"Sounds like you've been reading *National Enquirer*," Ott muttered.

Peavy ignored him. "So, one of the tenets of SOAR is what we call *relationships without walls*." Crawford could see what was coming. "We believe in relationships with anyone, anytime… as opposed to restrictive, antiquated relationships with just one partner."

"So, we're talkin' free love?" Ott said.

Peavy laughed. "You can call it that, Detective, and I won't fight you on it. But your tone seems kind of judgmental and derogatory."

"It was just meant to be factual," Ott said.

"Tell us about Christian Lalley and Marie-Claire Fournier," Crawford said, having heard enough about Ted Turner and his four-pack.

Peavy nodded. "First, would you agree with me, all systems are imperfect?"

"What do you mean?" Crawford asked.

"Well, let's take the police force. There's a code that, for example, you're never meant to use excessive force… or you're never supposed to accept a bribe…*bu-ut*…cops do sometimes."

"Where you going with this?" Ott asked impatiently.

Peavy held up a hand. "I'll illustrate it with an example: Marie-Claire and Crux had a very close relationship… in every sense. Yet Crux, in keeping with the *relationship without walls* tenet also had relationships with other women—"

"Sex, you mean?" Ott said.

Peavy nodded. "But Marie-Claire did not. She seemed to embrace the outmoded tenet—"

"—of being faithful?"

"Detective Ott, if you would stop interrupting me, please."

"Sorry, go on."

Peavy nodded. "So—and I think it was in a misguided attempt to make Crux jealous—one day, Marie-Claire started a very conspicuous affair with Christian. Christian tried to keep it low-key but that wasn't what Marie-Claire wanted. So, one time—and this is secondhand and I can't swear to all of it—but Marie-Claire and Christian ended up somewhere for drinks and they both had a lot of 'em"—Crawford recalled Vega telling him about Christian's fondness for 'blabbermouth soup' at Ta-boo—"then went back to her bedroom at Elysium." Peavy stopped to take a sip from his water bottle. "Only thing is they didn't end up in her bedroom."

Ott raised his hands. "So where *did* they end up?"

"Marie-Claire's bedroom, which is now Fannie Melhados's, has a connecting door to Crux's bedroom and she... she coaxed Christian into it. Crux's bed, that is. So, she and Christian were, ah, going at it, let's say, when—"

"—Crux walked in on them," Crawford said.

Peavy nodded. "Exactly. Which was very uncharacteristic of Marie-Claire, because for the most part, as I said, she was kind of old-fashioned and really kind of proper."

"But she wanted to get Crux jealous, and I'm guessing this is what got Christian exiled to fourteen-fifty?"

Peavy shook his head. "No, not at all. Crux was a little irritated that they were using his bed, but he had no problem with them making love. After all, *relationships without walls* was his concept."

Ott looked over at Crawford and tried to hide a smirk.

"So, an obvious question," Crawford said, "what was Lorinda Lalley's reaction to all this?"

"Well, that's the whole point. In a phrase... she was *really pissed off*. That her drunken lout of a husband had the gall to fu— make love with—a woman in the boss's bed. I mean, poor Christian was kind of a laughingstock for a while. And besides, Lorinda was never a full-fledged SOAR believer. She lived with Christian on SOAR property but had a regular job elsewhere."

"Not a SOAR job, you mean?"

Peavy nodded. "Correct. And about six months later, she filed for divorce and moved out."

"So, are you suggesting Lorinda Lalley killed her husband?" Ott asked.

"I'll let you be the judge," Peavy said. "She was overheard saying something pretty incriminating when she confronted him after the whole incident in Crux's bed."

"Which was?"

"'I could kill you, you stupid son of a bitch.'"

"I dunno," said Ott, scratching his head. "Sounds like the normal reaction of someone who just got cheated on."

NINETEEN

BACK AT THE STATION, Crawford saw he'd missed two calls while interviewing Leo Peavy. The first one was from Rose Clarke. He dialed her number and she picked up right away.

"Got a scoop for you, Charlie," she said.

No 'hi,' 'hello', or 'how are you.' Rose was too busy for that.

"Please be about my case, which is going nowhere fast," Crawford said.

"Well, it is… and it isn't. I'll let you decide," Rose said. "Guess who lives in one of those SOAR houses?"

"Who?"

"Torrance Grey."

"No kidding—" Then he snapped his fingers, remembering "I knew he looked familiar. Ott interviewed him. Now, what exactly was the story with him? I kind of forget."

Torrance Grey, the actor, had totally vanished from sight about ten years ago and that was about all Crawford remembered. Except there had been a major scandal of some sort.

"Don't you remember? His wife was killed in Beverly Hills. It was —depending on who you listen to—either a burglar or Grey did it himself."

"Oh, yeah, that's right. He was there when it happened. Claimed he was out by the pool or something."

"Yeah, at two in the morning," Rose said, dubiously.

"Right, but no charges were ever filed, correct?"

"True, but it turned out to be a career-killer for ol' Torrance. Don't you remember how brutal the murder was? They compared it to O.J."

"Yeah, I do now. Really vicious and they suspect it took place over a long period of time. Almost like she was tortured. I remember thinking after I read about it, why would a burglar take all that time? Wouldn't he want to get out of there as quick as possible?"

"I had the same reaction. Speaking of murders, you're not getting anywhere with Christian Lalley?"

"You didn't hear this from me, but no, not really."

"Your secrets are always safe with me."

"Thank you," Crawford said. "The people at SOAR, they're a pretty strange cast of characters."

"Like who are you referring to?"

"Well, there's the billionaire heiress and her brother, a guy who defrauded his company *and* the government for millions, a construction worker turned SOAR's assistant CFO, a mysterious and inscrutable Chinese guy, and now a movie star who may have killed his wife but certainly killed his career… and, of course, a partridge in a pear tree."

Rose laughed. "What a line-up. Who's the construction worker?"

"His name is Larry Swain. Lives with that guy, Bemmert, you told me about who ripped off his company and now—lo and behold—turns out to be SOAR'S CFO."

Rose shook her head slowly. "Well, I just thought I'd let you know about Grey. A bunch of us were talking about a movie of his and someone mentioned he was living there."

"Thank you, Rose, I appreciate it."

"You're welcome. Just trying to do my bit to take criminals off the streets of our fair town."

"I'll tell Mort he spent fifteen minutes interviewing the star of *Seven Suspects* and didn't even realize it."

"And don't forget, *Harpers Bizarre.*"

That movie was one of Crawford's all-time favorites.

"Later, Rose."

"Bye, Charlie."

His other call-back had been from Vega. He dialed her number and she picked up right away.

"Hi, Charlie."

"Hello, Vega, how are you?"

"I'm fine," she said. "Your message said you wanted to ask me about Xi Kiang?"

Crawford chuckled. "Yeah, I thought I'd ask you about him now, so we don't clutter up dinner with a bunch of shop talk."

"How very thoughtful of you. So, what do you want to know about Xi and his yellow shirts?"

He already knew a fair amount about the man.

Xi Kiang was in his mid-50's and Crawford had interviewed him briefly at Elysium. At that time Kiang was either very circumspect or didn't speak English very well. Crawford suspected it was the former. One thing he said, however, had gotten Crawford curious. It was in answer to a question Crawford had asked him. The question was, "What do you do in SOAR?" He couldn't tell if Xi either didn't under-stand or didn't want to answer the question. But Crawford persisted, asking it a little differently. "Most people have a function in SOAR, something they're particularly good at. What is it that you contribute?"

His answer had been terse. "I help with organization part."

"Organization part... were you involved in something like that in China?"

Xi nodded.

Crawford pressed harder. "What exactly?"

"A religion."

"What is it called?"

"Falun Gong."

Crawford asked him to spell it. It sounded vaguely familiar. From there, the interview sputtered badly, with Xi not volunteering anything further and answering most of Crawford's question with 'yes' or 'no' responses.

Back at his office, Crawford had then Googled Xi Kiang. There were five long paragraphs about him on Wikipedia. He and two others had started a religion call Falun Gong back in 1992 and it had grown to an astonishing seventy million in number. But apparently it got so big that the Communist Party viewed it as a threat exactly because of its size. Seemed like the proverbial elephant in the room, its independence from the Communist party and anti-establishment teachings anathema to them. What followed was that the state-run press ran negative articles about the Falun Gong. Then, in July of 1999, the Communist government made it clear that they wanted to eradicate the "practice," as they called it, and went on to denounce it as a "heretical organization."

What followed was years of human rights abuses on a massive scale, including torture, forced labor, and psychiatric mistreatment. Worse of all, though, was an estimated ten thousand people who were killed to, allegedly, supply China's widespread organ-transplant industry.

Crawford shifted his cell phone to his other ear. "So, I looked into the Falun Gong," he told Vega, "and Xi's involvement in it—"

She interrupted. "More than involvement, he was one of its major architects."

Crawford put his feet up on his desk. "So, I'm trying to put two and two together and I think it adds up to Crux recruiting him to help do for SOAR what he did for Falun Gong."

"I am impressed," Vega said, "just that you even know about Falun Gong."

"I just know that they got on the wrong side of the Communists. Never a good move."

"You probably know more about it than me."

"I'm just amazed at SOAR's membership. I mean, it's an international line-up of peculiar characters."

"I'm not quite sure Xi is peculiar. More like a man who was persecuted for having an idea that got too big."

Crawford churned through the line-up of SOAR members and did a quick count in his head. Indeed, a good portion of the SOAR membership could definitely be described as peculiar. Or maybe just extremely diverse.

"But, as far as you know, did Crux recruit Xi to ramp up your membership? To put it on the map as quick as possible? Maybe even pattern it on the Falun Gong model?"

Vega didn't respond right away. "I'd answer that this way. Yes, yes and I'm not sure."

"You're not sure he wanted to make it similar to Falun Gong?"

"I'd say similar in certain respects."

Crawford didn't say anything for a few moments. "Wow," he said at last.

"Wow what?"

"Wow, this is all a hell of lot to absorb."

"What is?"

He went through the whole litany again of SOAR members and their unique histories and characteristics but left out the partridge in a pear tree.

"It is quite a list, isn't it?"

"Yeah. It's like you're one of the few normal ones."

Vega laughed. "Oh, I wouldn't go that far," she said. "Okay, my turn to ask you a question."

"What's that?"

"So, I've always wanted to go to a cop bar."

"Really? Somehow you don't strike me as a cop bar kinda gal."

"But I've always been a curious kinda gal, and I'm dying to see what a cop bar looks like. I figured you probably hang your hat at a good one."

"*Good one* might be stretching it. But I do have one I go to. It's called Mookie's Tap-a-Keg."

"You had me at Mookie's," she said. "Let's go."

"So, you want to bail on Grease Burger?"

"Yeah, Mookie's just sounds much more colorful."

"All right, consider it done. But let me just warn you, instead of the best burger in town Mookie's specializes in those big jars of pickled eggs. You know, the kind that look as though they been sitting there festering for a couple of years. The other culinary delight it specializes in are Slim Jims."

"What's a Slim Jim?"

"Are you kidding? You don't know what a Slim Jim is?"

"Heard the name before, but sorry, don't know what it is."

"Okay, well, let's start with the ingredients—"

"Is this going to make me gag?"

"Maybe."

"The question is, how would you even *know* what ingredients are in a Slim Jim?"

"That's a very good question...let's see... how do I explain it? Sometimes when you hang out in a cop bar too long, nursing your fifth beer, you got nothing better to do than read ingredients on things. Want to hear what's in them?"

"Why not?"

"Okay, so their main ingredients are—and I quote—*mechanically separated chicken, maltodextrin, and extractives of paprika.*"

"That's disgusting… except I love paprika."

"Then you'd love a Slim Jim."

Vega was silent for a few seconds. "I think I'll just drink."

"That's probably a wise decision."

TWENTY

CRAWFORD GOT up and headed down to Ott's cubicle.

Ott had his cell phone up to his ear and was nodding a lot as Crawford waited to talk to him. Finally, he lowered his voice and said, "Gotta go, babe."

Crawford dialed up a big grin. "So, dude, not only do you call your friend Laura 'hon' but 'babe' too."

"How do you know her name's Laura?"

"Remember? Leo Peavy."

"Oh, yeah... so what's up?"

Crawford sat down in the chair next to Ott. "So, you're a movie guy...how come you didn't recognize Torrance Grey in the Elysium interviews?"

Ott thought for a second, then it hit him. "Holy shit, that's who that was. I knew he looked familiar. Said his name was Sidney something, though."

"Probably the name he was born with."

"Now there's a guy who has not aged well."

Crawford tapped his fingers in Ott's desk. "So, I looked into that guy Xi Kiang, who Simon Petrie mentioned?"

Ott nodded for him to continue.

"I pretty much came to the conclusion that Petrie was suspicious of him because he never smiles or says much. But, fact of the matter is, he hardly knew Lalley."

"So, you're ruling him out?"

"Pretty much. I just don't think there's anything there."

"It's just weird."

"What is?

"How you start out somewhere in China and end up in Palm Beach, Florida?"

"I agree with that," Crawford said, getting to his feet. "Come into my office. It's time to get out the trusty whiteboard."

The whiteboard was a standard part of many of their investigations. They had probably used it in a little over half their cases. It was pretty straightforward. Under "Suspects," Ott—who had the most legible handwriting— would write the names of potential perps. In one case, he'd run out of room on the whiteboard, but usually the number of suspects ranged from four to seven.

Crawford led the way into his office. Ott lifted the whiteboard from where it was resting up against the back wall and hung it on a hook. He picked up the black dry-erase pen and wrote 'Suspects.' Then: '1. Crux.'

"Too big," Crawford said. "You better make 'em smaller."

Ott nodded and erased '1. Crux' and rewrote it half the size. He turned to Crawford. "Okay?"

"Perfect. So, he's your first choice?"

"I don't really have one at this point," Ott said. "Just that he's first one that came to mind."

Leaving room below '1. Crux' he wrote '2. Bemmert', then '3. Swain', '4. Peavy', and then thought for a second.

"5. Lorinda Lalley," Crawford said. "Though I'm thinking she's a long shot."

Ott nodded and wrote it down.

"6. Gerster," said Crawford.

Ott looked over at him.

"He was Lalley's crooked client who went to jail and blamed him."

Ott nodded and wrote it down, then wrote, '7. Torrance Grey.'

"Why him?" Crawford asked.

"'Because I want to go back and get his autograph. No, 'cause if he killed once, he might have killed again. You never know."

Crawford shrugged. "*If*, in fact, he killed once. And I'd say he's about a hundred to one. Can't imagine what motive he'd possibly have."

"Yeah, I know. So, we're ruling out the Gong Show guy?"

Crawford laughed. "Yeah, I think so. I might just take one last look at him."

"Okay, anybody else?"

"Oh, yeah, the Melhados."

"Why?"

"I don't know," Crawford shrugged. "Just something about her."

"That's not a real good reason, but I'll put 'em down." Which he did. "I'm still leaving room for late arrivals."

"I noticed."

Next, they put a short phrase or two for their suspects motives besides their names. For Crux, Ott wrote simply, 'Whitmore thing.' For Bemmert, they had a discussion:

"I don't know. It's kind of like a fox in the henhouse thing," Crawford said.

"What do you mean?"

"I mean, he goes from some big money grab at that mortgage company to running the money at SOAR."

"Yeah, I hear you," said Ott. "But don't take this the wrong way, okay… we don't know for a fact that ever happened. That mortgage company thing. I mean, it *was* just a rumor that Rose heard somewhere."

"True. But she's got about a ninety percent record for accuracy."

"I know. She's pretty reliable."

"And being treasurer, CFO, whatever, of what seems like a pretty loosely-run billion-dollar organization presents a big opportunity."

"Yeah, except Bemmert and his friend are living in that dinky apartment. Driving around in that Sentra or whatever the hell it was. Worse than your Camry."

"Hey, that car has served me long and loyally."

Ott shrugged and wrote *$???* next to Bemmert's name.

Next to Swain, he wrote: 'Beats me.'

Crawford just chuckled.

They went through the rest of the list, ending with, '9. Freddie Melhado' and '10. Fannie Melhado," both of whom received question marks next to their names.

"I found out that guy Gerster got out of jail a month ago," Crawford said.

Ott turned. "Hmm. Perfect timing." He sat in his chair facing Crawford. "You gonna talk to him?"

Crawford nodded. "If he ever gets back to me."

AT 7 O'CLOCK P.M., Crawford drove to Elysium on North Lake Way to pick up Vega and take her to Mookie's Tap-A-Keg. He had a lot to pick her brain about, but he didn't want to start right in on it. When he picked her up, he noticed way up on the third floor a man looking down through a window. He thought it might have been Crux and was pretty sure he had a frown on his face.

CRAWFORD WARNED her that she might have to step over a body lying on the beer-stained floor at Mookie's, but turned out the coast was clear.

"Table or bar?" he asked her as they walked in.

"Bar, please," she said looking around, "That's where the colorful types hang out, right?"

"Some call 'em colorful, some call 'em strange."

Vega sat down and Crawford slid onto the barstool next to her.

Jack Scarsiola, the owner and barkeep, approached them. "Hey, Charlie, what's it gonna be?" Then nodding at Vega. "Ma'am?"

"Vega, I'd like to introduce you to the proprietor, Jack Scarsiola... but you can call him Scar."

"Hey, Scar. Could I have a pinot grigio, please?"

"Sorry, how about chardonnay?"

"That'll be good. Thank you."

"I'll take a Yuengling," Crawford said

"Coming right up."

A few moments later Scarsiola showed up with the drinks.

Vega took a sip of her wine and glanced behind the bar. "I see what you mean. Those eggs," she said, pointing. "Does the health commissioner know about those?"

Crawford laughed as he spotted someone at the end of the bar. "Don't look now, but remember me telling you about Slim Jims?"

"Yeah, made from 'mechanically separated chicken' and 'extractives of paprika.'"

"Good memory. Well, a guy down at the end is eating a Slim Jim sandwich."

Vega looked anyway. "How do you know it's a Slim Jim sandwich?"

"Because that's what he always has. Joe Wright's his name. I think he invented it. Scar lets him go behind the bar and make them. Wonder bread, Gulden's mustard, and Slim Jims."

Vega frowned. "Ew, that's really gross."

"No argument from me. So, you okay changing the subject?"

"Please do."

"Thank you. I'm curious about the SOAR hierarchy."

Vega took another sip of her wine and set it down. "Well, despite what you may have heard, it's pretty corporate."

"Corporate? What do you mean?"

"Okay, so Crux is the CEO. Guy Bemmert is the CFO, Frannie Melhado is the COO—chief operating officer—Leo Peavy is the CIO and CMO—"

"Wait, what do the last two stand for?"

"Umm, Chief Information Officer and Chief Marketing Officer," Vega said with a chuckle and a shrug of the shoulders. "And me, I'm nothing."

"Those are actual titles?"

Vega nodded, then something caught her attention at the other end of the bar. "You can smoke here?" she asked, noticing an older man puffing away on a cigarette.

Crawford glanced down to where she was looking. "Oh, no, that's just Scarpa. He's what you might call our local scofflaw."

"Is he a cop?"

"Was a cop. A damn good one."

"But he smokes in defiance of the law."

"Yeah, pretty much. Scarsiola kind of gave up on him."

Vega shrugged. "O-kay."

"So back to SOAR. Frannie Melhado is Chief Operating Officer?"

"Yup. My take is that getting that job was a little like buying an ambassadorship. All it takes is money."

Crawford nodded. "Because she's only been around about a year?"

"Exactly."

"Is there a lot of jockeying for power? Like in a corporation?"

"Oh, yeah, you bet there is. Maybe it's a little more subtle—" she paused and cocked her head "—actually, now that I think about it, it's not subtle at all. Then there's *ascendancy* and *descendency*."

"What's that again?"

"I forget who came up with it, but it's pretty much what it sounds like. No matter who you are, you're either *ascendant* or *descendent*."

"You mean, going up or going down the SOAR totem pole?"

"Right. And if you're *descendent* for long enough, you're out."

"Really? You can get kicked out of SOAR?"

Vega nodded enthusiastically. "Oh, yeah, except they call it, 'failing to maintain standing.'"

"And has anyone 'failed to maintain standing' recently?"

"Not that recently. But Charlie Blackwell got the boot about six months back. And Simon Petrie before him. By the way, did you hear about what happened to him?"

Crawford nodded.

"Of course, you did," Vega said. "And a lot of people thought Christian Lalley was headed for the door."

"What for, specifically?" Crawford asked though he had a few good guesses.

"Well, he was caught with Marie-Claire Fournier in Crux's bed. Did you hear about that?"

"Yeah, I did."

Vega smiled. "Plus, he was the failed treasurer. That's what they called the job before Guy Bemmert came along and they gave it a fancy name. Chief Financial Officer."

"There's also hierarchy in the houses, right?" Crawford asked.

"Sure is. Ties in with ascendancy and descendency. Obviously, Elysium is the top of the food chain. Then in order of clout: Seraphim, Vangelis, Callisto, and the place you don't want to end up, Ganymede."

"I've heard some of those names before. But can you repeat them, please?"

And she did. Crawford wrote the names down on a cocktail napkin that had *ascendency* and *descendency* already scribbled on it, along with *CEO-Crux, CFO- Bemmert, COO- Fannie* and *CIO + CMO- Peavy.*

"So is it possible to go from, say, Ganymede"—he looked down at the names—"to Callisto, to Vangelis, to Seraphim, then to Elysium."

Vega nodded. "Yes, you can work your way up like that, but it's more common to go the other way."

"Meaning Elysium, Seraphim, Vangelis, Callisto, Ganymede, then out the door."

"Exactly."

"So, I'm guessing that if you're ascendant you're doing your job right. If you're descendent you're—"

"Screwing up. Or not playing politics very well."

"Or didn't give enough money."

Vega nodded. "Yes, that, too. And then there are the report cards."

"The what?"

"They're actually called *evaluations,* but everyone calls them report cards. You know, how well, or badly, the board thinks you're doing."

"Who's on the board?"

"Top secret, but it's some mix of the Chiefs."

"Meaning what you said. Executive, Operating, Financial, et cetera—"

"Yeah, what's that old expression? *Too many chiefs, not enough Indians?*"

He moved a little closer to Vega. "I'm curious about you. Why you decided to join SOAR?"

Vega sighed and looked down at her wine glass. "That's a good question. I was coming out of a bad relationship and a job that sucked. Crux seemed so damn earnest about helping people and I was kind of sick of my life being all about *me*. Maybe I was just sick of…me."

"Understand. So, are you pretty involved in the day-to-day at SOAR?"

"Yes, in kind of a behind-the-scenes way. People there solicit my opinion. I feel they value my slant on things—" she looked down the bar and frowned "Oh God, that Scarfa man is coming this way."

"Scarpa," Crawford said, turning to see Don Scarpa, a Winston dangling out of the side of his mouth, approaching them.

"Hey, Don," Crawford said.

"Charlie," said Scarpa, then with a nod at Vega. "Ma'am."

Vega started batting her hands, shooing away the smoke.

"Smoke bother you?" Scarpa asked.

"Matter of fact, it does. Smoking's illegal, you know."

"It is?" Scarpa said, feigning ignorance. "When did that happen?"

"Oh, about twenty years ago."

Scarpa reached for his cigarette. "Really? Jeez, Charlie, why didn't you tell me about that?"

He proceeded to stub the cigarette out on his left thumbnail.

TWENTY-ONE

RIGHT AFTER CRAWFORD dropped Vega off at Elysium, he got a call on his cell phone.

"Ray Gerster," the display said.

He answered, "Charlie Crawford."

"Yeah, Detective, it's Ray Gerster; you called me a few times."

"Thanks for getting back to me. As I said in my first message, I'm one of the lead detectives on the murder of Christian Lalley and I'd like to meet with you, ask you some questions."

"Why don't you just ask them now?"

"'Cause I'd like to be face-to-face with you."

A long pause. "Well, I guess that's okay if you don't mind coming up to the slums of Riviera Beach.

Parts of Riviera Beach could be a little dicey. "How is eight tomorrow morning?"

"That's fine. I'm an early riser."

"And the address, please?"

Gerster gave it to him and clicked off.

Crawford headed to the station on South County Road. It was 8:15 p.m. and the place would be quiet. It was time to do some research on a number of subjects.

FIRST AND FOREMOST, and long overdue, was Vega. His source on all things SOAR. Its history, its people, its scandals, its… everything. Of course, everything she told him was subjective, colored by the way she saw things. Or maybe the way she wanted *him* to see things. She could spin the facts exactly how she wanted to.

In some respects, she seemed like just a somewhat lonely person, happy to spend time with a man and have an audience, but in some ways… well, he just wondered.

There wasn't much about her on the Internet, but then finally he found something in an obscure corner of LinkedIn that, literally, made his jaw drop in astonishment.

THEN HE TOOK one last look at Xi Kiang just to be one hundred per cent sure he was not his man. After twenty minutes of research, he decided that Kiang was in the clear. Crawford went over to the white board and erased his name.

A few minutes later, he heard footsteps and in walked Dominica McCarthy, looking—as she always did— like a million bucks.

"Hey," Crawford said. "What are you doing here so late?"

"Oh, just catching up on a few things. What about you?"

He motioned to a chair. "Working on Christian Lalley," he said. "Have a seat."

"You getting anywhere?"

He sighed. "Slowly."

She sat down then put one of her long, shapely legs up on Crawford's desk. "Maybe you need me on the case. Like that one a year ago… Pawlichuk."

Dominica had gone undercover back then, posing, convincingly, as a hedonistic party girl. What she'd discovered helped crack the case.

"You have any interest in joining SOAR?"

"What's SOAR?"

He gave her a three-minute explanation

She nodded. "So, I'd play an eager recruit. Get the inside scoop for you."

"I don't know. It could be dangerous."

She didn't hesitate. "Danger's my middle name."

"Thank you, Austin Powers," he said and bumped her on the shoulder. "Hey, is your mother still in town?"

She smiled. "Why? Are you getting—"

"Yup," he said with a smile. "Let me think a little bit more about you going undercover. I'm not quite ready to throw you into that den of weirdos yet. Maybe never."

"I like weirdos," she said. "Mom leaves tomorrow."

"Dinner the day after?"

"You're on."

HE HADN'T YET LOOKED DEEPLY into Fannie Melhado. He'd only had the one long and revealing interview with her.

He Googled her. The first thing that caught his attention was that she had gone to Brown University and had been magna cum laude there. He guessed that's what she meant when she told him she was "almost" a Mensa.

Then he read about something called the Palm Beach Prayer Group. It was a group Fannie had apparently been a member of a few years ago. The *Palm Beach Daily Reporter,* aka, *The Glossy,* made a vague reference to a "friendly takeover" of the Prayer Group some time back, engineered by a "heiress and her minions." Something told Crawford the heiress might be Fannie. Apparently, the evangelistic-leaning Prayer Group had started out with noble philanthropic aspirations but had evolved into a handful of gossipy dilettantes who had a few hours to kill in the afternoons. It seemed rosé and pinot grigio had crept into the picture, making benevolent deeds less of a priority.

Fannie Melhado was quoted in *The Glossy*: "At the end of the day, all I'm trying to do is help give a little direction which Phoebe had once so capably provided."

A not-so-subtle slap in the face of Phoebe, whoever she might be.

Reading between the lines, Phoebe, obviously the former leader, had, according to Fannie's inference, lost her way. *Once* said it all. Crawford figured that the pinot grigio and rosé might have been a contributing factor in Phoebe's loss of direction. What was interesting to Crawford was that Fannie Melhado seemed to now be repeating a similar pattern at SOAR, but on a much larger scale.

Crawford decided to find out Phoebe's last name and put her on his interview list. Try to get to her by early-afternoon before the pinot grigio bottle made its appearance.

He looked at his watch. It was almost 9:45 and he hadn't had dinner. It was looking like he'd be cracking open a can of scrumptious Hormel Corned Beef hash. *Hey, it could be worse*, he thought, remembering Joe Wright's Slim Jim sandwich from a few hours earlier.

He decided it wasn't too late to call Rose Clarke. He knew from experience he could call her up to ten, but never before eight in the morning. He dialed her number.

"Hey, Charlie. What's up?"

"I got a quick real-estate question."

"Shoot."

"Do you know where Coquina Way is in Boca?"

"Of course. I had a listing there once."

"Would you happen to know the house at 702 Coquina Way?"

He heard her clicking her keyboard.

"Oh, yeah, sure, the real modern one."

"Yup. Can you look up the owner?"

Rose had a database that listed all houses in Palm Beach County and their owners' names.

"Sure, hang on a second."

A few moments later, she said, "Alton and Cynthia Kirkwood."

Damn.

"Is that helpful?" Rose asked.

"No... but I still love you," Crawford said. "Well, thanks, I appreciate it."

"Oh, by the way, sometimes it takes a while for a new owner to show up on my database."

"Gotcha. Well, thanks again," Crawford said. "Hey, want to come over to my place and share a can of Hormel corn beef hash?"

She laughed. "The *my place* was tempting. The *corned beef hash*... umm, not so much."

"Got succotash, too."

"You're on your own, Charlie."

TWENTY-TWO

BEFORE CRAWFORD LEFT FOR HOME, he looked a little deeper into Torrance Grey. What he found did not eliminate the man as a murder suspect, but he still remained a long shot. What conceivable motive could there be?

Reading between the lines in one incident, Grey had been harassed in a Palm Beach restaurant, though it was unclear what the issue was, then had gotten in a fistfight with a man one table away. The man he fought with had pressed charges and—apparently seeing a big payday from the former A-list actor— followed it up with a ten-million-dollar lawsuit, which evidently went nowhere. Grey and the other man ended up getting wrist-slaps.

Then, two years ago, Grey was arrested for shoplifting. *How the Mighty Have Fallen* screamed the headline in *The Glossy* as it recounted the story: He had apparently gone to the Costco in Palm Beach Gardens, and as he was going through the check-out line, a Costco manager had approached him and asked him what he was palming in his left hand. Reluctantly, Grey turned his hand over, opened it up and there was a fifteen- hundred-dollar Raymond Weil Freelancer watch. He was ignominiously arrested as shoppers around him pointed and whispered, "That's the guy who was in…" and "Isn't that the actor…"

He claimed he had just forgotten it was there and fully intended to put it on the conveyor belt and pay for it.

Two months of community service this time, and he was told by the judge that next time he was arrested he would do time.

Crawford got home at 9:50 and sat down in front of the TV at 10:40 with a plateful of corned beef hash and succotash on a tray table. He remembered the words from his mother that eating dinner a short time before going to bed was bad for you. He couldn't remember the reason why, though.

———

CRUX WAS WEARING blue silk pajamas as he slid into the Pizuna satin sheets in his colossally oversized bed. For a change, no one would be joining him. He had made a few overtures—Lena in Callisto, hinting that her presence in his bed might lead to relocation to Elysium, and an oldie-but-goodie, Vega—who had had turned him down without an excuse or explanation.

His mind bounced from one subject to the next, which usually made falling asleep at least a one-hour process. He couldn't get the two homicide cops out of his mind. All he could think of was the cliché, *dogs with a bone,* how they were fixated on the incident involving Holmes Whitmore and the two boys. *Jesus, give it a rest.* Okay, so what if he had orchestrated the whole thing...? No one had died and Whitmore was a piece of shit anyway. Ruined his old man's life, and his mother's. The guy deserved to be drummed out of town in disgrace. Then, as his head flopped from one pillow to another, he thought about Xi Kiang. The man—even in his late sixties—seemed quite effective at teaching that exercise regimen, whatever it was called, but the jury was still out whether he could deliver the big numbers for SOAR as he had done for Falun Gong.

Crux heard a barely audible noise but didn't think anything of it. His mind shifted to Fannie Melhado. The woman's ambitions seemed limitless. He couldn't figure out if that was a good or a bad thing. A good thing, he concluded, as long as she didn't forget who was the boss. He considered all the money she and her brother had committed to SOAR. But he wasn't in it for the money, rather what it could achieve for SOAR. He had no interest in being like that Indian religious leader who had twenty-three Rolls Royces or the scam man in Albany who had taken the Bronfman sister for a hundred-million-dollar ride. Those men were clearly in it for the sex and money.

Sure, he'd take those things, but what he really was after was at least a chapter or two in the history books. 'Religious visionary'... now that was something that had a really nice ring to it. Or for that matter, anything with the word 'visionary' in it.

He heard another noise. It seemed to come from across his bedroom. Like a creaking floorboard.

And then, suddenly, he felt two hands around his neck.

TWENTY-THREE

HE TRIED to yell but nothing came out. The man—there was no question it was a man because of the body mass and the sound of his grunting—was on top of Crux, trying to strangle him. Crux swung his elbow up at the man's head but missed. He was starting to panic because the man had tightened his two-handed grip to the point where Crux could hardly breathe. He tried to scream again but it came out as a flat hiss. He guessed the man weighed fifty pounds more than him.

Do something quick or you're a dead man.

He suddenly rolled hard to his left, hoping he could buck the man off. The man's body shifted but he still maintained the chokehold and stayed on top. Crux rolled with all he had in the opposite direction and this time he slipped out of the grasp of the larger man. The man's hands loosened and Crux started to scream. But then, out of nowhere, the man smashed him hard in the left cheek. That was surprising, since it was pitch-black in the room. How could his assailant have targeted him? A lucky punch? Whatever it was, Crux saw something that looked like the flash of fireworks, then fade to black.

"THOSE FUCKERS ARE AT IT AGAIN!"

It was Ott, calling on his cell.

Crawford just knew it was somewhere between 11:35 p.m.—when he'd turned off the TV—and daybreak.

"What's up, Mort?" he rasped.

"Someone tried to kill Crux, the SOAR guy."

"Jesus, is he okay?"

"He's gonna live."

Crawford looked at his white-faced alarm clock. 12:30.

"Any suspect?"

"Nope."

"All right, I'll see you there in twenty minutes."

"Very inconsiderate. These cultist douchebags."

CRUX HAD angry red marks all around his neck, a swollen left cheek, and a blackened right eye. He was still wearing blue silk pajamas that had splotches of blood above his chest from a bloody nose. He, Ott, and Crawford were sitting in a sun porch on the first floor. It was just past one in the morning.

"Guy reeked of booze," Crux said. "Like he had just taken a bath in a vat of bourbon or something."

"So, you couldn't make out any of his features," Ott said, "except he weighed a lot more than you."

Crux nodded. "Yeah, he was straddling me, and I couldn't get him off me."

"You were asleep when it happened?" Crawford asked.

"On the verge," Crux said. "I remember hearing something in the room but didn't really think anything of it."

Crawford was not looking forward to another night of interviewing Elysium residents. As before, they had all been woken up and ushered into the living room by two uniform cops who had gotten to the scene first.

"What kind of a sound was it you heard?" Ott asked.

"Ah, like a creak in the floor."

Ott eyes shot to Crawford, then back to Crux. "Do you have mice here?"

"Is that a joke?"

"Not at all. Just if I heard my floor creak, I'd want to know what it was."

Crux eyed him with mild spite but said nothing.

"So, you have absolutely no idea who it could have been?" Crawford asked.

"Absolutely none."

Crawford's eyes shifted to Ott. "Let's talk to the others."

Ott nodded.

"Okay," Crawford said to Crux. "You sure you don't want to go to Good Sam?"

"Yes, I'm fine. Well, not fine," he said, gingerly touching his cheek, "but nothing's broken or anything."

"That's good," Crawford said, standing up.

The three of them walked into the living room where the others were.

Crawford saw Fannie Melhado across the room. She stood and walked up to them.

"I think I know who may have done this," she said matter-of-factly to Crawford.

"Can you follow us, please?" Crawford said, turning to walk out of the living room.

Ott, Crux, and Fannie Melhado followed him back to the porch and they all sat down.

"So, who do you think it was?" Crawford asked.

"A man named Bartholomew Moulton."

The strange thing was the name was familiar to Crawford but from way back. From where he grew up in Connecticut. How many Bartholomew Moultons could there be?

"Who's he?" asked Crux.

Fannie slouched in her chair and didn't answer right away. Then, barely audibly. "An old boyfriend of mine."

"Why the hell is an old boyfriend of yours attacking me in my bed?" Crux asked, outraged.

"Let us ask the questions, please," Crawford said.

Crux threw up his hands. "I just want—"

Crawford held up a hand. "Tell us why you think that," he said to Fannie in an even tone.

And Fannie Melhado proceeded to lay it all out.

Bartholomew Moulton—she said he didn't allow anyone to call him Bart—was a man from a so-called "good family," who was handsome, athletic, formerly rich but no longer, and always held doors for ladies and wrote thank-you notes.

She had met him at a charity ball several years ago in Palm Beach, and shortly after that they had started dating, or "seeing each other," as she said. He didn't take long to propose to her.

"It was at a time when I was going through what my brother refers to as my... metamorphosis."

"Your what?" Ott asked.

"Metamorphosis," Fannie clarified. "Back when I met Bartholomew, I was still attracted to handsome, witty men"—she glanced at Crawford—"but over time realized that they were, for the most part, superficial and shallow. Not to mention, I had a strong sense Bartholomew was after my money."

Crawford cocked his head. "So, after this, ah, metamorphosis—"

"I was more interested in brains and character, not pretty faces."

Crawford nodded, but this information didn't explain why Bartholomew Moulton had ended up in Crux's bedroom. "Ms. Melhado, why—"

"All right, I know, I know," she cut in. "I'm getting to it. So, about a year ago, I broke up with him. I think he was pretty crushed. He kept calling and emailing, but I never got back to him. I mean, it was over. So, he called my brother, who he kind of had become friends with, and talked Freddie into letting him in."

"Let him inside Elysium, you mean?" asked Ott.

She nodded and her eyes dropped to the floor. Like she had suddenly decided she didn't want to finish the story. Or there was a thorny detail or two she'd just as soon skip over. She looked up and caught Crux's eye, then quickly looked back down. "You remember, right?"

Crux nodded, as if whatever she was referring to wasn't a pleasant memory.

Crawford shrugged. "My partner and I are in the dark here. How 'bout filling us in?"

"Well, so... Freddie told Bartholomew downstairs that I didn't want to see him, and Bartholomew just lost it and ran up to my room." She glanced over at Crux again. "I wasn't in my room... I, I was next door in—" She nodded at Crux. "In his room."

"Son-of-bitch attacked both of us," Crux cried out. "I had no idea who he was or what it was about."

"But that was a year ago...why—" Crawford began.

"He started calling me again a few days ago," Fannie said in a rush, then exhaled slowly, "asking me if we could give it another chance. I said no as emphatically as I could, but he didn't give up. I said I didn't want to see him under any circumstances and thought that was the end of it."

"But it wasn't?" Ott asked.

She shook her head. "He called Freddie—again—and told him he had a present for me."

"When was this?"

"Today," Fannie said. "My brother, who's kind of a soft touch, let him in and went up and got me. I said, no way was I going to see him. Freddie said, 'It's all right, he just has a present for you.' I said, 'It's not all right, the man scares the hell out of me.' Anyway, I finally agreed to see him—Freddie was going to be there, so I figured it would be safe— and went downstairs. Bartholomew had a package in his hand and was giving me this off-kilter grin. I asked him what it was, and he said, 'Why do people always ask that? Just open it.' So, I did, and it was this needlepoint pillow that used to be on his bed that said, *Miss you, babe.* I looked at him and he still had that off-kilter grin, so I said, "Bartholomew, I don't want to ever see you again. Just stop it; it's been over for a long time.' He said, 'It's that guy, isn't it?' I told him it didn't matter, just please leave."

"So, what happened?" Ott asked.

"He ran out. I think he was crying."

"But you think he came back tonight," Crawford said. "You think he was the one who assaulted Crux."

She nodded. "'Cause my brother stopped by my room after Bartholomew was here and asked if I'd seen his keys. Thought he might have left them in my room when he came up to get me."

Crawford nodded. "I get it, so you think Bartholomew ended up grabbing Freddie's keys?"

"After I heard what happened to Crux, yes, that's exactly what I thought."

"The keys, what do they look like?"

"Just keys, but—oh wait—there was this embroidered Irish setter keychain. Freddie's old dog."

"So, Bartholomew figured Crux was the man you were seeing?"

Fannie nodded.

"But he wasn't?" Crawford asked.

Fannie shook her head.

"So, who is?" Ott asked.

Fannie turned on him and gave him a dirty look. "It's none of your damn business, but as of this moment… no one."

TWENTY-FOUR

MOST OF THE other Elysium residents hadn't heard a thing until they were awakened by the siren from the car of the first officer on scene, then the pounding on the front door when no one answered after the cop pressed the buzzer. Nothing in the interviews of the other seven Elysium residents made Crawford and Ott suspect that any of them had anything to do with the attack on Crux.

They walked out of Elysium at 3:35 a.m. They'd learned where Bartholomew Moulton lived from Fannie Melhado—in a little rental on Seabreeze—and were heading there now. Ott had suggested that it could wait until later that morning, after they got some sleep. Crawford had simply said, "It's time to put someone in jail, even though this guy probably had nothing to do with Christian Lalley."

Halfway down North Lake Way, Crawford turned to Ott: "I knew this guy in another life."

"Moulton?"

"Yeah, we grew up in the same town in Connecticut. Greenwich. He was a year older than me—what they used to call a Big Man on Campus. Guy was a jock who always got the girls. One of those older guys you look up to."

"Weren't you kind of like that, Charlie?"

"Hell no, man. I was a fat-faced kid in high school. Didn't start growing until I was a junior. But this guy Moulton had it all. I heard he ended up being a model when he was like twenty."

Ott pulled into the driveway of the address Fannie Melhado had given them. There were no lights on.

"Hey, by the way, remind me to tell you about Vega when we get done with this."

Ott turned to Crawford. "Something good?"

"Maybe... I'll let you be the judge."

They got out of the Crown Vic and Crawford walked over to an older-model Mercedes parked in the driveway. He put his hand on the hood. "Warm."

Ott nodded.

They walked up to the front door.

"Think we need weapons?" Ott asked, his voice lowered.

"I doubt it," Crawford said. "Be ready, though."

Ott put his hand on his holstered Glock as Crawford rang the doorbell.

After a minute or so they saw a light snap on. A few moments later a man came to the door. He was shirtless and wearing only boxer shorts. Crawford recognized him right away. Probably forty years old to Crawford's thirty-nine, a little stoop-shouldered and with a slight case of early-stage jowliness. But still handsome. His eyes, which Crawford remembered as electric, azure blue, were still striking but somewhat dulled, as if a few cirrus clouds had drifted across a brilliant, bright blue sky.

"Mr. Moulton?" Crawford asked, even though he knew it was.

"Yeah, what the hell is this?" Moulton asked.

"I'm Detective Crawford, this is my partner, Detective Ott. May we come in?"

"What do you want?" He glanced at his watch. "It's four o'clock in the goddamn morning."

"Yes, we know," Ott said. "May we come in?"

"Hold on," Moulton said. "I gotta get my pants."

He walked away.

Ott chuckled.

"What?"

"All you Connecticut boys wear boxers?"

Crawford smiled. "Just certain parts of Connecticut."

"The non-tighty-whitey parts, huh?"

Moulton came back wearing khakis, a yellow sport shirt, and no shoes. He gestured at the pair. "Come on."

They followed him back to a living room. The best you could say about it was that it was dated, but more accurately, the furniture in it was tired and shopworn. Everything about it was faded and dismal.

Moulton sat down and let Crawford and Ott decide where they wanted to light. Crawford ended up on an orange couch, the kind with big black buttons, though this one was missing a few. Ott sat in a white leather chair from the 1950s that could have used a scrub with some Comet and a hot sponge.

Moulton leaned closer to Crawford as something seemed to register. "You look familiar. Have we met before?"

Crawford didn't hesitate. "No, we haven't. Mr. Moulton, we have reason to believe that you went to 1500 North Lake Way earlier tonight and assaulted a man there."

His blue eyes seemed to darken. "What in God's name—"

"The same house you went to earlier today to see Fannie Melhado," Ott said.

"When you brought her a pillow that said, *Miss you, babe,*" Crawford added.

Moulton sighed and looked away.

"Mr. Moulton, would you mind emptying your pockets?" Crawford asked.

"Why? What the hell for?"

"To prove we got the wrong guy."

Moulton groaned, reached into his pockets, and pulled out a checked handkerchief, some change, and a several keys on a chain that had an embroidered Irish setter dog.

"What do those keys go to, Mr. Moulton?" Crawford asked, pointing.

Moulton looked at them like he'd never seen them. "Ah, a friend's house."

"And why do you have them?"

His brow furrowed as if he was concentrating on a very difficult question. "Because she's out of town and asked me to water her plants and, ah, feed her cat."

"What's the address?" Crawford asked.

"In West Palm."

"Street and number?"

"Murray Street, um, 61 Murray Street."

"Okay, let's go there now," Crawford said.

There was a look of panic in Moulton's eyes. "Why in God's name—"

"Those are Freddie Melhado's keys to 1500 North Lake Way, aren't they?"

Moulton didn't answer.

"Where were you earlier tonight between midnight and 12:30, Mr. Moulton?" Crawford asked, getting to his feet.

Moulton still didn't answer.

"There are cameras up and down North Lake Way, including several right around 1500," Ott exaggerated, as he stood.

"We're arresting you for assaulting Lucian Neville earlier tonight," Crawford said. "Please stand up. My partner's going to read you your rights."

Shakily, Moulton got to his feet and finally spoke, addressing Crawford. "That bastard was sleeping with my girlfriend. How would you feel?"

"You're wrong on both counts," Crawford said.

"What are you talking about?"

"One, she's not your girlfriend, and two, I don't think she's sleeping with him these days."

"Yeah, you got the wrong guy," Ott chimed in, then read Moulton his Miranda.

"Put your hands behind your back, please, Mr. Moulton," Crawford said. "I'm going to handcuff you."

Moulton, just a few feet away, eyed Crawford like he was trying to place him. "Are you sure we don't know each other? From Greenwich, I'm thinking?"

"Greenwich where?"

"Connecticut."

"Never heard of it."

TWENTY-FIVE

THE ARREST of Bartholomew Moulton didn't stop there. Crawford and Ott drove to the station and had a nice, long talk with him in a not-so-nice, small interrogation room. When it became clear to Moulton that they had a mountain of circumstantial evidence as well as the strong possibility of catching him on a security camera, he confessed, going from a small room to an even smaller one…with bars.

It was five o'clock when they put Moulton in the cell. Ott decided to go home and get a few hours of sleep, Crawford elected to stay at the station, mainly because he had an appointment with Ray Gerster up at Riviera Beach at eight o'clock. He also was eager to interview Phoebe, whose last name he still didn't yet know, the apparent creator of the Palm Beach Prayer Group. He figured she might be able to give him some insights into Fannie Melhado, as it seemed obvious Fannie had tried to hijack Phoebe's group and make it her baby.

Finding Phoebe's last name was easy. All he did was Google "Palm Beach Prayer Group." The first thing that came up was a short article in *The Glossy* from twelve years ago. "Phoebe Lilly," the article started out, "who you see tooling around town in her 'sensible car,' a Prius, is the primary force, and founder, behind the Palm Beach Prayer Group. Phoebe—worth hundreds of millions—has no problem being referred

to as a 'born again Christian' and professes to have a 'special relationship with Jesus.' Her group presently has more than thirty members
and her immediate objective is to establish other chapters throughout
Florida (Vero Beach, Boca Raton and Naples are only a few.) So, if you
see a car decal with a subtle cross or a not-so-subtle Born², chances are
it's either Phoebe or one of her fellow Prayer Group members."

Crawford looked at his watch. 5:45. It was too early to be calling
Phoebe Lilly but not too early for the Starbucks on Worth Avenue. Or
so he thought. He needed a shot of caffeine and drove there. He
double-parked and walked to the Starbucks inside. It was closed and
didn't open until 7:00.

Bummer.

Just another reason to patronize Dunkin' Donuts, or Dunkin' as
they were trying to call it these days. It was always open, or at least the
one on Okeechobee always was. Why wasn't there one in Palm Beach?
he wondered. He knew the answer: too downscale, not in keeping with
the highfalutin' Palm Beach image. Same reason there wasn't a
McDonald's or Burger King.

He drove over the bridge to the Dunkin' Donuts—which he was
never going to call just Dunkin'—on Okeechobee. He ordered his
standard go-to, a medium extra-dark and two blueberry donuts.

He took his first sip. Ah, heaven. No comparison. In his opinion,
it was way better than the Seattle alternative, plus he didn't have to
listen to their schmaltzy music. Michael Bublé and that skinny guy
who played the sax…He walked back to his car with his breakfast. He
chuckled to himself about the time he had tried to convince Dominica
that the two blueberry donuts were health food.

She'd rolled her eyes and replied, "You mean because each one has
three blueberry specks which you can't even see unless you use a
microscope?"

But Crawford wasn't going to give up without a fight. "Well," he
said, examining one of the donuts, "I'm counting at least six specks in
this one alone."

"Jesus, Charlie, you're right. It's practically a salad."

He'd laughed at that. "I knew you'd see it my way."

He turned the ignition key and backed up. It was still dark, but there was the faint light of the sun coming up. He decided to go to one of his favorites spots and watch the sun rise. It was down near the town docks, where some of the biggest boats were docked. There was a bench on a lawn where people walked their dogs—and very scrupulously cleaned up after them—that Crawford had discovered and found to be a good place to simply sit and think. Or, in this case, watch the sun come up over the Intracoastal. It was six-fifteen when he plopped onto the empty metal bench and turned his mind to the case.

Then he flashed back to Bartholomew Moulton in his boxers a few hours before. One would never guess he was the high-scoring wing on the Greenwich Country Day School hockey team who went on to become the MVP on the Choate team. Crawford was pretty sure he had gone on to Williams or Wesleyan from there, one of those small but academically rigorous New England colleges. Then… who knew, exactly? Crawford had heard that he had been in a bar, or maybe it was a party, when a scout for a modeling agency had approached him about becoming a model. Crawford even remembered seeing Moulton's handsome visage in a beer or liquor ad. Fitting, he'd thought. Moulton had also become the spokesman for some hotel chain in TV commercials, but Crawford couldn't remember which.

He'd also heard rumors about Moulton's drinking. How he ended up at one of those rehab places out in Minnesota, where they all go. Or maybe it was Silverhill in Connecticut, with their all-star line-up of celebrity graduates. Then he'd lost track of the man.

As he watched the gold glimmer peek out over the horizon, he thought about others he had gone to school with. The really smart guys who seemed to have stalled out in the corporate world. Or the really, *really* smart ones who had their own jets and yachts. The so-so students who became Silicon Valley dynamos. The many who took the train every day to jobs they hated. The few who didn't give a damn about money and were either selfless teachers or working for a cause they were dedicated to.

Then there was him: Charles J. Crawford.

Greenwich Country Day School. Taft School. Dartmouth College. A homicide detective. Of everyone he knew, he had probably started more tongues wagging than anyone else. How could a guy who went to twelve years of exclusive private schools, then an Ivy League college, end up a cop? Especially one who'd had three generations of prominent Wall Street bankers precede him and a nice job waiting at Morgan Stanley when he graduated.

He had told a few friends about the single incident that had re-routed his career but most of them didn't really get it.

One of his friends told another one:

"Charlie told me how a buddy of his from the Dartmouth football team got killed the night before graduation. This black dude. And how the cops knew who did it but couldn't get enough on the guy to arrest him. Something like that. So, Charlie hung around that summer in Hanover, New Hampshire, playing amateur detective, trying to get the guy. Never did, though."

"That's it? That's why he bailed on Wall Street? Gave up his future?" the listener asked.

"Yeah, plus his father's suicide. I guess his father told him once how he'd spent thirty-five years at a job he basically couldn't stand."

"Yeah, but still… a *cop*?"

"Hey, I'm just telling you what I heard."

There were times when it didn't make sense to Crawford himself. His lame apartment overlooking a grocery-store parking lot. The fact that he hadn't taken a vacation in forever. His Camry beater… okay, he wasn't a BMW kind of guy, anyway, but come on….

But there were also the times when he knew he had done the right thing. Like when he put really bad people—murderers—away for life. It resonated with him when Rose described the rush she got making a colossal real-estate deal. The amazing high. Well, maybe it wasn't exactly a high he got, but something pretty close. An exhilarating feeling that lasted a while. A feeling of accomplishment. Of doing something that maybe no other person could do as well or as consistently.

Because, like Rose Clarke, he was damn good at his job. And fuck 'em if they didn't get it.

But still, he thought, maybe it was finally time for a housing upgrade.

TWENTY-SIX

THE SUNRISE WAS spectacular and so were the blueberry donuts.

He went back to the station and found Ott there.

"Couldn't sleep," Ott explained.

Crawford told him what he had found out about Phoebe Lilly and the prayer group she started.

Ott smiled and put down his coffee. "I saw this bumper sticker the other day. Know what it said?"

"What?" Crawford asked, apprehensively.

"Jesus Loves You...."

"Yeah?"

Long, dramatic pause. "'But Everyone Else Thinks You're An Asshole,'" Ott said. "Oh hey, that reminds me, I was supposed to ask you what you found out about Vega."

"Oh yeah, so get this, she went to Yale and... get ready for it... belonged to Skull and Bones there."

Ott's eyes got big. "No shit, that secret group of... wannabe spooks?"

Crawford laughed. "That pretty much nails it," he said. "So ever since I found that out, I've been thinking about her."

"What do you mean? What about her?"

"Like the fact that she's about the only member at Elysium who doesn't have a big job. Or a title. You know, just about everyone else there is either a COO, a CEO, a CIO, or some damn thing. Or at least very involved with SOAR. Vega is just kind of a ... I don't know, resident. She knows everything that goes on in SOAR but isn't like a... participant. Kind of detached."

"So, you mean, like... passive?"

"Yeah, exactly," Crawford said, then after a few moments. "I've got a theory I'm working on."

"Okay, let's hear it, bro."

"Came up with it after I found out about the Skull and Bones thing."

"Okay, okay," Ott said, motioning with his hand, "come on, out with it."

"I think she might be Crux's spy. That he's a little paranoid, maybe it goes back to that Holmes Whitmore thing with his mother and father, or maybe he was just born that way."

"Yeah, keep going."

"So, Vega... she seems to get along with everyone and because she's not threatening and because she clearly doesn't miss a trick, Crux saw her as the perfect spy. She can keep him informed about everything, be his eyes and ears. Like if Fannie Melhado's planning to try to take over, or, I don't know, Christian Lalley's talking to that reporter..."

"Shit, Charlie, I like it. It's a damn good theory."

"And to take it a little further, she might also be spying on me. Trying to find out what we've got, or steering me in a certain direction, or away from another one."

"Yeah, innocent little Vega, who knows everything," Ott said, then he started shaking his head. "That Skull and Bones outfit...another weird Ivy League thing."

He relished opportunities to take potshots at Crawford's alma mater.

Crawford raised his eyebrows. "Hell, us Dartmouth guys just guzzled grain alcohol and passed out naked in snowdrifts."

"Good clean fun," Ott said. "Seriously, what's with that Skull and Bones shit?"

"How would I know? It's secret."

"Yeah, but you know about it."

"Not really, I just know that some famous people were in it," Crawford said, and he typed up Google on his MacBook Air.

"Like who?"

"Hang on a sec." He started scanning the results. "Well, like both George H.W. Bush and George W. Bush, John Kerry, William F. Buckley... another president, William Howard Taft—"

"He was the really fat one, right?"

"Yet another *un*-politically correct comment."

"Sorry, how 'bout morbidly obese?"

"Now this is interesting," Crawford said, still reading about Yale's most famous secret society. "These are other names Skull and Bones goes by... The Order... Order 322 and... The Brotherhood of Death."

"No shit, so three presidents were members of a thing called *The Brotherhood of Death*," Ott said. "Speaks well for the office."

Crawford cocked his head to one side. "Well, doesn't mean they actually killed people."

Ott chucked. "Phew, that's a load off my mind... so what are you gonna do about Vega?"

"I don't really know. Just watch her closely. I change anything and she'll pick up on it."

Ott nodded.

Crawford glanced down at his watch. "All right, I'm gonna head up to Riviera Beach."

"Sounds good," said Ott. "Probably too early for the gangbangers to be making their rounds."

———

CRAWFORD CHURNED through all his conversations with Vega on his way up to Riviera Beach. She had done most of the talking, but she also—in her own subtle way—had gotten information out of him. More importantly, she had masterfully directed conversation to where, it seemed in retrospect, she wanted it to go. And had made it easy for Crawford to reach conclusions. The conclusions she, no doubt, wanted him to make.

Crawford always thought Riviera Beach got a bad rap. Bimini Lane had a number of very nice houses and Ray Gerster's was one of them.

Crawford was looking out the back window of Gerster's home. Behind, it had a small pool, next to a channel with a dock. Docked was what looked like a sportfishing boat.

"What kind is it?" he asked Gerster.

Gerster looked more like a middle-aged surfer than a tax-cheat. He had blonde hair and a perfect tan that Crawford suspected may have been bronzer enhanced.

"A Rampage 38."

"Nice," Crawford said, and sat in a white leather chair that bore a striking resemblance to the one he'd sat in at Bartholomew Moulton's house only five hours before.

He'd expected a man who had spent two years in prison to be living a little more modestly and not have such a nice tan.

"So, as I said, I'm the lead detective on Christian Lalley's murder and would appreciate whatever help you can give me."

"Hey," Gerster said with a shrug, "Christian was my friend and accountant. Whatever I can do to help, I will."

"But he was a friend and accountant who testified against you. Correct?"

"Yeah, but I forgave him for that. He got squeezed by the IRS. I would have gotten convicted with or without his testimony."

"You're pretty forgiving."

"I've had a long time to think about the whole thing."

"But his wife said you threatened to kill him."

"Did I?"

"That's what she said."

"Well, I didn't mean it," Gerster said. "Hey, that's just not me."

Crawford nodded. "So, as I understand it, he testified you ran a Ponzi—"

"Don't call it that," Gerster protested. "I got in a jam where investors were pulling their money out of my fund all at the same time. I needed new investors to make the old investors whole."

Crawford cocked his head. "Isn't that the definition of a Ponzi scheme?"

"A Ponzi scheme is when early investors are getting money that they think are profits and returns but it's really just money from new investors coming into the fund."

Crawford didn't want to get into a debate about it. "Okay, whatever. I'm really more interested if you know of, or if Christian Lalley ever told you about, someone he may have feared, someone who may have threatened him; you know, someone who might've killed him."

"Like I said, when you're in the slammer you have a lot of time to think."

"I gotcha. So, what did you come up with?"

Gerster tapped the arm of his chair. "You ready for a longshot?"

Crawford leaned in. "Sure, whatever you got."

"You ever heard the name Andy Barrow?"

Crawford shook his head.

"I'm not surprised," Gerster said. "So, Andy is a caddy at some fancy club like the Poinciana in Palm Beach, except it's not the Poinciana. And he met Christian's daughter, Samantha, a year or so ago in a bar, I think it was. Anyway, they hit it off and after a while it got serious, then Christian heard about it. He was not happy. Told me once, 'I'm not about to let my daughter marry a goddamn caddy, especially one who was a high school drop-out.' But it was too late, his daughter, who was a dental assistant, was already engaged to Barrow and wanted to marry the guy. So, Christian put heavy pressure on her to break it off. I think his wife, Lorinda, got pretty involved too."

"How old were they? Andy and Samantha?"

"I think she was like twenty-five and he was a few years older. Anyway, it sounded like the guy was gonna be a caddy for life, or until his knees gave out." Gerster paused and took a sip of coffee. "So, Chris and Lorinda were real persistent and finally Samantha caves and cancels the engagement. So, Andy goes to Chris, who he's never met before, and tries to plead his case. But all Christian's sees is the kid's mullet and hears him call him 'man.'"

"What did he say exactly?"

"I don't know, something like, *I love your daughter... man*. So, Chris tells him he doesn't want him marrying her and Andy kind of snaps, grabs Chris's shirt with one hand and says, 'This ain't the end of this.'"

"Really?"

Gerster nodded. "Flash forward to a week after Christian gets killed—"

"The two get married?"

"How'd you know?"

"I've seen that movie before... or maybe its sequel."

TWENTY-SEVEN

As THEIR CONVERSATION was winding down, Ray Gerster remembered at which club Andy Barrow was a caddy: a fancy place called Blowing Dunes.

After he left Gerster's house, Crawford called the country club and asked for the golf shop, then got transferred to someone else, who he asked to be connected to Andy Barrow.

"Uh, AB's out loopin'," the man said.

Crawford, being an experienced but less-than-average golfer, knew that "looping" meant caddying eighteen holes.

"When he gets back in, ask him to call Charlie Crawford, please," Crawford said, electing to leave out 'Detective.' No sense in getting the person who answered suspicious, or Barrow in trouble. "Tell him it's important. He left his number."

Next, he called Phoebe Lilly, whose number he got by Googling the Palm Beach Prayer Group again. He didn't have any better luck there and left a message.

Then he called Rose Clarke, who always answered his calls. Not this time, though. He left her a message, too.

After Rose was Vega. No luck again. He left another message. 0 for

4. He was beginning to feel unloved, but then Rose called back a few minutes later.

"Hey, Charlie. You rang?"

"I know you don't touch a buyer who's looking for a house for under five million," he said. "So, I wondered if maybe you could recommend an agent who can show places for between three and four hundred thousand."

She was silent for a few moments. "I'm guessing the prospective buyer might be you?"

"Yeah, I'm looking for a condo. I don't want to mow grass or pull weeds and I'd really like a nice view."

"That Publix parking lot got old, huh?"

She had been to his place on more than one occasion.

"Yeah, the ocean would be great. Got somebody you can recommend?"

She didn't hesitate. "Yeah, me."

She'd totally be slumming it, taking him around to dumps barely up to the standards of her cleaning lady, but *if she was game....*

"Do you even know what a condo is?" he asked.

She laughed. "There're plenty of five-million-dollar condos. There are even some for over ten."

"Yeah, well, drop a zero or two. Plus, your commission is gonna be about forty-eight bucks."

"Charlie, I would be honored to squire you around. There's a pretty good selection on the market right now. It's a buyer's market. I'm thinking of something on North or South Flagler would be good for you. You can get some amazing views there. The Intracoastal in the foreground, then Palm Beach, and the ocean off in the distance."

"You sure you don't mind?"

"It would be fun. I think you can probably get two bedrooms, two baths in that price range. Only thing is the bedrooms run pretty small. Square footage would probably be between eleven-hundred and twelve-hundred square feet. Something like that."

"That's plenty. I think my rental's around a thousand. Hey, I really appreciate it. The best broker in Palm Beach taking me around in her shiny white Jag. What an honor!"

Rose laughed. "How about financing? Are you going to need a mortgage?"

"Nah, I got cash. Us homicide cops pull down the big bucks. Truth is, I never spend money on anything."

"That's not true. You took me out to dinner at Buccan once."

"Yeah, 'cause I had an ulterior motive."

Rose chuckled. "And, as I recall, it worked."

TWENTY-EIGHT

They agreed to go look at condos on Sunday. Rose said she would email him a bunch of listings in his price range in buildings on Flagler, with an emphasis on ones that were on high floors and had good views.

A little while later, Phoebe Lilly called back. "Did I do anything wrong?" she asked in a friendly tone. "It's Phoebe Lilly. I don't have detectives calling me all that often."

"No, ma'am, you're good. I'm working on a case and just wanted to stop by and ask you a question or two. Background information, really."

"On what subject, may I ask?"

"Fannie Melhado."

A pause. Then, a change of tone. "Oh, Fannie. Well, she no longer belongs to my group."

"I know. Do you have any time this afternoon?"

"Sure. How's three o'clock?"

"That's perfect. And the address, please?"

BEFORE HE MET with Phoebe Lilly, Crawford decided to go over to West Palm—specifically Flagler Drive, which ran along the Intracoastal—and drive up and down it, looking at buildings that had good views. He was getting more and more into the idea of having a nice place, one that looked out over not one, but two, bodies of water. He also started thinking about getting a new car. The Camry had served him long and loyally, but it was time. Then he went a level deeper and wondered why it was that, since he'd left New York, he had always had a shitty car and lived in a shitty apartment.

He could have afforded something better, quite a lot better.

It was odd. *He* was odd.

Was he rejecting his childhood? His entire privileged background? Was that it? Growing up rich—well, maybe not rich, but certainly well-off—in one of the richest towns in the country?

If so, why? What was the point?

He came to the realization that, if not for the one big incident in his life—his friend getting run down on purpose the night before his Dartmouth graduation—his whole life would have turned out vastly different. He would have taken the job that had already been offered him at Morgan Stanley and probably worked in some branch of finance for the rest of his life: a banker, a trader, or maybe a hedgefund honcho. That was where many of his friends, along with his brother Cam, had ended up. Chances are he would have bought a co-op somewhere in New York City, a summer place—Nantucket, Martha's Vineyard, the Hamptons—and, odds were good, still be married to Jill. Because that was the life that she'd wanted. The one he hadn't given her.

He looked up at twin buildings on Flagler and saw a sign that said Rapallo. He pulled up in front and studied the structures. They looked to be about twenty stories high and were facing due east. The views from the high floors had to be spectacular.

He drove ten minutes north and saw another building on the right with a sign that said Placido Mar. Again, he pulled over and looked up. It, too, looked like it had jaw-dropping views and was even taller than the Rapallo buildings. He imagined seeing tanker ships miles off on the horizon, puttering along in the ocean. Or seeing Crux's new yacht down on the Intracoastal making its maiden voyage.

He looked at his watch. It was 1:50 p.m. He was going to be late for his meeting with Phoebe Lilly at 611 Island Drive on Everglades Island. He did a U-turn and caught the Placido Mar building in his rearview mirror. He liked the name. He could picture himself living there.

But enough of that... A condo and new car could wait. He was spending way too much time on personal stuff. The killer of Christian Lalley was still out there, not where he belonged—behind bars.

As HE DROVE up to Phoebe Lilly's house, he imagined that if he had taken the route in life he'd been destined for, he could reasonably have expected to one day own a house like hers. Hell, he knew guys his age —late thirties, early forties—who already had them.

He chuckled to himself.

Nah...a nice two-bedroom at Placido Mar with a killer view will be just fine.

He figured Phoebe Lilly to be around sixty as she walked him out to the covered back porch of her house on Island Drive. She turned, shaded her eyes, and looked up at him. "Have a seat." She motioned to a padded chair that looked out at the Intracoastal. "I'll give you the one with the nice view."

He imagined being up on the twentieth floor of his place in the Placido Mar, looking down at Lilly and himself. Two little specks a few miles away.

"So, what would you like to know about Fannie Melhado?" she asked once they were seated. "And the bigger question is why are you investigating her, but you probably won't tell me that."

Crawford tapped the arm of the chair and looked off in the distance at two tall buildings. He was pretty sure it was the Rapallo buildings he had gazed up at only a half-hour ago.

"I'm one of the detectives working on the case of the man killed up on North Lake Way earlier this week—"

"Christian Lalley."

"Yes, did you know him?"

"No, I didn't, but, of course, I read all about it. And knew that Fannie's a member of that group he was in."

'That group' had a distinctly disdainful ring to it.

That was when he noticed that Lilly was chewing gum. It was so incongruous, this woman in a crisp, light blue dress and expensive-looking shoes with little bows on them. Crawford seemed to remember they were called Belgian shoes. Rose had a pair, maybe two, maybe ten. Phoebe sported perfectly-coiffed but unmistakably bleached-blond hair and a patrician accent. She was almost a stereo-type of the many rich, elegant, WASPs who had a winter house in Palm Beach, not to mention two or three others scattered around the country or the world. Crawford had heard her type of accent referred to as Locust Valley lockjaw.

Gum? he thought again. *Really?*

"Ms. Lilly—"

"I'm old-fashioned. Mrs. Lilly, please.'

"Mrs. Lilly…could you tell me a little bit about Fannie Melhado's time with your group?"

Phoebe nodded. "Sure. I knew Fannie before she was in the group. She's a smart woman, outspoken, not very good at suffering fools. Gets kind of impatient. Anyway, I think she was looking for a project. She wasn't cut out to be a mere dilettante all her life."

"She told you that? About looking for a project?"

"No, not in so many words, but I could tell. By the way, I apolo-gize for the gum, but I'm trying—for the umpteenth time—to quit smoking."

Crawford nodded. "Well, good luck with that. So, according to what I read, Ms. Melhado tried to… is it safe to say, take over your group? Make it into her vision, was the way I read it."

Phoebe stopped chewing her gum and thought for a few moments. "Yes, I suppose that's safe to say. I remember thinking at the time it was like she wanted to be queen with as many subjects as she could assemble. It was weird. I mean, all I was really trying to do was bring together like-minded people who could join me in forming as close a bond with Jesus as possible."

"So, what finally ended up happening?"

"Well, two things, really. The first came one day when I played this CD of Billy Graham." Phoebe stopped chewing. "You know who he is, right?"

Crawford nodded. "Sure. The evangelist. Died a while back."

Phoebe nodded. "Yes. The CD was a collection of his sermons. Teachings, I guess you could call them. Anyway, Fannie was totally mesmerized by them. She asked me if she could borrow the CD. I said sure and gave her a few others I had too. In our next meeting, all she did was rattle on about how brilliant and what an incredible visionary Billy Graham was."

"Like what did she say specifically?"

"Well, like he had almost become… Jesus Christ himself to her. She told us, the group I mean, all about how Graham had been close with Martin Luther King. And Queen Elizabeth. And just about every president for the last fifty years." She cocked her head. "You know much about the man?"

Crawford shrugged. "Not much."

"Okay, here are a few tidbits that I remember from what Fannie told me: Lyndon Johnson asked him to be a member of his cabinet. Richard Nixon offered him the ambassadorship to Israel. He was the fourth person in U.S. history to lie in state at the Capitol rotunda in Washington—" She smiled and nodded. "And last but not least, he has a star on the Hollywood Walk of Fame."

"Hmm. That's quite the resumé."

"I'll say. A lot of people think he was the greatest preacher since Jesus."

"Including, it sounds like, Fannie Melhado," Crawford said. "You mentioned two things. What was the other?"

"SOAR. She felt it was going to go a lot further than my little group. And she was absolutely right. I never had aspirations of my group being, you know, the next big thing. And, from what I understand, they've got very ambitious goals."

"How do you mean?

"Well, like how they want to have a huge presence in the world as a major religion, one day."

Crawford shrugged. "Interesting. I know what you mean. It does seem as though they've got big goals."

He flashed on Xi Kiang and the Falun Gong.

"Not to mention, they've got a lot of money and brainpower."

"Oh, you mean the Mensa thing?"

"Yes," she said with a little laugh, "But I never quite got the Einstein vibe from Fannie. Don't get me wrong, she's smart, but I don't know about top two percent. Ambition, though... top one percent, without a doubt."

TWENTY-NINE

CRAWFORD WAS at the exclusive Blowing Dunes Country Club in Palm Beach Gardens conducting an interview in a golf cart. Definitely a first.

He had driven up there hoping he'd catch the caddy, Andy Barrow, in between "loops." As it turned out, Barrow had just completed eighteen and was in the 'caddy shack,' which was hardly a shack at all, but instead a nice, air-conditioned room at the rear of the clubhouse that had two wide-screen TVs—one tuned to the Golf channel, the other ESPN.

Not wanting to get Barrow in trouble with anyone, Crawford asked a young man coming out of the caddy room if he would tell Barrow a family friend had dropped by to see him.

A few moments later, a tall, rangy, man with broad shoulders, a skinny waist, and a perfect Coppertone tan walked out. He was clearly in shape and could probably do three loops a day if daylight allowed.

Crawford put his hand out. "Andy? I'm Detective Crawford."

"I go by Andrew."

"Okay, I'm lead detective on the murder of Christian Lalley."

Barrow gave him a fish-grip handshake, which contrasted mightily with his musclebound physique. "Okay, so what do you want from me?"

"Just have a few questions."

Barrow looked around apprehensively. "Okay, well, just so my... colleagues don't wonder why I'm talking to a guy with a bulge at his hip, why don't we step into my, ah, mobile office."

Barrow pointed to a golf cart behind Crawford and started walking toward it. He slid into the driver's side of a golf cart. Crawford walked around and got in the passenger's side. Barrow turned the key and drove them down a cart path in the direction of a practice putting green and driving range.

There, with nobody around, Barrow pulled to the side of the cart path and turned to Crawford.

"Okay, Detective," he said with a smirk, "is this maybe the scenario you dreamed up in your head? Christian Lalley didn't like his daughter going out with a caddy, and really didn't like her being secretly engaged to one. So, he gets on her case to dump me. And me, being wildly in love with his daughter, goes crazy and sees killing him as being the only solution."

Crawford cocked his head. "Well, you tell me. Is that what happened? You wanted to remove an obstacle?"

Barrow laughed sarcastically. "Not even fucking close. It was Samantha's idea to get engaged. It was Samantha who, more or less, asked me out on our first date. It was Samantha who was in a big hurry to get married. What I'm trying to tell you is the fact that Chris didn't consider me a catch wasn't something I gave much of a shit about. 'Cause if not Samantha"—Barrow shrugged—"well, there're plenty of women out there. Know what I mean, dude?"

Crawford glanced over at the putting green and saw a rotund man with white, hairless legs putting. "Yeah, I guess I do."

He was not warming up to this man.

"Tell you a little bit more. I'm not just a *caddy* caddy."

"What do you mean by that?"

"Heard the name Blake Caldwell?"

"No. I don't think so."

"Well, he's a guy on the Korn Ferry Tour. You know, the guys just below the PGA tour."

Crawford nodded. He did know what the Korn Ferry Tour was. Prior to that, it was the Web Dot Com Tour. He followed golf.

"Anyway, dude's won a couple of times on Korn Ferry and I'm his caddy. Just a matter of time 'til he breaks into the big leagues."

"I get it. And you'd make, what, ten percent of his winnings, right?"

"Yup, So this gig here—"

"Is just temporary, I guess is what you're saying?"

"That's exactly what I'm saying," Barrow shrugged again. "So, I don't know what more to tell you."

Crawford slouched down in the golf cart seat. "So that scenario you thought I might have concocted: You took out Christian Lalley because of your fear he would squelch your relationship with Samantha—"

"It just don't compute, man. 'Cause, like I said, there're millions of women in the Sunshine State." Barrow gave him a cocky snort. "I'd just move on to the next."

Crawford's first reaction was to give Barrow a restrained backhand, or maybe not so restrained. He was not a fan of men who were cocksure of themselves for no apparent reason. "Okay," he said instead, getting out of the golf cart. "Thanks for the ride. Good luck on the pro tour."

———

CRAWFORD WENT STRAIGHT BACK to the station. First thing he did was Google Billy Graham. Second thing he did was ask Ott to come join him. He brought Ott up to speed on his conversations with Andy Barrow, and before him, Phoebe Lilly, and what she'd said about Fannie Melhado's preoccupation with Billy Graham.

"This whole thing's starting to really drive me crazy," Crawford said, shaking his head.

"What do you mean? How?"

"It's just... everything's so bizarre. I mean, just go down the line-up of suspects." He pointed at their whiteboard. "We got a billionaire woman obsessed with a dead preacher who's got a star on the Hollywood Walk of Fame—"

"And who Nixon wanted as Ambassador to Israel."

"And a Chinese ex-pat who's supposed to bring in fifty million followers to a start-up religion. A weirdo who knows more about our lives than we do."

"That would be Leo Peavy?"

Crawford nodded.

"And a short, squirrely dude from New Zealand who's giving people nicknames out of fuckin' *Star Trek*," Ott said.

"Not to mention trying to buy Bethesda church and a megayacht." Crawford exhaled long and loudly. "This whole damn thing has gotten *way, way, way* the hell out there."

"I hear you."

"I mean, Christ, can't we just have a few normal suspects? You know like a jealous husband or a crooked lawyer or a corrupt politician or a homicidal maniac. Instead of a kleptomaniac ex-movie star, two guys living in a modest garage apartment and driving around in a shit box while they manage a billion dollars, a caddy who thinks he's master of the universe—"

"And let's not forget our Skull and Bones gal, Vega; God knows what she's up to. And that funny-looking, smiley dude who's an authority on all our girlfriends, past and present—"

"I said him already."

"Oh, yeah, right." Ott nodded.

Crawford looked up at the list of suspects on the whiteboard and shook his head. "And the list goes on...."

"Yeah. Where are they when we need 'em? Those jealous husbands, crooked lawyers, corrupt politicians and... what was the other one?"

"Homicidal maniacs."

"Yeah, I really miss those guys."

THIRTY

It was re-interview time. Crawford needed another round of questions with both Fannie Melhado and Vega. They answered his calls and he set up back-to-back interviews that afternoon: three p.m. for Fannie, four for Vega.

He pulled into the driveway of Elysium just before 3:00, right behind another car. It was a boxy, nondescript Mini, from which Fannie Melhado emerged. He was not surprised by her choice in cars, even though she could afford a fleet of Bentleys.

He reached into his glove compartment, quickly slipped something out, put it in his pocket, and opened the door of the Crown Vic.

"Hello, Detective," she said with a smile as he slid out of his Crown Vic.

"Ms. Melhado," he said. "Nice to see you again."

"Thank you." She gestured, instructing, "Follow me."

They walked through Elysium, out to the back terrace, and sat down next to the pool. Crawford imagined looking down at her and him from a 27th floor, two-bedroom condo at Placido Mar directly across the Intracoastal. He imagined tossing a rock from up there and landing it in the pool. It would make a big splash.

"So, how's your friend Vega?" Fannie asked with an impish grin.

"She's fine. I'm meeting with her after here. Why do you ask?"

The impish grin got wider. "No reason. She just told me she was 'seeing' the cute detective. And I figured that she *didn't* mean your partner."

Crawford smiled. "Oh, I don't know, I think he's pretty cute," he said, loyally. "And, just for the record, I'm *seeing* Vega just like I'm *seeing* you."

"Don't get defensive, Detective," Fannie said, then she snapped her fingers. "Oh hey, I noticed Vega's wearing a fancy new suit today. Chanel, I believe."

"So?"

"Just a wild guess, but maybe she's… dressing up for you."

Crawford just sighed and gave her a quick eyeroll.

"Oh, and another thing, she got herself a flashy new car."

"Really? I thought she was a bicycle gal?"

"Not anymore. Big old BMW, I think it is."

Crawford filed that under, '*hmm.*'

"And while I'm dishing—which I don't often do—do you know who Christian's secret squeeze was?"

"You mean, after Lorinda?"

"During and after."

"No, but I know you're going to tell me."

"Once again, Vega."

"No kidding. I knew they were friends."

The news was not a big stretch, but this was the first he'd heard of it.

"Bosom buddies," she said with a naughty smile. "Well, actually, there's another phrase for it that's more accurate but I'm too prim and proper to say it… *blank* buddies."

"Ah… I think I can fill in that blank," Crawford said. "So, to do a complete one-eighty, I understand you're a big fan of the evangelist Billy Graham."

She laughed. "Wow, talk about non sequiturs. I'm going to guess you spoke to Phoebe Lilly, huh?"

Crawford nodded.

"Billy Graham was one of the greatest Americans to ever live,"

Fannie blurted unabashedly. "He had more influence on this country and made more positive contributions than anyone I can think of."

Plus, there was that star on the Walk of Fame thing.

"Why do you ask?"

"I guess I just wondered whether he was an inspiration to you, and you've clearly answered that."

"An inspiration. A mentor. Someone who I'd like to model my life after. Did you know that man preached to live audiences of 210 million people in over 185 countries in his lifetime, including a television audience of over 2.5 billion people worldwide?"

"Pretty impressive," Crawford said.

"Impressive. He was without a doubt the most admirable Christian leader of the 20th century. Not only that, more than 3.2 million people have responded to the invitation of Billy Graham's Crusade to accept Jesus Christ as their personal savior."

Crawford nodded, not quite sure how to respond. "He lived a nice long life, I read."

Fannie nodded. "Ten months shy of 100. I went to his funeral up in Charlotte, North Carolina."

She was clearly much more than just a *big fan.* "Oh, did you?"

She nodded again. "A very solemn event. Trump was there. I sat next to Rudy Giuliani."

Again, Crawford wasn't sure how to respond. "On another subject, when we spoke last time, you told me about how members of SOAR all had skills they contributed. Based, in many cases, on professions they had before they became members. So, I was just wondering, what is yours?"

No hesitation. "I don't need a skill. I've got lots of money." For a moment, she looked like she wanted to reel that back in. "Sorry, that sounded really arrogant. Actually, I do have a job, which I take very seriously. It's simply spreading the word about SOAR. Speaking of Billy Graham, I'd like to emulate his success in spreading the word. So, my job is telling as many people as I can about SOAR and how it can enhance and broaden their lives."

"Sounds like a very admirable goal."

"I remember you telling me you were a lapsed Unitarian," Fannie said. "Any chance we can bring you into the fold?"

Absolutely none, he thought. "Maybe when my life slows down a little," he said instead.

"Well, you know where to find us."

———

VEGA INSISTED they meet at Green's Pharmacy. Because she was craving a cup of their coffee, she said, though Crawford doubted that was the real reason.

Still, Vega took a big sip and pretended to savor it.

"The coffee here is marginally better than the stuff at my station," Crawford said.

"Yeah, I know. There are just a lot of big ears at Elysium," she said, confirming his suspicion.

"Like who?"

"Well, like Fannie. Your last interview."

Crawford took a swig of water. "So, do you have any scoops for me today?"

"Not that I know of."

"Speaking of Fannie, tell me about her predecessor."

"Marie-Claire?"

Crawford nodded. "Did she play an active role in SOAR, like Fannie is?"

Vega thought for a second. "Um, I'd say Marie-Claire spoke softly but carried a big stick."

Crawford cocked his head.

Vega nodded. "I know, that's a little vague. What I mean is, she stayed out of the day-to-day, but weighed in on certain big things."

"Like?"

"New people. Specifically, new people with power. Give you an example… there was this guy who came along, used to be a preacher at one of those stadium churches."

Crawford motioned for her to go on.

"Well, his pitch was that we should build a hundred-thousand seat church out west of here somewhere and he'd preach the gospel of SOAR. Get people to come from miles around, fatten up the membership. So, Crux asked Marie-Claire to meet this guy and listen to him. Her first question to this preacher was, 'Okay, what exactly is the gospel of SOAR?' The guy mumbled some answer, but clearly had no clue. Marie-Claire stood up, said, *Thank you very much*, and walked out of the room."

"And that was the end of the preacher man?"

"Exactly. I guess I'd say Marie-Claire acted like Crux's second opinion on big stuff. Any time she thought he was getting a little loosey-goosey about people he let in, she stepped in and nipped it in the bud."

"I get it," Crawford said with a nod. "Somebody mentioned that she had two daughters, and that one lives around here?"

Vega nodded. "Yup, down in the estate section. I forget which street. Her name is Patrice Lord."

Crawford typed it into his iPhone.

"Thank you. That's helpful." He looked up at Vega. "I have another question about Fannie Melhado."

"Okay?"

"Does she have a boyfriend?"

Vega was silent for a moment. "Sorry, I don't know anything about that. I mean, Crux... but, no, not really."

"And Leo Peavy? You said to check him out. Why'd you say that?"

"'Cause I just get the sense he's hiding something. He talks about working at that advertising agency, Interworld, and boasts about how he was a big honcho there. But Christian kind of let it slip that Peavy was involved in something before he worked there that he didn't want anybody to know about. Like a chapter he wanted to expunge from the record. I wasn't sure if Christian didn't want to tell me about it, or just didn't know what it was. I have a theory, though, and when I brought it up with Christian, he didn't deny it. Just changed the subject."

"So, let me guess, Christian told you this during happy hour at Taboo?"

"Yup," said Vega. "But just about everything he told me turned out to be true. 'Cause one of the jobs of being treasurer was Christian had to dig around and dredge up people's personal histories. Crux wanted him to interview 'em before they got the nod to join SOAR, just to make sure they didn't have any skeletons in their closets. So Christian also had some guy he hired to nose around and find out stuff."

"You mean, like a private investigator or something?"

"Yeah. I could find out his name if it would be helpful."

"It sure would. So, Leo Peavy... exactly what did Christian find out about him?"

"He was a creative director at that place I mentioned, Interworld. A big ad agency like Young & Rubicam or Ogilvy and whatever, one of the international ones. He was the branding guru. So if you wanted to go from unknown Company X to a household name, he was the guy. The brains behind that sports apparel company, Under Armour, and Tesla, I think it was. Put 'em on the map."

Crawford nodded. "So, if you wanted your product to break out of the pack, Leo was the man you went to?"

"Exactly," Vega said. "As far as Leo's mysterious past, every time I'd bring it up with Christian, he'd change the subject. I have a theory about that, too."

"And what is that? Your theory?"

"That there was something pretty murky way back there."

Crawford cocked his head. "That doesn't help much."

"How about dark and murky?"

"Still doesn't help much."

"How 'bout dangerous and deadly?"

"Much better."

THIRTY-ONE

ALL VEGA COULD RECALL about the private investigator who did occasional jobs for Christian Lalley was that his name was Maxwell. She thought it was his last name but wasn't absolutely sure. They finished up lunch and stood up to leave.

"So, I understand you have a fancy new car?"

Vega looked bushwhacked, but quickly recovered. "Oh yes, my little splurge."

"What is it?"

"A BMW."

"Which one?"

"M760."

"Wow, that's a beauty."

Ott had pointed out a few driving around Palm Beach.

"I'll take you for a spin some time."

"I'd love that."

Then they split up and Crawford went back to the station and did some more research. The PI wasn't hard to find. His company was called Maxwell Investigations. "Max got the facts," one testimonial on his website read. "Satisfaction to the Max," read another one. Something told Crawford that Max himself might have been the author of both quotes. It sure wasn't some creative wunderkind at Interworld or Young & Rubicam.

He dialed the number for Maxwell Investigations.

"Maxwell," a voice answered.

"Detective Crawford, Palm Beach PD. That your first or last name?"

"Everyone calls me Max," the man said. "I heard of you. Homicide guy, right?"

"Yup, working the Christian Lalley murder."

"And you found out I knew the guy, huh?"

"What are you doing in fifteen minutes, Max?"

"Ah, waiting for you in my executive suite?"

"I appreciate your cooperation. I've got your address," Crawford said, clicking off, and looking down at his watch. It was 5:15.

Before he left, he looked up the number of Patrice Lord, the daughter of Marie-Claire Fournier. He found E. and P. Lord on 151 Via Bellaria, which was in the so-called "estate section" of Palm Beach. He dialed the number, but it went to voicemail. He asked Ms. Lord to call him back.

Fifteen minutes later, he was walking up the steps of a dingy three-story building in a West Palm Beach industrial park. Max had buzzed him up to the second floor and was waiting for him at the top of the stairs. Crawford was looking up at Max, just as he had looked up Crux in his throne, but Max was much less regal looking. He was a large man wearing flip flops with a heavy gold chain around his neck that couldn't be good for his posture.

He pointed toward an open door. "Come on in, Charlie. Don't mind if I call you Charlie, do ya?"

"Nope."

They walked into Max's office, which rivaled Crawford's apartment for worst view in West Palm. Max's was of a loading dock for UPS trucks; Crawford's, of course, was of a Publix supermarket parking lot. The view was probably a toss-up, but Crawford's office itself was way better. Mainly because behind Max's badly-scarred wooden desk was a set of barbells—Crawford guessed about a hundred pounds—resting on a rickety steel frame that probably would have collapsed if he added another ten pounds. Off to the side was a small brown refrigerator on a white wicker table which, Crawford took a wild guess, contained a six-pack of beer, half a day-old pizza, and maybe a jar of dill pickles.

"Get ya a water or something?" Max asked, motioning toward the refrigerator.

"No, thanks," Crawford said, as Max took a step toward it and opened its door.

Crawford tried to peek around him to see if he had been right. He saw a white pizza box and a bag of brownish carrots that looked like they were way past their expiration date. No beer or pickle jar in sight. One for three. But when Max, water in hand, stepped to his right, Crawford saw three bottles of Budweiser. Two for three.

"Have a seat," Max said, pointing to what looked like a bad knock-off of a Herman Miller Aeron chair.

Crawford sat down in it. It tilted back and was surprisingly comfortable. "Nice chair."

Max nodded. "Eighty-nine bucks at Wayfair."

"I might have to get me one."

"'Fraid the sale might be over now."

Crawford gave him an *oh, well* shrug. "So, I'd appreciate knowing about your relationship with Christian Lalley."

Max leaned back in his squeaky chair. "Chris was a good guy. I think he may have gotten in a little over his head."

"What do you mean?"

Max spread his hands on his desktop. "Well, he was in with all those Wensa people—"

"You mean, Mensa."

"Yeah, whatever. IQs off the charts. Chris was smart, don't get me wrong, but didn't seem to be in that league."

Crawford nodded. "But my understanding was that he was one. A Mensa, I mean."

"Maybe, but if so, on the low end, I'd say."

"Okay. Tell me about the first time he contacted you?"

"Yeah, sure. He called me up and said that he was treasurer of this company and wanted me to do background checks on people coming on board."

"He called it a company?"

"Yeah, as I remember it. And the fact is, I do a lot of that kind of work. You can put any damn thing you want on a resumé, but it can all be a hundred percent bullshit. Me, I'm a bullshit detector."

"And a damn good one, I bet."

"Well, thank you Charlie, most people making hires don't want to spend a whole lot of time checking out every little detail."

"So, who did you check out first?"

Maxwell looked away, then his eyes snuck back to Crawford's. "You know this is all supposed to be highly confidential."

Crawford knew 'supposed to be' was his opening. Maxwell needed some gentle arm-twisting. "I understand, but your client *is* dead."

"Yeah, but I still do the occasional job for Guy Bemmert."

"The CFO?"

"Yeah."

"Seems like that's the same job as Lalley's, but with a new, fancy title."

"That guy Peavy came up with the title thing. Told the head guy they should all have hokey corporate titles."

"Speaking of Leo Peavy, I'm assuming you did a background check on him."

"Sure did."

"And?"

"Come on, Charlie, you know I can't—"

"I just need to know a little about his past. I know he worked for a big ad agency before he joined SOAR. World champion branding expert, supposedly. Went to some fancy college, summa cum... whatever."

Maxwell seemed like a man who wanted to keep his cards close to his vest but might be persuaded to give you a little peek. "And you want to know what he did after college, right?" Maxwell asked.

"Yeah, exactly."

Maxwell put his hands together and rested his chin on them. "Tell you what, Charlie, I'll make you a deal. I'll fill in the gap for you if you tell me about one of your cases. I follow 'em in the *Post*." He laughed. "Cop groupie, guess you could say."

Crawford thought for a second. "I think I can do that. As long as it's not active."

"It's not," Maxwell said, cocking his head. "From a few years back. That former police chief who bought it."

"Oh, yeah, you mean Clyde Loadholt."

"Yeah, that's it. So, like I said, I was following that case in the *Post* and on TV news. Guy had a rep as a pretty nasty cop. Violent fucker. So, I figured the guy who did it had to be either that gay dude he crippled or maybe the son of that burglar he shot. But it turned out to be his granddaughter who ran that casino in New Orleans. So, my question is, how the hell did you ever get to *her*?"

Crawford leaned way back in the Herman Miller Aeron chair knock-off. "Well, as you know, half the time a homicide is in the family. But it took us a long time and a few breaks to get wind of the granddaughter. Turned out she had a history of getting abused by good 'ol Gramps and some of his poker buddies. She was a strange one and we had to go all over the map—New Orleans, Charleston, South Carolina, then down the South Carolina coast to finally track her down."

"We, meaning you and your partner Ock or something?"

"Yeah, Mort Ott. Best birddog in the business."

Maxwell nodded. "And how'd she kill the guy? I forget."

"Put one in his chest from ten feet away, then dumped him over the side of her yacht. Guy was fish-bait."

"Girl did pretty well for herself, as I remember," Maxwell said.

Crawford nodded. "Sure did, managed a big casino... 'til she became a murderer, that is. Okay, your turn, Max."

Maxwell unclasped his hands and raised his head. "You never heard a word from me, okay?"

"Never met you before in my life."

Maxwell smiled and shot Crawford a thumbs-up. "Okay, so here's the story: Leo Peavy went right from college into military intelligence. Army, I guess it was. Got recruited 'cause he had a totally off-the-charts IQ and wanted to do his thing for God and country. Something like that anyway." Crawford nodded. "Then, after about two or three years, he ended up in something called Blackwater. Ever hear of it?"

"Oh, yeah, sure. Badass mercenaries. Did a bunch of under-the-radar work in Iraq and Afghanistan. Kind of a private military company." Suddenly Crawford remembered something. "There was an incident that blew up on them in Baghdad, I think it was. They killed a bunch of people without any provocation."

Maxwell nodded. "You got a good memory, Charlie. It was a place called Nisour Square. Seventeen people were killed by Blackwater"— he did the finger quote thing—"*security contractors*, was what they called themselves. They were up in the air in two choppers."

"And, as I recall, a bunch of them were tried for manslaughter or murder."

"Yeah, one of 'em got life."

"So, what does any of this have to do with Leo Peavy?"

Maxwell cleared his throat. "Leo Peavy was one of 'em."

"The shooters?"

Maxwell nodded.

There was no way in hell, Crawford thought, that this could be the same Leo Peavy he had met with twice. The sweater-clad Mr. Rogers of *won't you be my neighbor?* fame looked more dangerous than Leo Peavy.

"You're kidding. You sure we're talking about the same guy?"

Maxwell nodded.

"Was he ever tried for it?" Crawford asked.

"Nope."

Crawford leaned back in his chair again and shook his head.

"I know what you're thinking," Maxwell said. "How the hell is it possible that weaselly little dude was a Blackwater thug?"

"Yeah, exactly what I was thinking."

"Seems like after the whole thing went down, someone pulled a few strings for Leo. Hustled him out of Baghdad on the next plane."

"How do you know all this?"

"He told me."

"You're kidding," Crawford said with a puzzled look. "Why would he do that?"

Maxwell shrugged and thought for a moment. "I don't know exactly. It almost seemed like he was proud of it."

Crawford's eyes narrowed. "Of killing seventeen innocent people."

"I think I know why. Or at least have a good guess."

"Let's hear it."

"You've met the guy. Looks like some runty, little college professor with dopey-lookin' sideburns, right?"

"Yup."

"I think being a guy with a big gun made him feel all macho. Know what I mean?"

Crawford thought for a moment. He knew exactly what Maxwell meant.

"So, he got rushed out of Baghdad," Maxwell said, "and next thing you know he's at that ad agency in New York."

"Somebody else pulled strings for him?"

Maxwell nodded. "I guess."

"That incredible," Crawford said. "What about a woman named Marie-Claire Fournier?"

"Is she someone in SOAR?"

"Yeah."

"I don't know that name."

Crawford realized there was no reason why he would. She had been in SOAR since the beginning. Unlikely Maxwell would have been tasked with checking her out.

"Or what about a woman named Fannie Melhado?"

"The billionaire?"

Crawford nodded.

"Clean as a whistle. Couldn't find anything gnarly about her."

"Nothing at all?"

Maxwell shook his head

Crawford nodded.

"And that guy you mentioned, Guy Bemmert? He have any dirty laundry?"

"No. He was clean, too. Used to be a guy high up in some big mortgage company. He's married to a younger guy."

"I know. Larry Swain. What about him?"

"Choirboy from what I could tell."

"So Peavy's the only one who's got a past."

Maxwell nodded.

"Okay, so let me ask you this," Crawford said. "You've looked into a lot of these SOAR people. If one of them killed Lalley, who would you put your money on?"

Maxwell put his hands together and rested his chin on them again, then lowered his voice. "Jesus, I don't know."

"But you've thought about it, I'm sure."

"Yeah, I have. Thought about it a lot after Chris bought it," Max said, scratching the side of his face.

"And?"

"I really have no idea."

IT WAS 6:20 when Crawford left Maxwell's office. He got a water for the road from the brown refrigerator. Maxwell offered him a piece of vintage pizza, which he declined.

In his Crown Vic, he dialed Rose's number.

Maxwell's grungy office had reminded him of his grungy apartment and added urgency to his desire to, like The Jeffersons, move on up.

"Hello, Charlie."

"Hey, Rose. I'm getting kind of itchy to move. Any way we can look at some places now?"

She didn't answer right away. Then, "Um, I'm going through the list in my mind.... Three of them are vacant, so let's go look at those. How 'bout we meet in the lobby at 5200 North Flagler at six forty-five?"

"Perfect. See you then."

ROSE WAS WAITING for Crawford inside the building's lobby. He walked up to her and gave her a kiss on the cheek.

"Only problem with this building is they don't have anybody at the front desk." She laughed. "Actually, they don't even have a front desk."

Crawford shrugged. "Why's that important?"

"Security. To accept packages. Someone to say 'good morning' to you."

Crawford smiled. "You, know, it's not that critical that I have someone say good morning to me." He followed Rose over to the bank of elevators.

She hit a button and the elevator door opened. "They've got two banks of elevators, at least."

"What floor?" he asked, looking at the floor buttons.

"Twenty-seven."

"Practically in the clouds, huh?"

Rose nodded. "Wait 'til you see the view."

"You've seen this one?"

"Just on the internet. Looks fabulous."

The elevator stopped and Crawford followed Rose to a door. She opened a lockbox, took out a key, let them in.

They walked through the living room.

"Oh, my God," Rose said. "Look at that. It's even better in real life."

They walked out onto a balcony. It was truly a breathtaking view: the Intracoastal directly below, then Palm Beach island, then the ocean beyond.

Crawford focused on the Intracoastal. There were seemingly hundreds of boats—mostly sailboats— moored in the thin body of water below. "Damn flotilla down there."

"Yeah, no kidding," Rose said. "You can't get a view anywhere near as good as this in Palm Beach"—she checked her listing sheet—"and it's only $275,000."

Crawford turned back inside and looked down at the floor, disapprovingly. "Plus, this lovely mud-brown marble floor comes with it."

Rose frowned. "Yeah, that is kind of an eyesore. So, what do you think?" she asked, following him into one of the bedrooms.

"I love the fact that all the bedrooms have balconies too," Crawford said.

"Yes, that's pretty unusual. I noticed there was no exhaust fan in the kitchen."

"Ain't no deal killer," Crawford said with a chuckle. "You know how much I cook."

She nodded. "Take-out Charlie."

They spent another ten minutes poking around in walk-in closets, opening cabinets, and admiring the incredible view again, then headed down to 2600 North Flagler.

This building did have a person manning the front desk and was also five minutes closer to the Palm Beach police station. The apartment was on the seventh floor and had a nice view but was by no means as dramatic as the one on the twenty-seventh floor of the building before. It had a nice layout and generously proportioned rooms, but also a monthly maintenance charge of over eight hundred dollars.

Crawford did some quick math. "That's almost ten grand a year."

Rose's expression didn't change.

Crawford chuckled. "Yeah, I know, chicken feed to you and your clients, but not to a lowly cop."

Rose feigned indignance. "You're a highly-decorated homicide detective, Charlie."

"Gee, thanks, Rose. Let's go check out the other two."

Rose nodded. "They're both in the same building. Rapallo North."

"Is that the one just south of the middle bridge?" he asked, recalling his earlier drive by.

"Yup. It's a great old building."

In Rapallo North, they looked at apartments on both the fourteenth and seventeenth floor. The one on fourteen was two bedrooms that needed work but had a nice southeast view across the Intracoastal.

"How much to replace the floors and renovate the master bath?" Crawford asked Rose. "Ballpark."

"Um, I'd say around twenty-five thousand."

"Which means I could get it done for twenty."

"Yeah, if you know how to lay tile and change out plumbing fixtures."

"Ah, not exactly," Crawford said. "But I figure you're quoting Palm Beach contractor prices, not West Palm ones."

"Okay, okay, maybe twenty-two, then."

Then they went up three stories to see a one-bedroom apartment described as a "stunning designer renovation with breathtaking views." The view was nice but nowhere near as jaw-dropping as the first one they'd seen.

"So?" Rose asked as they both looked across at Everglades Island.

"I don't know. What do you think?"

"I think this one if you just want to move in and do nothing. It's pretty perfect the way it is. The question is do you need an extra bedroom?"

Crawford shrugged. "I don't know, it's not as though I got a hell of a lot of people coming to visit."

The one time his brother Cam had come down, he'd stayed at a high-end hotel.

"Well, there you go. Of the ones we've seen, I'd say this is perfect for you."

"Does the building take dogs?"

Rose cocked her head. "Dogs? Since when do you have a dog?"

"I don't. But I'm thinking of getting one."

"Jesus, Charlie. You got all kinds of life changes goin' on. New pad. New dog."

"An old pad and an old dog would be okay, too. I'm thinking about getting one from the Humane Society."

"Wow, so it wasn't just a passing thought?"

Crawford shook his head. "I've been thinking about it for a while."

"You know, you've got to walk a dog so it can pee and poop. Take it to the dog park and all that. Those little plastic bags. You got time to do all that stuff?"

He thought for a second. "Yeah, those are drawbacks."

"What about a cat?"

"I hate cats."

"A hamster?"

Crawford laughed. "So, do they take 'em in this building or not? Dogs."

"I think so, but I'll find out for sure."

"I saw this one at the Humane Society. Part Labrador, part…I-don't-know-what."

"Big dog?"

"Pretty big."

"Cause the buildings that take 'em like to limit the size. Twenty pounds or so is typical."

Crawford thought for a second. "I'd say this pooch would have to go on a diet. Lose about thirty pounds."

"Hm." Rose considered that. "What about a goldfish?"

THIRTY-TWO

A FEW MINUTES past 8 a.m., Crawford and Ott were nursing mugs of office rotgut in Crawford's office. Crawford filled in Ott about what Maxwell had found out about Leo Peavy. Ott had said 'no shit' three times and whistled once while shaking his head so hard Crawford thought something might fall out of it.

"Oh, I forgot to tell you, I snuck my GPS tracker under the trunk of Fannie Melhado's Mini."

Ott raised his fist. "Attaboy. Why is it the richest people in the country drive those little shit boxes?"

Crawford shrugged.

"I'll tell you why… to broadcast to the world that—down deep—they're just modest, ordinary folks."

Crawford chuckled. "The world according to Ott."

"That would make a good title to a book," Ott said.

"Already taken."

Ott shrugged. "So, which bug did you use?"

"That little black one."

"Good old SpyTec."

"Yeah, and if I had another one with me, I would have put it on

Vega's new BMW. Maybe I'll swing by there tomorrow and slip one on it."

"Better wear a disguise."

"Nah, I'll be alright. The lot at Elysium is separate from the house."

"That's true," Ott said. "So, you suppose Fannie Melhado buys her groceries at Winn-Dixie and her clothes at TJ Maxx?"

"Unlikely. But I guess we'll find out." Crawford sat back and tapped his desktop for a few moments. "It's time, Mort."

Ott frowned. "Huh?"

"We've dicked around with this thing long enough. Gone down a bunch of roads that went nowhere. Had a bunch of suspects that were dead ends. It's time to wrap this damn thing up."

Ott didn't react at first. Then, "That's easy for you to say, but aside from this guy Leo Peavy who's seems to have experience at killing people, who we really got?"

Crawford pointed at the whiteboard behind Ott. "Let's look at the board again."

Ott turned around and looked at it. "Okay, so I think we can rule out Lorinda Lalley, Gerster and the movie star. And the caddy, too, though he never made the whiteboard."

"Yeah, so do I," Crawford said. "You think everyone else is still live."

"Yeah, but nobody's popping out except for Peavy and we don't have a clue what his motive is."

"Think we should add Vega?"

"Sure. Why not? Make it an even seven. But why her? Got any more theories?"

"I'm fresh out."

"What do you think, should we bring in Norm again?" Ott said. "Remember last time around… what was it… 'even a busted clock is right twice a day.'"

Crawford laughed. "Close."

Ott shrugged. "What was it again?"

"Even a blind squirrel finds a nut once in a while."

"Oh, yeah, right."

Crawford picked up his landline phone and punched in three numbers.

As he often did, Chief Rutledge answered with a question, his voice testy. "Solved the sucker yet?"

"Not yet. But with your brilliant insights we probably will."

"I'll be right there," Rutledge said, then, as an afterthought, "And how 'bout losing the sarcasm."

"Yes, boss," Crawford said sarcastically.

A few minutes later they heard they heavy, thudding footsteps spaced far apart. Ott referred to it as the 'caveman walk.'

Rutledge's face appeared at the door.

"Hey, Norm," Ott said.

Rutledge grunted and sat in the chair next to Ott, across from Crawford.

"We've talked to every suspect who could possibly have done it," Crawford said, pointing to the whiteboard, "and these are the finalists."

For the next twenty minutes, Crawford summarized what they had discovered about SOAR and its members in the last few days.

"I'm going with Fannie Melhado," Rutledge said at the end, without hesitation.

"Why?" Crawford asked.

"I don't know, I just have a hunch."

Crawford glanced at Ott, who fought mightily not to roll his eyes.

"Or that guy Peavy… but he seems too obvious. Who you guys going with?"

Crawford looked at Ott. "I don't know."

Ott shrugged.

"Well, that's just fuckin' swell," Rutledge said, raising his arms. "By the way, why the hell do we have people like that living in our peaceful, little town?"

"Well, actually, Bemmert and Swain live in Boca."

"Good," Rutledge said. "Keep 'em there… but that Blackwater guy, Peavy, lives here, right?"

Crawford nodded.

"By the way, Norm," Ott said, "Did we ever tell you that SOAR tried to buy Bethesda-by-the-Sea?"

Rutledge threw up his arms. "You're making this shit up."

"Nope."

Rutledge shook his head. "This is turning into a bad science fiction movie."

"Or something you'd see in the West Palm library," Ott said.

"What?" Rutledge said.

"Nothin'," Ott mumbled.

Crawford got a call on his cell. *Patrice Lord*, it said on the display. He held up his hand and took the call, telling Patrice that he had questions about the death of her mother. She seemed a little surprised but agreed to see him later that afternoon.

"So, you're saying you've definitely ruled out family members, relatives, business associates, all the usual?" Rutledge asked.

"Yeah, definitely. Nothin' there," Crawford said, and laid it all out for Rutledge.

Rutledge nodded. "Gotta be Peavy."

"What happened to Fannie Melhado?"

"I changed my mind."

"And his motive?" Crawford asked.

"You figure it out," Rutledge said, getting to his feet. "But just make it happen, will ya? I don't much care how you do it. But, come on, this is taking forever."

"Got news for you, Norm: the only place they catch guys fast is on *Law and Order*," Crawford said.

"An hour, to be exact," Ott added.

"Well, minus the commercials, it's more like forty-five minutes," said Crawford.

CRAWFORD HAD JUST SCHEDULED BACK-TO-BACKERS. First, Leo Peavy, then he'd wedged in Marie-Claire Fournier's daughter, Patrice Lord.

When Crawford called him, Leo Peavy asked to come into the

station. Said he'd "never been to a police station and was dyin' to scope one out."

Crawford obliged him and met him at the front desk, then led Peavy back to his office. He'd buzzed Ott ahead of time to alert him that Peavy'd arrived. Ott had wisely reminded Crawford to hide the whiteboard before he brought their suspect back.

When Crawford and Peavy stepped into his office, Ott was already sitting in his designated chair. He didn't bother to get up but shook Peavy's hand. "Mr. Peavy," he said. "Always a pleasure."

"Backatcha, Detective," Peavy said, sitting down. "So, what are we going to talk about this time, fellas? Pretty much exhausted every subject, haven't we?" He rubbed his hands together like he was prepared to enjoy himself. His muttonchop sideburns looked even thicker than they had last time. Dense as a ficus hedge. As Crawford studied him, the man's eyes seemed even more yellow and rheumy. The last thing he looked like was a mercenary who had helped mow down seventeen defenseless people on a street in Iraq.

"So, we understand you were in Blackwater?" Ott started right in.

Suddenly, Peavy looked as though he wasn't enjoying himself quite so much. Like he'd been gut-punched. His skin pallor went from yolk white to ghostly pale.

"What's that got to do with anything?"

"And that you were there when those seventeen people got killed in Bagdad?" Ott said.

Peavy rolled his eyes and coaxed out a dramatic sigh. "You ever been to war, detective?"

"No."

"You should try it sometime." It was a decent comeback and he added, "If that's what you got me here to talk about then I'm out of here."

Crawford raised a hand. "Relax, Mr. Peavy. We were just curious," he said. "Since we last met with you, have you heard anything that might be helpful to our investigation? I mean, people talk, people theorize, people confide in other people.... Have you heard anything at all?"

Peavy gazed first at Crawford, then Ott next to him, then at the wall over Ott's shoulder, then back at Crawford. "You guys have a funny way of doing things. Your partner insults me, then you ask me for help. So, I'm guessing today you're playing the good cop"—then turning to Ott—"and Smiley here, the bad cop."

Ott gave him a look, clearly not loving his new nickname.

Crawford put up his hands. "Hey, I just asked you if you heard anything. Presumably, you don't want a killer wandering around in one of your houses."

"Have you checked into Fannie Melhado? Or are you just wasting all your time on me?"

"What specifically would we have found if we had looked into her?" Crawford asked.

"Well, the fact that Christian Lalley had something on her, for starters."

"Okay, and what was that? If you could be a little more specific... since Lalley's not around to tell us."

"Something so kinky it would make the Marquis de Sade blush," Peavy said. "Lalley had a guy look into her private life."

"Oh, really. You know the identity of the *guy?*"

"All I got is general info," Peavy said with a smirk. "It's up to you guys to do your job and get the specifics."

"Just thought you'd want to help," Crawford said. "You know, clean up your house."

"My house *is* lily-white. Fannie Melhado's... ah, not so much."

Ott leaned toward Peavy. "You know, Mr. Peavy, you might have a little credibility if your past was lily-white, but I just don't remember reading about your Eagle Scout days."

Peavy got up and headed for the door. "I've had enough of your bullshit. I didn't come here to get insulted."

And he was gone.

Crawford eyed Ott. "You gotta think about biting your tongue every once in a while, Mort."

"Sorry, I just—"

Crawford raised a hand. "Don't worry about it, we weren't gonna get anything out of the guy anyway. He was making shit up on the fly."

THIRTY-THREE

ON THE WAY to Patrice Lord's house on Jungle Road, Crawford told Ott that the PI Maxwell had said Fannie Melhado was "clean as a whistle." And that whatever it was that was reputedly 'kinky," as Leo Peavy described it, hadn't showed up on Maxwell's radar screen.

"Maybe he was only giving you half of what he knew?" Ott observed.

"Or maybe trying to throw me off the scent."

"Also, possible."

51 Jungle was just off of South County Road and merged with South Ocean boulevard to the south a few blocks. As with many of the houses in the so-called estate section, Patrice's house was Mediterranean in style, beautifully landscaped, and huge. It was dark brown stucco with hedges that rose up the full height of the two-story house.

One time when Crawford was riding around with Rose in her white Jag convertible—doing his damnedest to pick her brain on a case—Rose had launched into a tutorial about celebrated Palm Beach architects. She told him her favorites were John Volk, Maurice Fatio, and Marion Sims Wyeth. Based on the Fatio houses she had pointed out during their drive, he was pretty sure the Lord house was one of his. As he remembered it, Fatio had designed more than two hundred Palm Beach homes.

"Nice pad," Ott said, as they drove in over the Chattahoochee pebble driveway.

Not exactly how Rose would have described it, but certainly accurate.

They got out of the Vic, walked up to the front door, and Ott pressed the doorbell.

A few moment later the door opened and a woman who looked to be in her mid-twenties greeted them with a wide smile. "Hello detectives, come on in. I'm Patrice."

"Detective Crawford," Crawford said, shaking her hand.

"I'm Detective Ott," Mort said, stepping into the foyer.

"Can I offer you a drink? Water, Coke, lemonade, anything?"

"No, thanks," Crawford said.

"I'm good," Ott said.

"Well, come on into the living room," Patrice said, leading the way.

As he followed her, Crawford wondered what a woman in her mid-twenties was doing in what he figured was easily a fifteen-million-dollar house. But the answer was obvious: a simple thing called inheritance. A rich relative dies, you get money. In this case, her mother, Marie-Claire Fournier. Crawford took secret solace in the fact that the $300,000 condos he'd looked at had way better views.

He and Ott sat in an overstuffed chintz sofa, facing Patrice. Not that Crawford had ever sat on a cloud, but this would be what he'd expect one would feel like. His most comfortable *sit* in a long time, Maxwell's faux Aeron notwithstanding.

"Mrs. Lord, as I mentioned," Crawford said, "we'd like to ask you some questions about your mother."

"Yes, sure," Patrice said. "When I got your call, I just wondered what took you so long."

Crawford shot Ott a quick quizzical glance, then back to Patrice. "Sorry, but I'm not sure what you mean?"

"Well, when mother died, I expected there to be at least some kind of investigation. I mean, she was the picture of health one day and the poor thing died the next."

"So, it sounds like you were suspicious... about your mother's cause of death? Is that accurate?"

"Not so much suspicious, just surprised that *nobody* seemed eager to look into it. I mean, Lucian Neville's biggest concern seemed to be where her money was going. You know him, right? Calls himself Crux?"

"Yes, sure, the head of SOAR, where your mother was a... congregant?"

Patrice laughed. "Congregant? I always hated that word."

"What would you prefer?"

"A cultist."

Crawford didn't need to look at Ott to know a big grin had just surfaced on his leathery face.

"Neville manipulated my mother for twenty years, and as hard as I tried, I couldn't change her way of thinking. 'Course I was pretty young."

"Mrs. Lord, was there anyone else who you felt should have looked into your mother's death who didn't?"

"Yes, the coroner, or medical examiner...whatever he's called."

Ott caught Crawford's eye, then looked back at Patrice. "Was his name Hawes? Robert Hawes?"

"Yes, that's him."

"So, he examined your mother at the time of her death?" Crawford asked.

"Yeah, and it took all of about ten minutes."

Crawford leaned forward. "Are you saying that you think your mother died of something other than a brain aneurism?"

"No, I'm not," she said, pushing a strand of hair behind her ear. "I'm just saying that when I went to Neville right after she died, he told me that she had been complaining about how bad she had been feeling. Well, that was news to me 'cause she never said a word about it, and I had talked to her at least three times in the week before she died."

Crawford tapped his foot on the hardwood floor. "When you

talked to her, did she bring up anything... I don't know... different from what she usually talked about?"

Patrice thought for a second. "No, not that I can think of—" she snapped her fingers "—wait, she did mention meeting with a man who wanted to join SOAR. This was two days before she died."

Crawford leaned closer. "What exactly did she say about him?"

"Mostly how she really didn't like the man."

"Do you remember his name?" Ott asked.

"No, I just remember her telling me that Neville wanted her to interview him. Tell him what she thought."

"Did she tell Neville?"

"My guess is she never got the chance," Patrice said. "She told me the man was a crook. Ran a company he got fired from for embezzling or something like that."

Crawford's eyes met Ott's. "How'd she know that?"

Patrice smiled. "My mother may have belonged to a cult, but she was a smart woman and always did her homework."

"Can you explain, please?"

"Well, she felt Neville was a little slapdash about letting people into SOAR. She told him a while back that if she was going to keep funding SOAR, he had to be more careful about who he let in. I think that's why Neville had her interview this guy right before she died."

Crawford exhaled deeply. "This is very helpful, Mrs. Lord," he said, looking over at Ott, who nodded his agreement.

"It sure is," Ott said. "Do you happen to remember what this man your mother interviewed was going to do at SOAR? I'm assuming he was bringing some skill, or money, to the table, right?"

"Probably, but I don't recall anything specific. I just remember he'd be pretty high up."

"No particular specialty, then, that you remember?" Crawford asked.

"Sorry."

Crawford sat back in the plush sofa. "When your mother looked into people— investigated them, I mean— how would she do it?"

Patrice rubbed her chin and thought for a second. "I guess the way most people do. You know, start with Google, Wikipedia, or one of

those. If you're anyone of any consequence—you know, good or bad—
your whole life story's right there. Then she'd make some calls to
people, find out even more."

Crawford nodded. Yup, couldn't beat good ol' Google and Wikipedia—unless it was giving Rose Clarke a call.

"HOLY SHIT," Ott said, exuberantly, as they walked across the Chattahoochee pebbles to the Crown Vic. "Sure sounds like Guy Bemmert."

Crawford already had his cell phone out.

"Yup. Timeline coincides. Bemmert joins SOAR right after
Fournier dies. Only thing that doesn't jibe is that the PI, Maxwell,
said Bemmert and Swain were clean. I gotta go brace that guy
again."

"But it could have been someone else altogether… who Fournier
spoke to. Someone who never got into SOAR."

"Yeah, true. But, if it was Bemmert who Fournier interviewed she,
obviously, never got around to telling Crux what she thought of him.
And we can assume Bemmert knew a negative review from Fournier
was gonna kill his chances of getting in."

Crawford dialed a number, held up his hand to Ott, and waited.

"Mr. Bemmert… hey, it's Charlie Crawford… so my partner and I
are in the Boca area and just wondered if we could stop by with a
question or two… great, oh I don't know, how 'bout in an hour or
so…? Perfect, see you then."

He clicked off. "So, we got an hour to figure out how we're gonna
play it."

"But it's only a half hour to get there"

"Yeah, I know. I want to check something out before."

As OTT SAID, they got to Coquina Drive in Boca in just over a half
hour.

"So now what?" Ott asked, as they turned onto Coquina.

"Park the car a block from the front gate, then we're gonna take a little walk."

Ott shrugged. "Okay, I have no clue what we're doing."

"Just trust me."

A minute later Ott parked the car a block away from 702 Coquina and Bemmert and Swain's garage apartment. They got out of the Vic and, as they neared the main house, Crawford held up his hand and stopped. Ott stopped just behind him.

"Let's get behind that banyan and just watch," Crawford said, pointing to a tree to the left of the driveway to the main house and garage apartment.

"Okay…." Ott said.

"My latest theory," Crawford said.

"You have 'em every five minutes."

"Not quite that often," Crawford said, stopping at the banyan. "Get behind it, so no one can see us."

Ott nodded. They just stood there and watched. Five minutes. Ten minutes. Fifteen minutes. They heard the sound of a door opening.

Crawford pointed.

Ott nodded.

Bemmert and Swain walked out of the enormous main house toward the garage apartment, walked up its stairs, opened the door and went inside.

"I'll be damned," Ott said.

Crawford pointed to a security camera on the street. "We need to take a look at the tapes on that. Going back to the murder last Wednesday and the night Simon Petrie was assaulted."

Ott nodded. "Got it."

───────────

As HAD BEEN the case more than a few times in the past, Crawford and Ott were prepared to wander off the reservation to get their killer. Not way, *way* off the reservation, but well outside their jurisdiction. That was something Norm Rutledge would never openly sanction, or encourage, but—fact was—that was of lot less concern to Crawford and Ott than it had been when they first joined the force. Plus, as Crawford reminded Ott, Rutledge had been crystal clear about what he wanted at the end of their meeting earlier: *Make something happen. And I don't much care how you do it.*

They had found that sometimes they had had to adopt unorthodox methods to solve homicides in Palm Beach. This was because they'd quickly learned that murder suspects in Palm Beach were smarter, or covered their tracks better, or were unorthodox themselves... often in cunningly creative criminal ways. More so than the ones in New York and Cleveland, it seemed anyway, where Crawford and Ott had formerly pounded the pavement. There was one, a brazen billionaire who had even gone so far as to confess to Crawford that he had murdered someone, then arrogantly asked, *so what are you gonna do about it?*

It took a while but finally Crawford and Ott *did* do something about it.

It seemed to have evolved into an unwritten understanding with Norm Rutledge. He didn't press too hard to find *how* they got their man, or woman; all her cared about was that they did. The fewer questions asked the better. The unspoken part, though, was equally important: Don't get caught...wandering off the reservation, that is.

They walked back to the car, got in, and drove up to the driveway of 702 Coquina.

They pulled up to the barrier gate and Ott pressed the button.

"Hey, fellas," Swain said, through the annunciator, "welcome back."

The mechanical arm went up and Ott drove in.

They stopped in front of the garage apartment next to the same blue Sentra, got out of their car, and started up the stairs.

Ott was the unofficial door-knocker and Crown Vic-driver.

Larry Swain opened the door with a welcoming smile. Like he had really missed them. He was wearing a sleeveless black tank top and had a small tattoo on his upper right shoulder.

"Come on in, fellas," Swain said.

The three walked over to where Guy Bemmert was sitting.

Bemmert was in the same chair as last time. "Palm Beach's finest," he said jovially, making no effort to get up.

"Mr. Bemmert," Crawford said with a nod. "How ya doin' today?"

"Not bad. Have a seat, boys."

They did. The sofa was nowhere near as comfortable as Patrice Lord's.

"So, first question is about Marie-Claire Fournier," Crawford said, plunging right in.

Bemmert tried hard not to change his expression, but his eyes narrowed slightly. "What about her?"

"We understand from her daughter"—though Patrice Lord had never actually said Bemmert's name—"that you met with her before you joined SOAR?"

"Yes, I did."

"And how would you characterize that… meeting? Actually, it was more like an interview, wasn't it?"

"Ms. Fournier and I had a nice chat."

"As we understand it, again from her daughter, Ms. Fournier wanted to have a say about who was getting into SOAR. And apparently, she felt that because she was giving SOAR a lot of money, she wanted to approve any new, ah, congregants."

"I don't know about any of that. All I know is we had a nice meeting and that was that."

Bad cop time. "Mr. Bemmert," Ott said, "what we were told was that Ms. Fournier felt Crux was getting a little sloppy in his admission policy. And after she met with you, she was opposed to you coming on board SOAR. She did a little background check and found out about certain issues with your previous employer."

Bemmert shook his head vehemently. "I don't know what the hell you're talking about. That's complete bullshit."

"And," Ott went on, "the problem was she never got a chance to tell Crux what she discovered about you… because she died right after meeting with you."

"So, let me get this straight: are you suggesting I had something to do with that woman's death… even though the medical examiner said it was an aneurism. I mean, come on, I understand you're desperate to find a killer, but you're way off base. Trying to make a natural death a murder. Gimme a break."

Bemmert did indignance to perfection.

Ott glanced over at Crawford. Hand-off time.

"Well, I guess we're gonna find out," Crawford said.

"What's that supposed to mean?" Bemmert asked.

Crawford paused a moment. "Marie-Claire's daughter is going to exhume her mother's body. Have an autopsy done."

Bemmert gripped his chair arm tightly. "Okay, so what? What does that have to do with us?"

"Don't know yet," Crawford said. "But, like I said, looks like we're going to find out."

"Well, good. Then you'll see you're barking up the wrong tree."

"Let me ask you something else," Crawford said. "How friendly are you with Leo Peavy?"

Bemmert shrugged. "I mean, we're both officers of SOAR... what specifically are you asking?"

"Well, do you know anything about his background?"

"Just that he had a big job at that place, Interworld."

"And...." This was the first peep out of Larry Swain, who seemed to be looking at Bemmert to give him permission to proceed.

Bemmert smiled broadly. "Oh that... so I bet you don't know this... Peavy and Fannie Melhado were a thing. Until like... a week ago."

"Really?" Crawford said, glancing at Ott. "We didn't know that."

Crawford remembered Peavy's recent trash-job of Fannie and guessed maybe she had cut him loose. Which likely meant Peavy had developed an extreme case of sour grapes.

"Question is," Bemmert said with a smirk, "why did a woman with looks and money have anything to do with a funny-looking guy with goopy eyes and excessive nose hair?"

Ott laughed. "Maybe he's got a beautiful soul."

Bemmert glanced over at Crawford. "Are we done here? Because Larry and I have to go up to Elysium to attend to some business."

Crawford got to his feet and Ott followed. "Yes, we are, and we want to thank you for taking the time to meet with us."

"You're welcome," Bemmert said.

Larry Swain nodded.

As Ott walked past Swain to the front door, he took a fast glance at Swain's tattoo. Then he and Crawford walked out.

At the bottom of the steps to the apartment, Ott turned toward the garage. "Hold on a sec."

He walked up to one of the garage doors and looked through a window at chin height, shading his eyes. "Hey, check this out."

Crawford came over and looked though the garage window, too.

"Harley Davidson, huh?" Crawford said.

"Yeah, let's get back in the car."

They walked over and got in the Vic. Ott started it up and turned to drive out.

He turned to Crawford, clearly amped up. "I didn't want them to see us snooping around. Did you check out Swain's tattoo?"

"Yeah. Looked like a skull."

"It's the logo of a biker gang called the Outlaws. Started out in Chicago but has a big chapter in Cleveland. They don't get any more violent than those dudes. Worse than Hell's Angels."

Crawford shook his head. "This thing gets more bizarre by the minute. Now we got a happily-married biker and a Mensa."

Ott nodded. "I don't know if you saw it, but in small letters below the tattoo it said, ADIOS."

"Adios?"

"Stands for 'Angels Die in Outlaw States.'"

THIRTY-FOUR

"So, I guess ol' Larry goes from assistant treasurer to potential murderer?" Crawford said.

"Who the hell knows, man, but he sure fits the profile a lot better."

"Yeah, that he does."

As Ott drove up the on-ramp to I-95, Crawford took out his cell phone, dialed a number and put it on speakerphone.

"Rose," he said in response to Ott's inquiring look.

She answered, "Hello, Charlie."

"Hi, Rose, I've got you on speaker and Mort is with me, so keep it clean."

"I always do... except... when I don't."

"Tell us what you told me about Guy Bemmert."

"Well, for one thing the guy's cheap as shit... oops, sorry, Mort. I told you about him trying to shave a half million off the price of one of those SOAR houses because it had a little wood rot."

"Yeah you did, what else?"

"Well, as I told you, supposedly he embezzled or extorted—I don't really know the difference—a lot of money from that mortgage company where he was CEO. I don't think he ever got prosecuted for it, but he definitely got fired."

"I'm asking because I Googled him and couldn't find much except where he'd worked and how long he was there," Crawford said.

Rose was silent for a moment. "You know, I've heard if you hire the right people, they can clean up your dirty laundry. Kind of make all the bad stuff go away. On the internet and everywhere."

"Yeah, I've heard that too. But did you hear this stuff about Bemmert from a pretty reliable source?"

"Let me think... yes, actually I heard it from a New York banker who did business with Bemmert's company... at least until Bemmert screwed the pooch. Oops, sorry again, Mort."

Ott shrugged. "I don't even know what that means."

"Good," said Rose, "I wouldn't want to corrupt you."

"So, is that pretty much it?"

"Pretty much. Except he had to pay a big fine. Left him almost broke, as I remember."

"Thanks," Crawford said. "If you wouldn't mind checking again who the owner of 702 Coquina is.... You said it can take a while to record the new owner."

"I will when I get back to the office. By the way, with all this info I'm giving you, we must be up to at least three dinners you owe me."

"I'm looking forward to all of 'em."

"Me, too. Bye, boys, sorry 'bout my mouth, Mort," she said and clicked off.

RIGHT AFTER OTT turned north onto 95, Crawford got a call on his cell phone. "Hello?"

"Hello, Detective, it's Simon Petrie."

"Hi, Simon. I was just thinking about you. How you doing?"

"As well as can be expected, I guess, for a guy who's got holes in his chest and neck. I wanted to have a little chat with you. You haven't caught Christian's killer, right?"

"No, not yet. Are you still at Good Sam?"

"Yeah, I get out in a few days."

"How 'bout we come there in a half hour or so?"

"I'm not going anywhere."

Crawford clicked off and turned to Ott. "You get the gist of that?"

"Petrie's maybe got a tip for us?"

"I guess we'll soon find out."

They had one stop to make before Good Sam. Crawford had brought another SpyTec bug along with him. They drove up to Elysium on North Lake Way. The parking lot was separated from the main house by a ficus hedge that made their job easy. Crawford even had a cover story if Vega happened along: He had lost his gym locker key around the time he was last at Elysium.

He didn't need it, though. With Ott as lookout, Crawford simply went up to Vega's white BMW and attached the magnetic bug to the underside of her rear bumper, then casually walked back to the Vic.

"Maybe shoulda put one on her bike, too," Crawford said.

Ott smiled, stepped on the accelerator and five minutes later they were at Good Samaritan Hospital. Ott parked, they went up to the desk, then up to Petrie's room on the fourth floor. Two officers were still stationed at his door. Crawford and Ott nodded to them, then walked in.

Petrie, reading a magazine, set it down on a bedside table and smiled. "You chaps made good time."

"We're eager to hear what you got," Crawford said.

Ott nodded.

"So, I've had a lot of time to think since there's not a hell of a lot else to do here and I'm going to tell you something I swore I'd never tell anybody. 'Cause I think it might be important."

"Great," Crawford said. "Let's hear it."

"I swore to Christian I'd never tell a soul, but he's dead. So here goes: he said that Marie-Claire told him she had a conversation with Guy Bemmert and wanted to make sure he never got into SOAR. Because—"

"Yeah, we just found out about that," Crawford said. "We spoke to her daughter, Patrice Lord, just this morning."

"I'm thinking Bemmert found out Marie-Claire told Christian she was going to blackball him, then—lo and behold—the next day, she died," Petrie said.

"Was Christian the only one who knew about it?" Crawford asked.

"At that time, yes," said Petrie.

"Except Marie-Claire mentioned it to her daughter," Ott said.

"But her daughter had nothing to do with SOAR and had no reason to ever mention it to Crux, who she didn't like anyway," Crawford said.

Petrie shifted in his bed. "So, this is me filling in some blanks with all the spare time I've had on my hands," Petrie said, "but I'm guessing Bemmert might have offered Christian money to keep quiet. About Marie-Claire wanting him to be blackballed."

Crawford nodded slowly. "But did Christian ever tell you he got money from Bemmert to keep quiet?"

"No, we were friends but that's not something he'd ever tell me. Or anyone, for that matter," Petrie said, brushing back his hair. "But it makes sense, right?"

"It sure does," Crawford said.

"Or maybe it was the other way around," Ott said. "Maybe Christian went to Bemmert and demanded money. Extorted him."

"Yeah," Crawford said with a nod. "That coulda happened."

"So Bemmert got a two-fer," Ott said. "One, he offs Christian so he doesn't have to pay him, and two, he gets his job."

"If Christian was, in fact, extorting him," Crawford said.

Ott nodded, then to Petrie. "Anything else you thought of... lying here in bed?"

Petrie glanced over at him. "Isn't that enough?"

Ott nodded. "It sure is. But why would he tell you this in the first place?"

"Christian and I went way back. Plus, he'd tell me lot of stuff after a drink or two."

Crawford and Ott both nodded. They knew all about the notorious blabbermouth soup.

"But you're leaving out the obvious," Crawford said.

Petrie nodded. "I know. I was just about to get to that. You mean, if Bemmert found out Christian told me any of that, he'd have a motive to kill me."

"Absolutely," Crawford said. "First, he shuts up Marie-Claire, then Christian, then you... or tries to anyway."

"Except you were lucky...you had a ferocious dog," Ott said.

"Good old Chief," Petrie said with a smile.

Crawford nodded. "Well, thanks for all your insights. We'll keep you up to speed on where things go."

"Yes, please do. Things are pretty dull around here."

"Later," said Ott as they headed for the door.

They nodded at the uniform guards as they walked out.

"Well, that's very interesting," Ott said as they walked down the corridor.

"Sure is," Crawford said. "I'm going to do something I probably should have thought of a long time ago."

"What's that?"

"Check Christian Lalley's bank account. See if he made any large deposits after holding up Guy Bemmert."

THIRTY-FIVE

CRAWFORD KNEW from his search of Christian Lalley's room at 1450 North Lake that Lalley banked at PNC on Royal Poinciana Way. He was fortunate to get a court order in record time to examine Lalley's banks accounts and also find a cooperative banker at PNC who gave him access to Lalley's accounts.

And, surprise, surprise… seemed Lalley had made substantial deposits in the month preceding his murder.

The most interesting thing, Crawford found, was that the deposits got larger and larger. The first one was for twenty-five thousand dollars, the next one fifty thousand, and the third was a hundred thousand.

Crawford went by Ott's cubicle to tell him what he had found.

"So, your theory was right," Ott said. "Lalley was getting too greedy for Bemmert. But here's the bad news. I just took a look at those CCTV tapes on Coquina—"

"And?"

"They show that Bemmert and Swain came back to their house on Wednesday the day of Lalley's murder at a little before six and never went out after that."

"Shit." Crawford wanted to pound something.

"And the night of Petrie's assault they drove in at 3:30 and never left."

Crawford threw up his hands. "Christ, just when I thought—"

"Sorry, man."

"Yeah, me too."

Neither said anything for a few moments.

"Well, at least we got 'em for paying off Lalley. A hundred seventy-five grand, to be exact," Crawford said.

"Yeah, you want to go back down there and hit 'em with that?" Ott asked.

"Nah, let's dig around a little more and see what else we can come up with."

CRAWFORD DECIDED to take a ride out to the Maxwell Investigations HQ in the exclusive warehouse district of West Palm Beach. He figured he'd just show up.

He parked and walked over and hit the buzzer.

"Charlie," came Maxwell's voice over the intercom, "you decided you wanted a piece of pizza after all."

"Buzz me in, will ya, Max."

And he did.

Maxwell was waiting for him at the top of the steps.

Crawford walked up to the landing and eyeballed Maxwell. "I think you lied to me."

"What do you mean?" Maxwell said, gesturing with his hand to go into his office.

"For one thing, you told me Guy Bemmert had a clean record."

Maxwell gestured to the Herman Miller knock-off. Crawford sat down in it. "Well?"

"I don't know what you're getting at."

"I'll tell you what I'm getting at. I told you what you asked about my case and you lied to me about Bemmert. You withheld, too. Why?"

Maxwell let out a long, theatrical sigh. "Charlie, I could bullshit ya, but well… I'm just not gonna do that. I got too much respect for—"

"Cut the bullshit."

"Okay, this woman called and said she'd pay me a grand to say Bemmert was Mr. Clean, if someone ever asked."

"When was this?"

"Same day you came here."

"And you're gonna tell me you have no idea who she was, right?"

"Yeah, 'cause I don't. Honest."

"Bullshit. So, you just expected some unknown woman to pay you a grand?"

"Yeah, and know what? A messenger came by with an envelope full of ten Benjys."

Crawford chuckled. "And I'm guessing… 'Benjys' would be private dick lingo for hundred-dollar bills."

Maxwell smiled and nodded.

Crawford got to his feet. "You sure you don't know who she was?"

"Hundred percent."

"Okay, Maxwell. In the future, don't lie to a cop. It'll get you in deep shit."

"I'm sorry, Charlie, it'll never happen again."

Yeah, Crawford thought…until the next time.

THIRTY-SIX

OTT HAD JUST JOINED Crawford in his office where his partner had recounted his brief conversation with Maxwell.

"Think he really didn't know?" Ott asked.

"No, I bet he did. But what was I gonna do, beat it out of him? Some woman doesn't just call you out of the blue, say they're gonna pay you a thousand bucks… it just smells bad."

"I agree."

"So, it had to be either Fannie Melhado *or* my old friend, Vega."

"How do you figure?"

"Well, Fannie because when I asked Maxwell about her, he said she was 'clean as a whistle.' Which doesn't quite jibe with Peavy's little revelation."

"So, you're thinking that if Maxwell took money from her, he'd bury something like that?"

"Yeah, definitely. And Vega 'cause of my spy theory. That she's the ultimate *spinmeister*. Then again… I don't know, man, maybe neither one."

They were both silent for a few long moments.

"Maybe we should go rattle Guy Bemmert's cage again," Ott said. "About those payoffs to Christian Lalley."

"Yeah, I'm just not sure where that's gonna get us. I mean, for all we know Bemmert could just say that was money he was donating to SOAR."

"I hear you."

"I'm going to have a talk with Freddie Melhado. See what he can tell me about big sis and that dreamboat boyfriend of hers, Leo."

"You still thinking Leo's our guy?"

"If I knew he was handy with a knife, I'd say definitely. Right now, he's still just a leading contender. Up there with the boys from Boca."

"While you're doing that, I'm gonna check our GPS bugs to see if the girls are going anywhere suspicious."

"Let me know."

———

FREDDIE MELHADO BOASTED to Crawford that he had just done a hundred laps in the Elysium pool.

"Best all-around exercise there is," Crawford said.

There were still some beads of sweat on Melhado's brow as he sat down opposite Crawford in the Elysium living room.

"I used to play tennis, but I sucked at it, so doing laps is my thing now," Melhado said.

"I'd probably peter out after about three of 'em," Crawford said, then segueing, "Does your sister swim, too?"

"Nah, she still rides, but that's about it."

"Out in Wellington, right?"

Melhado nodded.

"She ever ride with Leo Peavy?"

Melhado chuckled. "So, you're up to speed on all the campus romances?"

Crawford smiled. "You hear a lot of stuff in my business."

Melhado nodded. "I bet. So, in answer to your question, far as I know, Leo's not a rider. But he's got a kayak down at our dock."

"Oh, there's a dock here?"

"Yeah, not a very big one."

"So, not big enough for the boat Crux is interested in?"

Melhado laughed. "Oh God no, not even close. Guy Bemmert's boat just barely fits."

Crawford's head jerked back. *Oh my God....* It was the proverbial lightbulb moment. He felt like dialing Ott immediately.

"So, Guy Bemmert's got a boat?"

"Yeah, a very expensive one, called a Pershing. Technically, I guess it's Guy's and Larry's."

"And he keeps it at the dock here?"

"Oh, no, he's got a dock down in Boca."

And there it was....

Crawford got to his feet. "Well, thank you, Mr. Melhado, I appreciate your time."

Melhado looked bewildered. "That's it?"

It was all Crawford needed to know.

"Yes, thank you. If I have any more questions, I'll give you a call."

Melhado shrugged. "Okay."

And Crawford was headed to the door at a walk just shy of a run.

———

"MORT," Crawford said into his cell phone. "Bemmert and Swain have a boat at a dock behind their house in Boca."

"No shit. I didn't know their place was on the water."

"The Intracoastal. We never saw it 'cause of that big ficus hedge behind their apartment."

"So, you're thinking... I got it," Ott said, amped up, "Instead of taking a car—"

"They took a boat."

Ott was nodding. "Now I got something for you. In fact, I was just about to call. So, speaking of Boca, guess who just went down to Coquina?"

"Who?"

"Vega."

"No shit. I'll pick you up in front of the station in ten minutes."

"I'll be waiting."

THIRTY-SEVEN

DESIGNATED drive-fast driver Ott jumped into the driver's seat, gunned the Vic, and turned to Crawford. "So, first, the boys took the boat up to 1450 and did Lalley, then the next night went up again and tried to do Simon Petrie? Swain being the guy with the knife, I'm guessing?"

Crawford nodded and said. "Yup, and I've been thinking about Vega's role in this. Know how she knows everything?"

"Yeah?"

"Maybe she found out that Bemmert and Swain were robbing the SOAR piggybank and wanted a piece of the action," Crawford said, watching a sign for Delray Beach fly by in a blur.

"Hmm," Ott said, "I like that, I like it a lot. Which would explain all the fancy clothes and the hundred-eighty-thousand-dollar BMW.... Hey, check the GPS and see if she's still at the boys' house."

Crawford checked it. "Looks like she's leaving."

"So, we can't round 'em all up at once," Ott said. "I just hope we don't have to chase her."

"Why?"

"'Cause that M760 would leave us in the dust. Zero to sixty in three point five seconds. Top speed two-hundred-five miles an hour."

Crawford nodded. "So, let's worry about Bemmert and Swain for now."

"Wonder what kind of boat they have?" Ott said.

"It's called a, ah… Pershing. Ever heard of it?"

Ott's eyes lit up. "A Pershing what? How many feet?"

"No clue."

"A Pershing, my friend, is my dream boat. In one of my *if-I-won-the-lottery* moments, and maybe after a cocktail or two, I surfed the Pershing website. Made by this Italian company and in this video, they kept talking about the "Pershing thrill," claiming that a Pershing was not driven, but like a fighter jet or a race car, it was "piloted. It's kind of the boat equivalent of the M760."

"205 miles an hour?"

"Not quite, but I bet it does forty-five knots."

"What's that in miles an hour?"

"Over fifty. Shit, man, sucker's got over 3,600 horsepower."

Crawford couldn't relate.

Ott told Crawford about a video he had seen about the boat. In it, it showed a smaller boat, called a tender, he explained, which could motor up to the swimming platform at the stern of the Pershing and moments later disappear *inside* the yacht. Like it had been swallowed up. Ott had been curious enough to want to know more and had called a yacht broker he knew. The broker explained that there was an "eye" built in on the bow of the tender and a "hook" attached to a cable inside the boat, and a "garage" effectively, inside the boat. Ott didn't need to be told any more to understand how it worked.: the big boat hauled the tender into the garage hydraulically. The whole process took no more than three minutes.

They were five minutes from the house at 702 Coquina Drive when Crawford's cell phone rang. He hit speakerphone.

"Hey, Rose."

"Charlie, I'll make this quick. Richard Guy Bemmert is the proud new owner of 702 Coquina Drive."

"Thank you, Rose. I can't thank you enough."

"Bye, Charlie. Go get him."

"On it," Crawford said and clicked off.

"Wow," Ott said, "top-of-the-line boat, waterfront mansion, wonder if he's bought a jet yet… so how we gonna play it?"

"We got enough circumstantial to take 'em in for questioning."

"So just arrest 'em, take 'em back to the station and work 'em over until we break 'em?"

Crawford nodded.

"Wonder whether they'll be in the main house or the apartment?"

"Good question," Crawford said. "We'll soon find out."

Three minutes later the Crown Vic eased up to the gate at Coquina Drive.

Ott pressed the buzzer to speak to Bemmert or Swain so they could get buzzed onto the property.

"Who is it?" Swain answered.

"Crawford and Ott, Palm Beach homicide."

They heard a click but the arm for the barrier gate didn't move.

"Try again," Crawford said.

As Ott pressed the buzzer, they saw Bemmert and Swain charge down the steps at the back of the main house, headed for the Intracoastal at full speed.

"Gun it!" Crawford shouted.

Ott floored the Vic and the gate's arm snapped like a brittle twig.

Bemmert and Swain cut to the right of a ficus hedge. Crawford was surprised—unpleasantly—how fast the older man was.

Ott had the car halfway down the driveway as Crawford drew his Sig Sauer pistol from his hip holster.

Below them, at the dock, Swain jumped onto the Pershing, turned, and pulled Bemmert on board. Then he unhitched the line and cast it aside.

The Crown Vic screeched to a stop at the end of the driveway, but Crawford had jumped out while it was still moving.

"Hands in the air or you're dead!" Crawford bluffed.

Bemmert dived to the deck of the boat as Swain jammed the accelerator forward on the Pershing. A line that Swain hadn't had time to untie snapped with a cracking sound and the Pershing engine roared like a racecar with the accelerator mashed to the floor. The big yacht picked up speed fast.

Crawford and Ott, his Glock out now, ran toward the dock. Neither was prepared to take a shot, but they wouldn't have had a clear line-of-sight even if they had. Swain was hunched down low behind the wheel and Bemmert still flat on the deck.

On the dock, Crawford pulled out his iPhone and hit speed dial. "Dispatch."

"Patty, it's Crawford, put me through to Cooper."

"Will do."

A male voice came on seconds later. "What's up, Charlie?"

"You in the chopper?"

"Yup. But I'm on the ground."

"I need you to fly down toward Boca. *Right now.*"

Crawford heard a clicking noise.

"You got it. Okay, I'm goin' up," Ronnie Cooper said. "Fill me in."

"All right. Go south on the Intracoastal. Keep your eye out for a silver boat. 'Bout, um, seventy feet long, sleek as hell, probably doing—"

"Forty-five knots, close to fifty miles an hour," Ott said.

"Hear that?" Crawford asked.

"Got it," Cooper said.

"Once you see it, fly over and keep going south," Crawford said. "We need a pick-up at the dock it took off from. 702 Coquina Way's the address, in Boca. You'll see us. There's a chance the boat might pull in somewhere in the meantime, but I hope the hell not."

"I'll fly low. See what I see," Cooper said.

"All right, man, we'll be waiting for you."

"Roger that."

Crawford dialed again. Patty answered.

"Me again," he said. "Rutledge there?"

"Yup. Want him?"

"Yes."

Crawford waited a few moments.

"Crawford," said Rutledge. "What's up?"

"Norm, I need two sharpshooters at the South Bridge. Quick as you can get 'em there. Or if they're not available, two officers with rifles."

"Roger that. Hold on a sec, I'm on it."

Thirty seconds, which felt like five minutes to Crawford, crawled by.

"Okay, they're on their way. What do I tell 'em the play is?"

"They're looking for a silver boat seventy feet long goin' fast, maybe close to fifty miles an hour. Two guys on it. One's wearing a yellow shirt. Tell the shooters to take a few shots into the bow."

"Not at the men?"

"No. Idea is to make 'em U-turn, so we get 'em hemmed in. Ott and I are gonna be comin' up behind 'em in the chopper."

"Care to elaborate on what this is about?" Rutledge asked.

"No time for details, but they did Lalley. Maybe someone else, too. Send out the police boats too. Tell 'em to go south and if they see the boat I described, keep their distance. These guys might have a small arsenal on board."

"All right, be careful and keep me updated."

"You got it," Crawford said and clicked off.

Ott chuckled. "Think he'll get out his old deer rifle and head down to the bridge himself?"

Crawford laughed. "Probably."

Ott turned serious. "What if these guys shoot at us in the chopper?"

"I don't know, man. Depends on how desperate they are."

"Probably pretty desperate."

"Yeah, I hear you. If they do, let's hope Coop knows some evasive moves."

"Damn well better."

Crawford's iPhone rang. "Coop?"

"Hey, I just flew over the boat. Few minutes from you."

"Okay, man, I'll keep the line open. Put the chopper down in the lawn next to the dock, east side of the Intracoastal. Ott's wearing a red shirt. We'll flag you down, then jump in."

"Roger that. I saw two guys in the boat. Hey, is that a Pershing?"

"Yeah, why?"

"Shit, man, that's my dream boat."

Ott nodded silently.

A few minutes later Crawford saw a dot in the sky, growing in the distance.

He pointed it out and Ott nodded.

"What's his top speed?" Crawford asked.

"I know it's a Bell Jet Ranger, just don't know which one. I think somewhere between one forty-five and a one-sixty."

"So, we can catch up pretty quick."

Ott nodded. "My guess is when they see the chopper coming back up, they'll figure it out."

"Yeah, they *are* Mensas. Bemmert, anyway."

"They'll want to pull into a creek or something, ditch the boat and take their chances on land."

Crawford nodded. "I like that scenario better than them shooting at us in the chopper."

"If they shoot at us, they'll know they're startin' a war, and we got a lot more guns and troops."

"Gonna be a tight squeeze anyway, gettin' that battleship into a creek," Crawford said.

"'Cause of the draft, you mean?"

"Yeah, I'm guessing it's five feet, maybe a little less."

The helicopter was a few hundred yards away, its propeller whipping up the Intracoastal water.

They ran over to the lawn between the dock and the guest house as the helicopter approached, twenty feet above the ground now.

Cooper brought it down expertly and Crawford jumped in the front seat and Ott the back.

"Welcome aboard, boys," Cooper shouted.

"Thanks for getting here so fast," Crawford said, raising his voice over the racket.

Cooper nodded.

"So, you gonna fly it if Coop gets popped?" Ott said to Crawford.

Cooper frowned as he maneuvered the chopper back up over the Intracoastal. He shot a glance at Crawford. "I forgot about your partner's lame sense of humor."

"Yeah, it gets worse all the time," Crawford said.

Cooper headed north and accelerated. "So, what's the game plan?"

"Best guess is, when they spot us, they're gonna want to get to land. The longer this goes on, the more guys we're gonna have surrounding them."

"Think they'll pull up to a dock?" asked Cooper. "'Cause a boat that size'll run aground real easy."

"Unless they find a deep-water inlet," Crawford said.

"If there even is one," Ott said.

Cooper nodded.

Crawford dialed his iPhone and got put through to Rutledge again.

"Got the guys down on the South Bridge," said Rutledge.

"Good," Crawford said. "The boat may never get that far. May figure their chances are better on land."

"All right, well, they're ready."

"Also, get a bunch of uniforms in cruisers headed south. As many as you can spare. Split 'em up, half on the west side of the Intracoastal, half on the east."

"Will do."

"If they beach the boat, I'll call you with the location and they can close in."

"So, they definitely did Lalley?"

"Yup, and probably another woman," Crawford said and clicked off.

"There they are," Cooper said, pointing.

Crawford saw the sun glinting off of the silver boat about a mile ahead.

Cooper turned to Crawford. "What's the play?"

"Just follow 'em but stay back."

"When they make their move, we can tell the cars running along the Intracoastal where they are," Ott shouted from the back.

"Our boats coming south should be on 'em pretty soon," Crawford said.

Cooper nodded. "Land, sea and air, huh?"

"Exactly," said Crawford as Cooper slowed the helicopter, dogging the Pershing from a safe distance behind.

Crawford pulled out a pair of binoculars from the console between

Cooper and him and looked through them down at the boat. It seemed to be slowing down, too. Crawford looked farther up the Intracoastal and saw two boats side by side. He recognized the black hull of one as that of a police boat.

He pointed. "Here they come."

Then he saw movement at the stern of the Pershing. And suddenly... almost like the big boat was giving birth, a small boat—a tender—squeezed out of the stern of the Pershing.

"Jesus, look," Crawford said, pointing, as the tender turned and shot forward.

In seconds it looked to be at full speed.

"Holy shit," Ott said, as Crawford pulled out his iPhone. "Just like I told you."

"You still there, Norm?"

"I'm here."

"Tell the guys in the boats, if they haven't seen it yet, the target is now a ten-foot white inflatable that just exited the yacht. Two subjects in it—" he paused to confirm its course "headed *south*. We're in pursuit."

"Roger that."

Cooper lowered the helicopter as the inflatable tender, now going almost as fast as the Pershing had been, aimed for an inlet that had two small docks on either side.

"Subject on course to enter an inlet on the east side of the Intracoastal," Crawford said, watching. "Just turned in now." He turned to Cooper. "Get as close as you can."

Cooper brought the helicopter down, so it was thirty feet above the water and descending.

"Subject's slowed down, in the inlet now, but not stopping at a dock—"

"Police boats have a visual," Rutledge said. "Report they're a half-mile from the inlet."

Crawford cocked his head. "Not sure they can get in." Then to Ott, "What's the draft on that inflatable?"

"Oh, shit, six inches, max? A lot less than the police boats."

"Okay," Crawford said, "then we probably have the best shot if the boats can't fit in there."

"Looks that way," Ott said, watching the inflatable speed past a few docks, as the helicopter descended to twenty feet above the water.

Suddenly, the inflatable, which had abruptly slowed, took a hard right and ran aground onto an open space between two thickets of palm trees. Swain jumped out, grabbed Bemmert's arms, pulled him out, and the two started running.

"Get us down!" Crawford shouted to Cooper, but he didn't have to say it, as the pilot dodged a tall pine and a wax palm, headed for a spot next to where the inflatable had run aground. "They're on foot now," Crawford warned Rutledge.

Swain and Bemmert disappeared into a wooded area. "Okay," he said into his phone, "I don't know exactly where we are but we're about to land and pursue on foot." He looked over at Cooper, who was concentrating hard on landing. "Once Coop drops us, he's going back up to try to spot 'em. Give you a location, too."

Cooper nodded as the helicopter skids touched down on terra firma.

Crawford, who had his Sig Sauer drawn, jumped out of the helicopter, and started running toward the wooded area.

"Right behind ya!" Ott shouted as he exited the helicopter, Glock in hand.

Crawford was the first to reach the wooded area but could hear Ott only a few steps behind him. He plunged in. It was swampy and his feet sank with every step. *Perfect location for snakes*, he thought… one of several fears he had that regularly tormented him since childhood. He heard a branch break behind him and heard Ott shout, "Motherfucker!" He didn't look back but kept scanning the woods ahead for Swain and Bemmert. The mud was getting thicker and deeper. Ahead, he spotted a blue, lace-less sneaker stuck in the mud.

He saw something off to his left. It was yellow and it was moving.

Bemmert.

He turned to Ott, still a few steps behind. "Pretty sure that's Bemmert."

"Yup, I saw. Want me to take him?"

"Yeah. I'll keep goin'. Try to run down Swain."

They ran another fifty yards and Bemmert was now only twenty ahead of them. Crawford could hear him panting for breath. Not stopping, he aimed his Sig. "Hands in the air, Bemmert! We got two guns on you."

Bemmert shouted something unintelligible.

"Hands in the fucking air!" Ott shouted. "Or you'll get one up the ass."

Bemmert raised his hands, then bent over, gasping for air.

As Crawford raced past Bemmert, he saw a cut on his face that was dripping blood onto his yellow T-shirt, which was already soaked through with sweat. He was only wearing one sneaker.

Ott came up behind him. "Okay, hands behind your back."

Bemmert did as he was ordered, and Ott cuffed him.

Ott turned him around and gave him a hard stare. "One down, one to go."

The woods had gone from muddy to swampy to ankle-deep muck, slowing Crawford considerably. He stopped to see if he could hear Swain ahead, but all he caught was the whir of helicopters blades above.

He mopped his sweaty brow with his shirt sleeve, then started running again. He wasn't at all sure he was even headed in the right direction.

The sudden crack of three gunshots in rapid succession told him he was. Another burst thunked heavily into a pygmy palm next to him. He dropped to the muck and aimed his Sig in the direction where the shots came from.

"Swain!" Crawford shouted. "You got no chance! I got cops in cars, boats, and choppers surrounding you. You got no way out, and you don't want to die in the middle of this swamp."

Another burst of gunfire was Swain's answer. Crawford heard one bullet slam into the tall grass a few feet away.

To make it clear to Swain he had no intention of dying in the swamp, he fired off a burst of three shots in the direction where he thought Swain was hunkered down. He had fourteen more bullets in his magazine, plus two seventeen-shot mags in his belt, so he wouldn't be running out of rounds anytime soon.

He cupped his hands around his mouth and shouted, "I can just stay here and wait you out, Swain! I got the cavalry coming, while you got nothing. Plus, we got Bemmert."

He heard what sounded like a branch snap. Swain was either running away or coming toward him. Crawford didn't see any movement ahead. But then he did. It was on the ground and it was one of his worst fears. A shiny, black snake with white and yellow bands. It was long—he guessed about six feet— and it was writhing…away from him, fortunately. Still, his first instinct was to unload a few rounds into the slimy bastard.

Calm, he told himself. *It wants no part of you….*

He looked up through the branches in front of him. He heard what sounded like another branch breaking, but this time farther away. Crouching low, he duck-walked forward, holding his Sig in both hands and leaving his slithering friend behind. He kept going for another fifty yards and saw and heard nothing. He was regretting not having shot his Sig in over a year, ignoring memo after memo reminding him about practicing at the range.

And then, there Swain was, in a clearing twenty-five to thirty yards ahead. He was wearing a camo shirt—how appropriate—and black jeans coated with mud up to his knees.

Crawford crouched down and aimed at his chest—center-mass— then shouted as loud as he could. "Drop your gun, Swain!"

Instinctively, Swain turned and squeezed off a burst. But Crawford had him sighted in and fired a single shot. It hit Swain in the upper chest below his shoulder.

Swain went down with a groan. Crawford feared the ex-biker becoming a desperate, wounded animal.

Still in a crouch, pistol in both hands, Crawford shouted again. "Toss your gun!"

No response.

He edged forward a few steps, then stopped.

"Toss it, Swain!"

Again, no response.

He crept forward a few more yards and stopped.

He could see Swain's jeans but not his upper body or his hands.

He took a few more steps and saw all of Swain's body: a large patch of blood in his upper right chest, pistol still in his right hand—a Glock, Crawford thought—and eyes shut.

He took a few more steps. Suddenly Swain's eyes popped open and he raised his pistol to aim, but Crawford was ready.

He fired three quick shots into Swain's chest.

Swain's arm and pistol fell to the mud before he could get off a shot.

THIRTY-EIGHT

A HALF HOUR LATER, a cluster of cops had gathered in the thicket where Crawford had killed Larry Swain.

Crawford had first called Rutledge and told him what happened, then found a clearing where Ronnie Cooper had eventually spotted him waving his white—and by now soiled and sweaty—shirt. First came Ott and his prisoner, Guy Bemmert, who looked down in disbelief and shock at the body of his dead partner. Then, two guys from the Marine Unit, who had docked their boat in the inlet. Then a uniform on an ATV, and finally two cops who had parked their car half a mile away.

While this was all going on around him, Crawford remained silent.

He hadn't killed a man in a long time. Since his days in New York.

There had been three up there.

It was not something he relished, and Ott could plainly see that.

"You okay, man?" Ott asked, going over to his partner, who was leaning against a tree, looking into the woods in an unfocused gaze.

"Not really."

"I hear you."

Crawford turned and caught Ott's eye. Ott had never seen the look before on his partner's face. It could have been despair. It could have been shock. It could have been regret. Probably a little of all three.

Ott, who never seemed at a loss for words, couldn't come up with anything he thought appropriate to say. Finally, he spoke quietly. "Probably time we both took a vacation. Got away from this shit for a while."

Crawford nodded an uncertain nod. "He just didn't want to get taken alive, I guess," he said, his gaze still distant.

"Yeah," Ott said. "Some are like that."

Crawford looked over at Guy Bemmert, who was kneeling next to Swain's body, surrounded by cops. It seemed like he was saying a silent prayer.

"I feel bad for the guy," Crawford whispered to his partner.

Ott nodded.

After a few moments, Bemmert looked up at them.

"Mr. Bemmert," Ott said, "we need to know about Vega."

THIRTY-NINE

ON THE WAY back up to Palm Beach, Ott checked the GPS tracker to see where Vega's BMW was. Their fear was that she may have heard on the news about the shoot-out and driven her high-powered vehicle off to parts unknown.

But no, she hadn't

"Her car's parked on Worth Avenue," Ott said, having just read it on the tracker.

"By the way, we need to get the judge to okay us looking at her bank accounts." Crawford said.

"One step ahead of you, I already called."

"Good man. Let's go find her."

―――――――

VEGA's white M760 was parked right in front of Ta-Boo at 241 Worth Avenue.

Crawford and Ott pulled into a space in front of the Jimmy Choo's across the street. They got out of the Vic and Crawford glanced at a pair of turquoise high-top sneakers in the window.

Crawford pointed "You'd look good in those."

"Yeah, probably set me back three hundred bucks."

"More," Crawford said as they crossed the street to Ta-boo.

They walked in and Crawford spotted Vega right away sitting at the bar. She had a drink in front of her in a long skinny glass with two olives in it.

The famous blabbermouth soup.

Crawford sat down beside her in a leather bar stool, Ott on the other side.

"Hello, Vega," Crawford said, as she turned to him.

"Hello, Charlie, I've been expecting you."

Crawford motioned to Ott. "This is my partner, Detective Ott."

She turned to Ott. "Hello, detective."

"Ma'am," said Ott.

She turned back to Crawford.

"So, you heard about what happened," Crawford said, "on the news?"

She shook her head. "From Guy Bemmert. He called from his boat. Said you were after him. You caught 'em, I guess?"

Crawford nodded. "Why didn't you run?"

"I thought about it, but I knew you'd catch me."

"You got a fast getaway car," Ott said.

Vega turned to him and laughed. "I never drive it over forty."

"What a waste," said Ott.

She turned back to Crawford. "Besides, I couldn't exactly picture myself as *The Fugitive.*"

Crawford laughed. "So, I'm guessing you found out Bemmert and Swain were stealing from SOAR and demanded money from 'em to keep quiet."

"Yes, I looked into Bemmert after I saw that fancy boat docked at Elysium. From what I had heard he had to pay a big fine to that company he had bilked and was, basically, broke. So, I said to myself, now he's got a million-dollar boat? How does that work?"

Ott leaned toward Vega. "I got news for you, ma'am, that's a two-million-dollar boat."

"Wow. Really?" she said, as the bartender approached them.

"Gentlemen," he said. "Can I get you drinks?"

"Oh, yes. Try a martini, Charlie?" Vega said.

Crawford looked up at bartender. "Coke, please."

"You're no fun," Vega said.

The bartender turned to Ott. "Ginger ale, please.""

"We're teetotalers," Crawford said with a smile.

Vega laughed. "You weren't when we were at Mookie's."

"So, I guess, with your Skull and Bones background, it was simple to find out what Bemmert and Swain were up to?"

Vega cocked her head. "How did you… oh, right, you're a detective."

Their drinks came and Crawford took a sip of his Coke.

"So, what's going to happen to me?" Vega asked.

"To be honest with you, I don't know. If there's a trial, I'll say you were cooperative. That is, if you are, and if you fill me in on everything you know and don't try to lead me astray. That was kind of your MO before. Like how you got your friend Maxwell to steer me away from Bemmert and Swain—" he took a sip of his Coke. "Also, if you testify against Guy Bemmert."

"And Larry Swain?"

Crawford sighed. "Ah, he's… no longer with us."

Ott leaned toward Vega. "Ma'am, speaking of Larry Swain—"

"He and Guy were a hell of an unlikely couple, right?"

"Yeah, I'll say. What do you know about Swain?"

"Not that much, except that supposedly he used to be in a motorcycle gang. He was always nice to me—hey, people change— but people said he had a nasty side."

"Did you ever see any weapons at their apartment?"

"I was only there twice. Today and, well, one other time, so… no, I didn't."

Crawford glanced over at Ott. "Something tells me when we go through that place, we will."

"Yeah, might find a bunch of cash squirreled away, too."

FORTY

VEGA, eager to be cooperative, spent the next half hour telling Crawford and Ott everything she knew they'd want to know. Fannie Melhado, with the exception of some twisted S&M escapades, was, as Maxwell the PI had said, clean as a whistle. Crux, with the exception of having been instrumental in the set-up of Holmes Whitmore, the falsely accused pedophile, was also in the clear.

And Leo Peavy…well, he just plain looked bad. But, with the exception of the sideburns and the plug-ugly watch, he couldn't really help it.

IN THE WAKE of the case, Crawford took Ott's advice and went down to the Keys for a few days. He had a friend who was an avid, almost obsessive, bone-fisherman and said how much fun it was catching the elusive fish. Crawford didn't really know what a bonefish looked like but thought he'd try it since his friend swore by it.

At the end of their first morning fishing, he still didn't know what a bonefish looked like because, even with the assistance of a man generally regarded as the best fishing guide around, they didn't catch one. A couple of times the guide pointed and said, *See over there.* Crawford swung around and looked but all he saw was water reflecting the sun.

The next day he took a tour of Ernest Hemingway's house on Whitehead Street in Key West. It was okay, a nice, old Spanish style, two-story house with lots of windows. Lots of cats, too, wandering around the house and grounds. They were reputed to be the great granddaughters and grandsons of Hemingway's original menagerie of cats. There were also plenty of photos and paintings of the man called Papa, along with his old typewriter and lots of old books, and for some inexplicable reason, framed photos of checks he had written. That was a head-scratcher. Crawford had no clue why anyone would think checks would be of interest. He left the house after half an hour, his takeaway being that he was still more of a Fitzgerald man.

Day three was dominated by a long walk around the funky town. He came to the conclusion he would have liked Key West better back in Hemingway's day. Too many T-shirt and ice-cream shops now. He also came to another conclusion: that he would have had a better time if he had brought Dominica along.

Night three he went bar-hopping. Beer was beer and rum was rum, but he had fun chatting up a few of the locals he met. One woman made it clear that she was available for the next chapter, but he wasn't interested.

He missed Dominica.

Rose, too.

FORTY-ONE

IT WAS SATURDAY. Crawford had arrived back from Key West the night before. He woke up, loaded three large teaspoons of Folgers finest into his Mr. Coffee machine and walked to his living-room window. He didn't know what was worse, having the Publix parking lot chock-a-block full of cars, trucks, and shopping carts or, as it was now… empty. Well, with the exception of a long-haired, bearded homeless man slowly dragging his way across the four football fields' worth of painted stripes, a tattered but colorful beach towel slung around his shoulders.

Just as it had been time to wrap up the Christian Lalley murder, it was now time for him to find a new place to live.

He waited until 9 a.m. to call Rose.

"Hey, Charlie," Rose answered. "So, congratulations are in order; you got your killers."

"Thanks, Rose," he said somberly. He was still having trouble getting over killing a man.

"That Bemmert guy," Rose said. "What a low-life."

"I'll tell him you send your regards. So, you got a full day today?"

"You want to look at places?"

"Yeah, if you can squeeze me in."

She thought for a second. "How about… four-thirty?"

"I got all day. No bad guys to catch. Four-thirty it is."

"Fine. Come on by the office."

"See you then."

A few minutes after he hung up with Rose, his cell rang. It was Ott.

"Whatcha doin'?" Ott asked.

"What kinda question is that? Sittin' here having a cup of coffee."

"Doesn't it feel weird having spare time on your hands?"

"I know. I'm going to look at condos with Rose later in the afternoon."

"Well, how 'bout a speed nine in the meantime?" Ott said. "Or, since you'll be doing it with me, let's just call it a… *relaxed nine*."

A *speed nine* was something Crawford had invented: it was a quick break from work and a form of recreation. In addition to going to his gym in West Palm Beach every other day, Crawford would play nine holes at the par-three golf course south of Palm Beach once a week or so. He had dubbed it a *speed nine* because he didn't take any practice swings and any putt within five feet of the cup was a gimme. It never took more than an hour and his record was forty-eight minutes. He usually played alone or with Dominica, who was a pretty decent golfer.

He liked speed nines because he could break up a day with a quick round, then go back to the office and work 'til late. The one time he played with Ott it took well over an hour and a half, as Ott insisted on taking two practice swings before each shot and scrupulously putting out every hole. So, Ott hadn't been asked back.

Dominica, on the other hand, got the idea fast and played even faster. Plus, she was a lot easier on the eye than Ott.

"Okay, man, you're on. But here are the ground rules: No practice swings—"

"I'm good with that."

"No shoptalk."

"That's easy, we got nothin' to talk about."

"And no farting when I'm about to putt."

Ott burst out laughing. "Why would I ever—"

"You did it last time we played. Twice."

"Same stakes as before?" his partner asked.

"Sure."

"Hey," said Ott. "Should we ask Dominica?"

"I was just about to say that. I'll call her," Crawford said. "Balls in the air—or, in your case, the water—at eleven?"

"Perfect. Then lunch and a libation or two."

"You got it. Better bring your A game."

"Ha, like I'll need it with you."

DOMINICA HAD to juggle her schedule but told Crawford she was eager for the opportunity to take his money. Then, she got serious. "How are you doing anyway?"

He knew what she was asking.

"I'm okay. Worst part of the job."

"I hear you."

There was a silence.

"All right. Enough of that," Crawford said, changing his tone. "I predict my game's about ready to return to its former greatness."

Dominica laughed. "Hm. Can't say I have any recollection of that."

"Now I'm really gonna kick your ass."

OTT DUCK-HOOKED his first drive on the 147-yard first hole into the water. He almost winged a seagull, which was drifting along minding his, or her, own business.

"See, if I had had a practice swing, I'd have been on the green," Ott said.

Crawford rolled his eyes at Dominica. "Here we go with the excuses."

Dominica chuckled as Crawford bent down, teed up his ball, then looked up at her.

She was wearing a short skirt with a swirl of abstract pastel colors over deeply-tanned and well-muscled legs...which would have been distracting enough. But then there was the upper half of this perfectly put-together woman.

Crawford, wearing tan khaki shorts and a blue polo shirt with no logo, addressed his teed-up ball and lashed at it. It started out fine, but then as if it had caromed off some invisible wall, it dived hard left and, after one skip, splashed into the same body of water that Ott's ball had found.

"Okay, boys," Dominica said, "you want to concede me this hole?"

"Not so fast, girl," Ott said. "There's plenty of room in that pond for another ball."

But Dominica hit a nice, straight drive that ended up on the apron of the green. She got her par and won the hole.

They went around in an hour and ten minutes, despite a few more water balls and unplayable lies.

But in the end, it was, surprisingly, Ott who won. He deposited his winnings—two twenties, a ten, four fives, and eleven ones into his previously skimpy wallet.

"Pleasure doing business with you," Ott said as the trio walked off the eighteenth green. "I might be able to retire if we did this every day."

"Typical," Crawford said, shaking his head. "Eke out a narrow victory and it goes straight to your head."

"Narrow?" Ott said. "What's narrow about me winning six out of nine holes. You're just a sore loser 'cause you came in third... behind a girl, I might add."

FORTY-TWO

CRAWFORD INVITED Dominica to join Rose and him on his condo search, and she accepted. He figured two women's opinions were worth a lot more than one of his.

Crawford picked up Dominica at 4:25 and drove to the Rapallo North building at 1701 South Flagler. They met Rose in the lobby of the building and Rose, pro that she was, didn't miss a beat when she saw Dominica.

"What an unexpected surprise," Rose said, walking over to Dominica and giving her a single-cheeker.

Crawford preferred single-cheekers himself because double-cheek kisses struck him as overproduced. Same with bro hugs.

"I hope it's okay I came along," Dominica said.

Rose nodded exuberantly. "Of course, the more the merrier. Gives us a chance to catch up." She gestured at the elevator. "Shall we?"

The three walked in, and Dominica turned to Rose. "So, how is the real-estate market?"

"Well, it depends. I'd say it's pretty strong, more sales than last year. But the condo market's a little soft."

Dominica turned to Charlie. "Music to your ears, huh?"

Crawford nodded and winked at Rose. "Look out, here I come: *Lowball Charlie*."

The first condo they looked at was the two-bedroom on the 14th floor they had seen before that needed some work but had a nice view southeast—out over Everglades Island.

"Do you really need a two-bedroom?" Dominica asked.

"It's not like I've got a lot of houseguests. Every once in a while, I guess I do."

Next, they looked at a one-bedroom, two-bath on a lower floor. It needed a fair amount of work, but the price was right. However, the view was only average, Rose pointed out.

Crawford shook his head. "After four years of watching people pushing shopping carts, it's all about the view."

"So, the one on fourteen?" Rose asked.

"Yeah, but I'm still trying to decide between a one-bedroom and a two," Crawford said. "What else we got?"

"A couple in Trianon."

That was another tall building just north on Flagler.

"How much?"

"Stretching your budget a little. Four-twenty-five and four-fifteen."

"Think we could get 'em in the threes?" Crawford asked.

"Yeah. I'd say high threes, maybe."

———

THE PROBLEM WAS they both were on low floors. Three and four. Both featured the same line-of-sight and had views more south than east—a long way from jaw-droppers.

Trianon was a notch above Rapallo as a building and only a five-minute drive to the station.

"There's another one in the building that has a view—I hate the expression— but it truly is, *to die for*."

"Can we get in?" Crawford asked.

"Yes, it's vacant. Problem is, you can't afford it."

"How much?"

"Seven-forty-nine. Two bedrooms, two baths, right around twelve-hundred-fifty square feet."

Crawford didn't hesitate. "Let's have a look."

"What's the point?" Dominica asked. "You'll just feel bad you can't have it."

Crawford shrugged. "Hey, it never hurts to look," he said. "They might be really motivated. You know, take like… three-fifty."

Rose laughed. "In your dreams."

They took the elevator up to the twelfth floor. It was apartment 1201. Rose opened the door, and the view was exactly as advertised. To. Die. For. Breathtaking. Jaw-dropping. Drop-dead gorgeous. Out of this world, and every other cliché you could come up with.

"Oh… my… God," Dominica said, as the three walked out onto the balcony.

Straight ahead was the Palm Beach Marina and some of the biggest boats around, many owned by Palm Beach's forty-three billionaires, no doubt. To the left, and slightly north, was the stately middle bridge, and a few miles beyond it to the northeast, the majestic Breakers Hotel rose in the distance.

Crawford looked to the southeast and saw Everglades Island. He thought he even spotted Phoebe Lilly's enormous British Colonial, an American flag flapping in the breeze. Then he looked straight ahead and pointed.

"That's the station," he said to Dominica. "I could wave to you from up here."

Dominica laughed. "You could if I had an office with a window."

Crawford patted her shoulder and turned to Rose. "I'll take it."

Rose's eyes bulged. "What?"

"Yeah, let's offer 'em seven hundred thousand…cash."

"But you…you haven't even seen the master bedroom yet."

"I'm sure it'll be fine," Crawford said, glancing at the new kitchen. "They obviously renovated the whole place pretty recently."

Rose looked over at Dominica. "He's been holding out on us. Not telling us about the Crawford millions."

"Yeah, I know," Dominica said to Crawford. "Can you buy me one too while you're it?"

Crawford smiled and turned to Rose. "How much is the monthly maintenance?" Then, he put up a hand. "Nah, don't tell me. Whatever it is, it's worth it for this view."

Again, Rose glanced over at Dominica. "Is this the same man we walked in here with? The man who said, 'Three hundred's my absolute cut-off. I can't go a nickel over?'"

Dominica smiled at Crawford, studying him. "Looks the same," she said. "I don't know what came over him. He did have a couple of beers at lunch...."

Crawford laughed. "What can I tell you? I thought things over a little... I'm going to get a new car, too."

"Oh, really," Rose said, reaching into her purse for her iPhone. "You want the number of the Rolls dealership?"

THE END

KILLING TIME IN
CHARLESTON EXCERPT

ONE

A YEAR after what happened in Boston, Janzek flew down to Charleston, South Carolina, for his college roommate's wedding. It took him about five minutes to fall in love with the place. Beautiful old houses, five-star restaurants on every block, streets crawling with killer women and, best of all, no snow in the forecast. What was not to love?

He had wandered off from his friend's wedding reception with Cameron, the twenty-eight-year-old sister of the bride. Together they discovered the culinary gusto of an out-of-the-way spot called Trattoria Lucca, then followed it up with some jamming music at a quasi-dive he figured he'd never be able to find again. Last thing he remembered was teetering down a cobblestone street, arm around Cameron's shoulder, looking for a place that had either Lion or Tiger in its name. That Cameron, what a handful she turned out to be.

The day after the wedding he canceled his return flight to Logan Airport, then on Monday morning walked into the Charleston Police Department on Lockwood Street. The résumé he had knocked out in his hotel room that morning had a typo or two in it, but that didn't seem to bother the chief of detectives who hired him on the spot.

Now, three months later, he was coming down the home stretch: Interstate 26, just north of Charleston. The first half of the trip down had been a little dicey, since the day he had picked for the move had turned out to be especially cold and windy. He was driving a U-Haul, his car on a hitch behind it, and had been wrestling the steering wheel of the orange-and-white cube the whole way down. A few miles before Wilmington, Delaware, a gusty blast blew him into the path of a rampaging sixteen-wheeler, which roared up on his bumper like an Amtrak car that had jumped the tracks. It was a close call, but things quieted down after he hit the Maryland border.

He had the window down now and was taking in the warm salt air, which reminded him of the Cape when he was a kid and life was easy. He was looking forward to the slow, Southern pace of Charleston. Kicking back with a plate full of shrimp and grits, barbeque and collards, or whatever the hell it was they were so famous for, then washing it all down with a couple of Blood Hounds, a bare-knuckled rum drink bad girl Cameron had introduced him to.

He was thinking about how he might get his lame golf game out of mothballs, psyched about being able to play year-round. One thing he'd miss would be opening day at Fenway, but he'd heard about Charleston's minor league baseball team and figured it would be good for a few grins. One thing he'd never miss would be staring down at stiffs on the mean streets of Beantown.

The ring of his cell phone broke the reverie. He picked it up, looked at the number, and didn't recognize it.

"Hello."

"Nick, it's Ernie Brindle. Where y'at?" Brindle was the Charleston chief of detectives, the man who had hired him.

"Matter of fact, Ernie, I'm just pulling into Charleston. A few miles north. Why, what's up?"

Brindle sighed. "Looks like it's gonna be trial by fire for you, bro. I'm looking down at a dead body on Broad Street... it's the mayor. The ex-mayor, guess that would be. How fast can you get here?"

Janzek had figured he'd at least get a chance to unload his stuff from the U-Haul before his first-day punch-in.

"Thing is, Ernie, I'm driving this big old U-Haul with all my junk in it. Can't I just drop it—"

"No, I need you right now. Corner of Broad and Church."

Janzek stifled a groan. "Is Church before or after King Street?"

"Two blocks east. Just look for a guy under a sheet and every squad car in the city. Not every day the mayor gets smoked."

"Okay, I'm getting off I-26. I see a sign for King Street."

"You're just five minutes away," Brindle said. "Welcome to the Holy City."

"Thanks," Janzek said. "Kinda wish it were under different circumstances."

Janzek rumbled down Meeting Street, breathing in the fragrant scent of tea olive trees. He got stuck behind a garbage truck and his first instinct was to lay on the horn, but something told him you didn't do that in Charleston. Up ahead, he saw a horse-drawn carriage jammed with gawkers. The garbage truck and the carriage were side by side—like blockers—creeping along at ten miles an hour. The smell of horse manure wafted through his open windows and replaced the sweet tea olive smell.

Janzek finally saw an opening, hit the accelerator, and slipped between the truck and the carriage. Broad Street was just ahead. He had never seen so many squad cars except at an Irish captain's funeral up in Southie. Ernie Brindle was keeping an eye out for him, and when he saw the U-Haul pull up, he directed Janzek past the long line of black-and-whites to a spot in front of a fire hydrant. Janzek got out and walked over.

Brindle, a short, intense guy with hair he didn't spend much time on, eyeballed Janzek's mode of transportation. "Jesus, Nick, not just a U-Haul but dragging a sorry-ass Honda behind it?" Brindle shook his head. "Thought you were s'posed to be a big-time homicide cop."

Janzek glanced back at the car that had served him long and loyally. "I'm not much of a car guy, Ernie."

Janzek looked down at the body sprawled half on and half off the sidewalk. Brindle pulled the sheet back. The late mayor was dressed in an expensive-looking blue suit, which was shredded and splattered with blood. A crushed gold watch dangled loosely from his wrist.

"So, what exactly happened?" Janzek asked, looking around at the cluster of cops, crime scene techs, and a man he assumed was the ME.

"According to a witness," Brindle said, "he was crossing the street when a black Mercedes 500, goin' like a bat out of hell, launched him twenty feet in the air."

"So... intentional then?" Janzek said.

"Yeah, for sure. Guy said he saw the driver aiming a gun."

"In case he couldn't take him out with the car?"

Brindle nodded. "I guess."

"Pointing it out the window?"

"Uh-huh," Brindle said.

"So, he was a lefty," Janzek said. "Guy say whether he fired it or not?"

"He didn't think so. Didn't hear anything, anyway."

"How'd he know it was a 500?"

"He's a car salesman," Brindle said. "On his way to the bank."

Janzek knelt down next to the body to get a closer look. It was clear the mayor had landed on his face. His nose was shoved off to one side, and his forehead and cheeks looked like a sheet of salmon.

The guy he figured for the ME, who'd been talking to two men nearby, came up and eyeballed him with a *who-the-hell-are-you?* look.

"Jack," Brindle said to the man, "this is Nick Janzek, new homicide guy." Then to Janzek, "Jack Martin is our esteemed, pain-in-the-ass ME."

"Good one," Martin said, crouching down next to the body, then looking up at Janzek. "So, how come you caught this one, Nick?"

Janzek didn't know the answer.

"'Cause I liked his sheet," Brindle said.

"Who you got him with?" Martin asked Brindle.

"Delvin."

Martin shook his head and glanced over at Janzek. "Urkel? Good fuckin' luck." Then he noticed the blue parka Janzek was wearing. "You plannin' on goin' skiing or something, Nick?"

Janzek glanced down at his coat. "Just drove down from Boston. Weather was a little different up there."

Martin nodded and kept looking Janzek over.

"Hey, Jack," Brindle said, "how 'bout examining the mayor 'stead of Janzek?"

Martin ignored him. "Boston, huh?"

"Yeah," Janzek said. "Massachusetts."

"Yeah, I've heard of it," Martin said, looking over Janzek's shoulder at the U-Haul. He shook his head, shot Brindle a look, and muttered, "Just what we need down here."

"What's that?" asked Brindle.

"Another frickin' wiseass Yankee."

Visit Amazon to continue reading
Killing Time in Charleston

AFTERWORD

Thanks for reading *Palm Beach Taboo*.

And to receive an email when the next Charlie Crawford Palm Beach Mystery comes out, be sure to sign up for my free author newsletter at **tomturnerbooks.com/news**.

Best,
Tom

ALSO BY TOM TURNER

CHARLIE CRAWFORD PALM BEACH MYSTERIES

Palm Beach Nasty

Palm Beach Poison

Palm Beach Deadly

Palm Beach Bones

Palm Beach Pretenders

Palm Beach Predator

Palm Beach Broke

Palm Beach Bedlam

Palm Beach Blues

The Charlie Crawford Palm Beach Mystery Series: Books 1, 2 & 3

The Charlie Crawford Palm Beach Mystery Series: Books 4, 5 & 6: Box Set #2

THE SAVANNAH SERIES

The Savannah Madam

NICK JANZEK CHARLESTON MYSTERIES

Killing Time in Charleston

Charleston Buzz Kill

STANDALONES

Broken House

Dead in the Water

For a current list of all available titles, please visit
tomturnerbooks.com/books.

ABOUT THE AUTHOR

A native New Englander, Tom dropped out of college and ran a bar in Vermont...into the ground. Limping back to get his sheepskin, he then landed in New York where he spent time as an award-winning copywriter at several Manhattan advertising agencies. After years of post-Mad Men life, he made a radical change and got a job in commercial real estate. A few years later he ended up in Palm Beach, buying, renovating and selling houses while getting material for his novels. On the side, he wrote *Palm Beach Nasty*, its sequel, *Palm Beach Poison*, and a screenplay, *Underwater*.

While at a wedding, he fell for the charm of Charleston, South Carolina. He spent six years there and completed a yet-to-be-published series set in Charleston. A year ago, Tom headed down the road to Savannah, where he just finished a novel about lust and murder among his neighbors.

Learn more about Tom's books at:
www.tomturnerbooks.com

Made in the USA
Coppell, TX
05 December 2021

67174444R00152